KILLER Beauty

THE CHAOS CREW
BOOK ONE

EVA CHANCE
& HARLOW KING

Killer Beauty

Book 1 in the Chaos Crew series

This is a work of fiction. Any resemblance to actual persons, living or dead, or actual events is purely coincidental.

First Digital Edition, 2021

Copyright © 2021 Eva Chance & Harlow King

Cover design: Temptation Creations

Ebook ISBN: 978-1-990338-20-5

Paperback ISBN: 978-1-990338-22-9

ONE

Decima

THE WALLS of my rooms were so thick that the screams of the dying couldn't reach me.

At least, I assume there were screams—and shouts and cries and the rest of the noises people make when they're facing their end, especially if it's violent. In my experience, hardly anyone goes silently.

But like I said, I couldn't hear them.

I was finishing up a pretty typical evening in my part of the house with no idea what havoc was being wreaked beyond my door. I'd worked out in the gym for a couple of hours before dinner, running through the new exercises Noelle had given me. After a gazillion years of workouts and assignments under my primary trainer's watch, it took a lot to bring the burn into my muscles. I threw everything

I had into the jabs, kicks, and flips until I'd broken a real sweat.

Slacking off wasn't an option. I had to keep pushing myself, keep stretching the time before fatigue started to set in. I never knew how long I might need to keep fighting or running to see a mission through, and a second's weakness could mean failure. A.k.a., curtains for me.

It was a dangerous world out there, and the only way to ensure survival was to be the most dangerous thing in it. I'd been doing a pretty good job of that so far.

Anna brought dinner at the usual hour looking totally normal, so the massacre mustn't have started until after that point. She'd set a novel on the tray beside my plate.

"I just finished that one," she said, tapping it with a smile. Anna gave out smiles easily—not like Noelle, who I only got a rare grin out of when I'd kicked ass particularly well. "I thought you might like it, Decima."

"Thanks," I said, practicing my smile in return.

I wasn't thrilled about the book, because I wasn't much of a reader. I got impatient with words strung together with so many details that hardly seemed important, characters meandering around with no idea what they wanted, so I'd start skimming and then lose track of the story. But Anna always tried her best to be kind to me, and she meant that kindness a hell of a lot more often than most people I'd encountered. I was grateful for that.

When I was little, once I'd figured out what a family was from books and movies, I'd wondered if Anna was my mother. She used to spend more time with me between my training sessions back then. She'd laughed when I'd asked her, looking a little sad at the same time, and said no, that my mother and father had been taken from me by the bad people out there right after I was born. But the household would stop those people from getting me too. The household would look after me. They'd make sure I was strong enough to handle the world outside our home when it was time.

And they'd definitely come through on that promise.

Hungry after the long workout, I wolfed down the lasagna and salad, and then I just couldn't settle down. My pulse kept thumping a little too fast as if the exertion of the workout hadn't worn off. Maybe some part of me sensed a shift in the air, a vibe of brutal chaos that seeped through the walls even if sound couldn't.

None of the movies or shows available on the TV—the nature documentaries, thrillers, and ridiculous comedies that Noelle had decided didn't have any lies distracting enough that they might interfere with my missions—caught my interest. I couldn't make it through two pages of Anna's book. I brought up a game on the new console she'd brought last year, which Noelle approved of for honing my reflexes and observational skills. Not even assassinating my way through an office building took the edge off the restless itch crawling under my skin.

Finally, I went into my bedroom, sprawled out on the bed, and dipped my hand between my thighs.

Getting off like this usually brought a rush of energy

and then a mellow lull that helped me relax after an intense mission or get to sleep. I kept my eyes shut and my mind blank, focusing completely on the physical sensations I summoned with the pressure of my fingers. If I let my thoughts stray, the chilling memories that would rise up might kill any chance of release. All that mattered was the slowly building pleasure and the thumping of my heart alongside it—

The whir of a lock disengaging jolted me off the bed. Every tingle of bodily enjoyment vanished in an instant.

With all my senses on the alert, I darted into the main room, instinctively sticking close to the furniture. Unexpected visits after dinner time were unusual. It could be Noelle coming with an urgent mission or with some kind of test, in which case I'd better show I'd prepared myself quickly.

But it was the other door that was swinging open, away from me into the room beyond. The door that led to the rest of the household.

No one *ever* came through there after dinner.

As I froze, bracing for the unknown, Anna staggered into view. Even clutching the door's outer handle, she was crumpling toward the ground. She'd always been so separate from the harsher parts of my training that it took my brain a second to process that the red all over her dress was *blood*.

The blood pulsed from beneath her other hand where it was pressed to the side of her neck. It seeped from a bullet wound that'd seared through her dress and stomach, and another at her hip. Holy hell.

I dashed to her, my mind automatically taking stock of the arteries and veins that were most likely severed, the amount of fluid she'd already lost, the odds of survival.

She was bleeding out. She'd *already* lost more blood than most people could have endured.

For both my safety and the rest of the household's, I wasn't supposed to leave the boundaries of my rooms without approval. I'd *never* crossed this specific threshold, only leaving by the outer door into the yard. When I reached the doorway, tension locked around my muscles. I stopped with my feet on the threshold and caught Anna just before her head hit the hardwood floor.

"Anna!" I said, her name coming out like a protest. My throat had constricted. I felt like I was choking.

I'd seen a lot of people dying before, but mostly people I'd killed with the full intention of doing so, and the others I hadn't known anyway. This—this wasn't right—how could this be happening?

Anna's grip on my forearm was weak. She couldn't lift her chin enough for her eyes to meet mine. She seemed to be staring at my running shoes braced on that uncrossable line between my rooms and the rest of the house. Her blood dripped in a rhythmic patter against the floorboards.

"Garlic milkshake," she croaked, or at least something that sounded like that, since the words I thought I'd heard made no sense. She coughed and sputtered. Her normally cheerful voice came out thin and warbled. "Leave. Find...

somewhere safe. I—I think they're gone... Played dead until—couldn't leave you locked away in here with no one—"

"Don't talk," I ordered. I meant to sound firm, but the words came out more frantic. "We have to—if I can stop the bleeding—"

But it was too late. I'd known that before I'd reached her, even if every cell in my body resisted the fact. As I moved to turn her so I could treat the wounds, her muscles went slack. Her body sagged, the last fragments of life slipping out of her.

I knew death well enough that I couldn't deny it when it was happening right in front of me. No amount of CPR was going to restart a heart that'd already lost twice as much blood as any living human being should. My hands itched to start the chest compressions anyway.

But what good would that do? It would only waste time, when—

The enemy had come here. To my own fucking home. What else had they done?

What was I going to do about it?

With my pulse thudding in my ears, I let Anna's limp body come to rest on the floor. My insides had tied into a string of knots from the base of my throat to my gut. I forced myself to stand, to take stock.

I had the door open in front of me, leading to a small room and a short hallway beyond it. It was the path to the rest of the house, a total unknown I'd never ventured into. Blood streaked the floorboards from around the corner, some of it in the shape of handprints. Anna had dragged herself here with her last bit of strength.

She'd let me out, given me permission to go, so I could —so I could do *something*.

The years of training kicked in with a wash of adrenaline, rolling back the haze of shock that had settled over me. My spine pulled straighter, my gaze flicking over my surroundings with an increasingly analytical sharpness. All my thoughts narrowed down to getting through the next however many minutes alive—and taking down the thugs who might still be lurking around, looking to add to their list of murders.

Unfortunately, Noelle always brought my mission kit to me before she sent me off on an assignment. I didn't have any firearms of my own in my rooms—no official weapons of any kind.

I walked to the trim wooden table where I'd eaten my dinner and snatched up the dinner knife. Blunt, but better than nothing. With a brisk motion, I smacked my water glass against the edge of the table just hard enough to crack it and pried out a long, deadly shard. My fingers clenched around it.

All right. Time to see what the hell was out there. Time to make whoever had invaded the safety of this house and riddled Anna with bullets very, very sorry.

I paused on the threshold, looking down at her lifeless body. The knots inside me tugged tighter. I had the urge to offer a gesture that would honor her in some way... but I had no idea how, and I didn't have much time to figure it out.

She'd thought the killers had left, but she could be wrong.

I stepped around her body with a silent, awkward apology and slunk through the room beyond. It was set up like a home office with a small desk and bookcases along the walls. One of those bookcases had swung out to reveal the door to my rooms. I hadn't realized they kept it quite that hidden.

With my ears perked, I stalked into the short hall, setting my feet down gingerly. No sounds reached me except a soft, distant rustling.

I peeked around the first bend and found a broader hall. Brass light fixtures gleamed, casting their bright glow over side tables and a geometric-patterned rug that ran the length of the hall. The furnishings had the same modern styling as in my rooms, but with a much more opulent feel to them that reminded me of the swanky hotels I'd run some of my missions out of.

The contrast was jarring enough that it took me a moment to notice the pair of feet protruding from a doorway at the other end of the hall.

I eyed the feet for a minute, but they didn't move. Keeping my back to the wall, I sidled toward the first doorway, much closer to me.

It opened to a dining room nearly as big as my entire main living space, with a gleaming ebony table that could have seated twenty people. It only held two at the moment:

a man and a woman face-down on the wooden surface, blood pooling beneath their lolled heads. And not just beneath their heads—one of the bullets had caught the man at just the right angle to spray more blood all over the wall behind him.

I walked closer. I didn't recognize either of these people, as much of them as I could see. But then, I hadn't had much contact with the household other than Anna and Noelle and the occasional temporary trainers who'd taught me skills that weren't in Noelle's wheelhouse. I *might* have met one or both of these two a decade or longer ago and simply not recognized their faces with the gore in the mix.

I patted them down out of necessity, but neither turned up any weapons or phones or anything else I could use. Offering them a silent benediction, I crossed the hall to the next room.

This one was a huge living room filled with white leather sofas and chairs, a large ebony liquor cabinet, matching side tables… and a whole lot of corpses.

"Fuck," I muttered under my breath, taking in the spectacle. Eight bodies lay scattered across the furnishings, their blood staining the pale leather and walls in every direction like some kind of sick abstract art. A meaty, metallic smell soured the cool air. Nothing moved except the swaying of a curtain where a draft was coming through a shattered window. That was the rustling I'd heard.

I'd killed a lot of people in my life, but I'd never made this much of a mess doing it.

I picked my way between the bodies, bile rising to the

back of my mouth, and realized the mess was purposeful. The style of certain wounds was distinctive—this man and that woman had clearly been shot to clip an artery for maximum spray while they were still moving around, before the killing strike. From the pattern of splatters around the guy over there, someone had neatly sliced his wrists and let him flail around before putting a bullet in his skull.

Whoever had done this had *wanted* it to look messy. Why?

I stopped by a woman sprawled in front of one of the sofas whose dark brown hair was streaked with gray. She'd taken not one but three shots to the face, which both struck me as excessive—a total waste of bullets—and had mangled her features into a fleshy pulp.

I swallowed hard. Was that Noelle? Had they managed to take even *her* by surprise? There wasn't enough left for me to tell for sure.

She wasn't the only body the killers had battered beyond recognition—and I was sure now that it was killers, plural. I could identify at least two different types of shot wounds reflecting different sizes of bullets from different guns. It'd have been nearly impossible for one to take down so many in the same space quickly enough anyway, especially with a knife in the mix.

A grim weight was forming inside me, pressing down on my stomach. Whoever had carried out this massacre was both very good at what they did and had reveled in the savagery. I didn't think I'd ever gone up against an opponent quite like that.

For all these years, the people of the household had looked after me and trained me so that I could hold the cruelty of this world at bay. But it hadn't been enough to protect them in the end. I hadn't even known this was happening.

I couldn't save them now, but I could ensure their killers were properly repaid. One last mission to set one small thing amid the awfulness out there right. To create some kind of justice for Anna and Noelle and everyone else who'd provided for me.

And then...

When I tried to think about it, my mind stalled, so I just didn't think that far.

The killers had left no trace of their identity that I could spot other than the unusual approach to their kills. Three more bodies lay in the space where I'd spotted the protruding feet, which was a music room with a sleek white piano and framed concert posters on the walls. Blood was splashed and smeared across all of it. Two of the bodies had been cut in an odd zigzag from their throat to the left side of their collarbone.

None of the bodies provided me with a gun or even so much as a pocket knife. Had the entire household really been unarmed, or had their killers removed their weapons afterward?

The latter seemed more likely. It was what I'd have done with a job anywhere near this big, to ensure anyone I hadn't taken down yet couldn't add to their options for striking back at me.

After making a circuit of the lower floor, I headed upstairs. The many bedrooms up there reminded me of the lavish penthouses where I'd carried out a few of my killings. There was one woman lying dead in her bed, her face smashed in with the impact of the bullets and the ivory duvet drenched red, but otherwise they were empty.

A quick search of the dressers and vanities turned up no weapons but a couple of wads of cash and several expensive-looking necklaces and bracelets, glittering with gold and gemstones. I stuffed what I could into the pockets of my track pants and dropped the rest into a tote bag I found hanging over the back of a chair. Missions took a lot of funding even when I knew who my target was. I wouldn't have the household's credit cards smoothing the way for me this time.

I wouldn't have the household at all. When I left here, it'd be for good.

The thought hit me hard enough to stop me in my tracks in the middle of the hall. A momentary chill flooded me.

I'd left the house plenty of times before, of course, but never for more than a week for a particularly complicated mission. Rarely for more than a couple of days. The rooms behind the bookcase had been mine for as long as I could remember. I'd barely talked to anyone other than Anna and Noelle except to get what I needed from bystanders in the middle of an assignment.

And in the blink of an eye, it'd all been destroyed.

My fingers curled around the makeshift blades I was holding until the pinch of the glass warned me to loosen my grip. None of this should have happened. I'd worked so hard—

I gritted my teeth. I'd keep working until the vicious assholes who'd done this were just as lifeless as the bodies they'd left behind.

When I was finished checking every inch of the house, I headed back to my rooms. I stuffed a box of energy bars and a couple of changes of clothes into the tote bag before pausing over the plush tiger toy perched on the headboard of my bed.

The stuffed animal's fur was worn from the many nights I'd gone to sleep hugging it when I'd been very young, and one of its glossy eyes was coming loose. But looking at it brought a sharp sense of possessiveness into my chest.

Damn it, it was *mine*. Somehow it felt like the only thing in this place that truly was, which didn't make any sense since it must have come from the household like everything else. Holding it had always given me a weird sense of comfort even though I couldn't remember who'd given it to me or when, I'd had it so long.

Without letting myself second-guess the impulse, I grabbed the toy and stuffed it into the bag with the rest of my belongings.

On my way out, I stopped by Anna's body with another twinge of regret. My practical instincts told me that I shouldn't let it be obvious she'd opened this hidden door.

My presence here was meant to be a secret. That might still matter to someone—it might matter to me. I'd have an easier time dealing with the pricks who'd done this if they didn't know I existed.

I eased Anna's body a couple of feet farther into the office room so I could push the bookcase and close the door. The bookcase swung back into place against the wall, concealing all trace of the entrance. I didn't know how to open it again—I couldn't have returned to my rooms even if I'd wanted to.

There was no way to go but onward.

I snuck out the back door I'd noted in my survey of the first floor and headed to the garage. Inside, a thick, oily scent laced the air that set off my inner alarm bells. I opened the hoods of each car in the row and found the engines' cables snapped, the compartments cracked by swift blows.

Of course. The killers had probably come through here before they'd entered the house so no one who managed to flee would have a vehicle to escape in. I couldn't repress a flicker of respect for their thoroughness, even if it made my jaw clench at the same time.

I'd just have to find transportation outside the property.

As I slunk across the expansive treed yard, the night's darkness cloaked my movements. Thick clouds blotted out the stars. A damp breeze licked over my face and my bare arms. It tasted like incoming rain.

The stone wall that surrounded the property stood a foot higher than me, but with a running leap, I clambered onto and over it. I dropped to the sidewalk outside with only the faintest rasp of my shoes on the pavement.

The whole rest of the city—the whole rest of the big, bad world—stretched out before me.

Clutching the tote bag close to my side, I touched the wall in silent farewell and set off through the shadows. Resolve hardened inside me.

The killers who'd descended on the household might be good, but they were going to pay the price anyway. They couldn't have counted on tangling with me.

TWO

Julius

BLAZE FLICKED between video feeds on his laptop's screen with the frenetic energy that rarely left his wiry frame. He'd mounted eight discreet cameras around the mansion's perimeter so we could monitor things after the job, and he zoomed in on one stream of video after another, each shrinking to join the row of smaller squares when he switched. He tapped his foot softly on the tiled floor of the deserted rooftop patio. The guy could never stay still.

Ages ago, his restlessness had irritated me, but now that he'd been part of the crew for years, I appreciated it. His mind was always in motion too, homing in on every important detail that could make the difference between a successful operation and a disaster.

The wrought-iron gate outside the mansion stayed

closed and the sidewalks along the stone walls totally empty. This late at night, that wasn't surprising. We'd counted on a lack of foot traffic. Out here in the suburbs, it wasn't as if there was much nightlife. And with the damp pressure in the air hinting at a rain shower to come, who would want to be out anyway?

Talon watched the screen too, his hands resting on the top of the chair next to Blaze's. "We didn't miss anyone," he said in his low, implacable voice. He glanced from the screen to the streets around us, although the long-closed restaurant we were camped out on top of was a few blocks from the mansion, too far away to really see without the cameras. The glow from the screen gleamed off his smoothly shaved scalp and glinted in his icy-blue eyes. "No hitches."

"Obviously no one managed to put out a call for help either," Blaze said with a grin, running his hand through the pale red hair that fit his chosen name, which fell to the collar of his shirt. Another tiny window on the computer screen was monitoring the police frequencies. "No cops, no nothing."

Garrison propped himself against the edge of the table next to the laptop, his lips curving with his typical cocky grin. "The Chaos Crew doesn't botch missions. Especially not when I've laid the groundwork."

Of course, Blaze couldn't resist arching his eyebrows at the youngest and newest member of our crew. "You mean like that time in Cairo," he said teasingly.

Garrison glowered at him, the hazel eyes that seemed

to shift in color depending on what he was wearing nearly black now in the dim light. "It was only my second time out, and *someone* forgot to fill me in on a key piece of intel."

Blaze smiled cheekily back at him. "I didn't forget. It was part of your training to see how you'd handle a gap. Good thing you recovered fast from that stumble."

"But I did," Garrison grumbled. "We got fucking paid. That's what matters."

"Enough," I said before they could take their scrap any further. That one word from me was enough for them both to fall silent. I nodded to the laptop. "We don't assume any mission is successful until afterward. We're going to wait a little longer, just to be sure."

I couldn't blame them for being keyed up. We all were after a job like that, exhilarated by the rush of the violence, the blood splattered in perfect disarray, the justice seen through. If sometimes I enjoyed the carnage itself just as much as the justice, there was no need to acknowledge that to anyone else. But after another half hour or so, we could pack up, go home, and leave this scene behind us.

Blaze sat up straighter, his shoulders stiffening. "Hey, guys."

As he clicked the trackpad to enlarge one video feed, the rest of us leaned toward the laptop screen. A woman had just stalked into view, walking alongside the stone wall, her arms tucked close to her sides and her head low. The waves of her long black hair veiled most of her face.

"A neighbor getting home late," Garrison said, flicking his shaggy blond hair away from his eyes. "No big deal."

"But she came out of nowhere." Blaze frowned at the screen. "She didn't show up on any of the other feeds, she was just suddenly there. I don't know where she came from."

"Look." Talon pointed at the figure just as she passed the camera, motioning to her T-shirt. In the darkness, the feed didn't show much in the way of color, but there was a dark smear on her chest that made my instincts ping in the same way my colleagues' must have. "Is that blood?"

Blaze zoomed in, but she'd passed by, now angled away from us and heading toward the edge of the camera's view. A tote bag bounced lightly against her back from where it was slung over her shoulder.

"She can't have come from the house, right?" our tech expert said. "We did two full sweeps—we caught everyone who was on the manifest."

We had, but I couldn't shake the sense that this woman wasn't just some random pedestrian either. It was too strange.

The Chaos Crew didn't leave loose ends. I couldn't *let* us leave them. That was how an operation could go to hell in an instant.

Talon lifted his gun. "We could kill her now."

I shook my head. "We don't have definite evidence she's connected to the job." Cutting her down would have been the easiest option, but it went against everything I stood for. We didn't have many rules, but those we had, we held to. And "Kill no innocent bystanders" was at the top of the list.

No one died because of us who didn't have it coming to them—not today, not ever.

But we couldn't let her just walk away either, not when she might not be remotely innocent after all.

I snapped my fingers, already moving toward the stairs. "Garrison, you're with me on foot. Talon, you and Blaze take the car. Keep me up to date on her movements. We'll see where she goes from here and then make an educated decision."

They sprang into action in an instant, taking my word as law. One of our other few rules was that no one challenged my leadership of the crew when I gave an order. It kept our team working as a unit. A highly sophisticated and efficient unit that didn't make mistakes.

Until, maybe, now.

That possibility sat uneasily in my gut as we hurried down to the street. Blaze's voice hummed through my headset. "She's crossed Blantyre Avenue, heading east."

"Acknowledged." I picked up my pace, Garrison following close behind. The woman had a substantial head start on us, but we could close the distance quickly. I set my feet carefully even as we hustled toward her location, making only the faintest patter.

Coming up on the next corner, we slowed and peered around the bend. "She's in our sights," Garrison whispered into his mic.

The woman we'd spotted had made it to the end of that

block, but she'd stopped by a sedan parked by the curb, which had given us more of a chance to catch up. What was she—

She yanked at something by the top of the window and then tugged on the door, which opened. She immediately dove into the driver's seat.

I muttered a curse under my breath. She'd broken into the damn thing. I headed along the street as quickly as I dared, sticking close to the shadows outside the shops on the opposite side of the road, Garrison right behind me.

If she noticed us, she'd probably bolt, and we weren't close enough yet that I was sure of chasing her down. If Talon and Blaze could get in place...

"Just coming around Carling St.," Blaze reported, and in the same moment, the car's engine revved.

"Fuck," I snapped under my breath, and broke into a sprint. "She's broken into a car and she's already got it running. Get over here *now*."

The stolen car's engine sputtered into silence and then roared back to life. The woman who'd hotwired it in a matter of seconds peeled away from the sidewalk. I'd never seen anyone take over a vehicle that fast. Who the hell was she?

The chances of her being innocent were quickly dwindling.

"She's getting away," I hissed into the mic. "Where the hell are you?"

Our car whipped around the corner before Blaze

needed to reply. It jerked to a halt beside us, and Garrison and I threw ourselves into the back seat.

The second Garrison had hauled the door shut, Talon hit the gas. The stolen car was just turning a corner up ahead.

"There," I said with a jab of my finger. "The dark gray sedan. Follow her."

Talon sped after her and swung around the same turn she'd taken. The sedan came into view a couple of blocks ahead of us, easy to spot in the gleaming streetlamps along this slightly broader road. Even here, traffic was sparse, only a few other pairs of headlights gleaming farther in the distance.

A heavy droplet of rain splashed on the windshield, briefly blurring the view. Another followed, and another, until Talon had to start the wipers going.

"You couldn't catch her on foot?" he asked over the rhythmic tapping of the drops.

I grimaced. "The bitch is fast. She must have set a record hotwiring that car. I don't even know how she broke into it to begin with."

"Not exactly your typical pedestrian out for a stroll," Garrison said in a wry drawl. "What are the odds that a woman who can hotwire cars in a split-second *isn't* involved in this?"

I didn't have an answer to that question. I narrowed my eyes at the car in front of us. Blaze licked his lips and clicked a few keys on his laptop, leaping from feed to feed. He was following along with the official traffic cams now.

There wasn't a government resource in this city he couldn't find a way to infiltrate.

"Not very good," Talon replied for me.

Garrison sank back in his seat. His breath was still a bit ragged from the jog to catch up with the woman—I'd have to remind him to get in more physical training on our days off. It wasn't his main area, but we all needed to pull our weight in every way possible.

"We should just kill her and get it over with then," he said. "Whether she has something to do with the job or not, she just committed a crime. So she's not innocent, so the rule doesn't apply."

Blaze swiveled in his seat with another of his heckling looks. "And by 'we,' I assume you mean anyone other than you with your weak stomach."

Garrison kicked the back of Blaze's seat. "I just know what I'm good at. And I know that every move that woman's made since the moment we saw her has screamed that she's up to something."

He was right, but at the same time, something about the situation still felt off to me. Killing the woman without sorting it out wouldn't necessarily mean we'd fixed the problem, only that we had no way of telling what else might have gone wrong.

"We catch her and talk to her first," I said. "Find out who she is and what she knows. Make sure there's nothing else we missed. It's no good tying off one loose end if that stops us from following it to a dozen others we didn't know about."

Garrison opened his mouth as if to argue but shut it immediately when I caught his gaze. He set his expression in a mask of indifference. Our social chameleon could put on whatever front we needed to get the players in position at the start of a job or ferret out information Blaze couldn't hack his way to. Even I couldn't tell which of the emotions that crossed his face were real. Were any of them?

It didn't matter. Nothing mattered except the security of this crew, and we couldn't know how the woman might threaten that without confronting her.

The rain picked up to a heavier downpour. It washed over the windshield between the swift flicks of the wipers. The stolen car slowed, and so did Talon, drawing up less than a block from her brake lights.

"Stay as close as you can without spooking her," I said. "We don't want to lose her. As soon as she stops, we have to be on her ass."

Even as I spoke, the woman took a sudden left turn. Talon fell back a little before following her. Two blocks later, she took an abrupt right. She hadn't signaled either time.

Blaze spoke up cautiously. "Are we sure she hasn't already gotten spooked? Did she see you before she grabbed the car?"

"We were too far back," I said. "I made sure she didn't see us—I hadn't expected her to take off that quickly."

"She was going straight ahead until a minute ago," Talon pointed out.

The stolen car veered through a gas station's lot and

out the other side. Talon gunned the engine to hurtle after her.

Garrison folded his arms over his chest. "This is ridiculous. We should force her to pull over now instead of chasing her all over town."

If we'd already been made, that was our best course of action. I exhaled roughly, and just then, one of the parked cars along the curb swerved into the street in front of our target.

Too fast, too close. The woman must have pulled hard on the steering wheel to avoid crashing into the other car, and the slick surface of the road sent her vehicle skidding. It careened across the road and rammed hood-first into a telephone pole. The screech of crumpling steel cut through the drumming of the rain on our roof.

THREE

Decima

THE HOUSEHOLD HAD BEEN thorough in my training, which meant I'd gotten a lot of driving practice in to prepare me for the occasional missions that required I get behind the wheel of various vehicles. I hadn't been on the road at night all that often, though. Or in the rain. The combination of the two, with the droplets slipping over the windshield with increasing frequency, made my hands tighten on the steering wheel.

Thank God the streets were pretty empty at this time of night. I could manage to navigate the periodic streetlights and the rows of parked cars along the side of the road just fine.

Which was good, because my mind kept wandering. The image of Anna's bloody body lingered in the back of my head.

Was there something more I should have done for her? For all of the people in the household? At the time, it'd seemed like leaving quickly was the best thing I could do, but now a pinch of guilt dug into my stomach. I hadn't felt guilt over a dead body in a long time, even all the ones I'd been responsible for.

I was totally alone now. I had nobody left. How could it be normal to leave behind the only home I'd ever known just like that?

But then, there was obviously nothing normal about the massacre I'd walked into.

I sucked my lower lip under my teeth and let my mind shift to the practicalities. I had too many questions that I needed to answer, and emotions would get me nowhere.

Who had done this? More importantly, how was I going to find them? And in what way would I end their lives? Would I make their deaths long and painful, allowing their arteries to spew blood for minute after minute before they died? That was how they'd killed everyone in the household, after all. It would be *fitting*.

I suspected I'd like that style of poetic justice very much.

Where would I start? I'd never been assigned a mission with so little preparation and such a vague objective. Noelle had always come with weapons, supplies, and a dossier of everything I needed to know to locate and take down my target. I'd never had to think about anything other than how to get into a specific building, evade bodyguards, or make a swift escape.

Right now, I had nothing but a stolen car, a bag of clothes and jewelry, and the knife and chunk of glass I'd tossed on the seat with the bag, which barely counted as weapons. I had no idea where I was going or who I needed to find. The possibilities spiraled away from me, so endless my mind froze up trying to process them.

It was probably shock. I couldn't be blamed for that, right? Discovering that everyone around you had been brutally murdered was pretty fucking shocking. I just needed time to think.

Headlights gleamed in my rearview mirror. I glanced at the mirror and realized the black car I'd noticed behind me earlier was still heading in the same direction. It'd pulled closer, only about a block away.

There wasn't anything so strange about that. I was on a fairly major street. I'd walked several blocks from the household before I'd found a car I could steal, and I hadn't seen anyone tracking me from there. I'd stuck to the speed limit and followed the traffic laws to a tee, so I shouldn't have raised any red flags for anyone who'd seen me drive by after.

But it was arrogance to assume I'd done everything perfectly. The car *could* be following me for one reason or another, and that meant I should act as if it was.

I slowed, monitoring the car behind me, and took an abrupt turn. They hadn't put on their signal, but they appeared behind me around the bend several seconds later. They left enough space for another car to pass, but… was this a coincidence?

The rain pelted my windshield. I frowned, squinting at the road ahead. There was a little side-street right there.

I swerved quickly but not violently, my heart jumping when the tires skidded on the wet pavement more than I'd expected. With a jerk of the steering wheel, I managed to straighten out the car. There. They'd drive on by, and I'd see I was just being paranoid and—

Headlights flashed behind me. The damn car had made the same turn again.

Apprehension gnawed at my stomach. This definitely didn't *feel* like a coincidence now. What were the chances that someone just happened to take this exact same route, when there was hardly anyone on the roads at all?

I had to lose them. That was all there was to it.

Spotting a gas station on a corner up ahead where the side-street met another larger road, I pressed slowly on the gas to increase my speed. The moment I came up on the station, I whipped to the side, careered past the pumps with my pulse beating in my throat, and flew onto the road on the other side.

That might not be enough. I had to take the next turn that—

A parked car I hadn't been paying attention to pulled out into the road right in front of me. I was going too fast. I hit the brake, but the tires screeched and slid in the rain. Shit.

I hauled on the wheel before I slammed right into the asshole who'd cut me off. The car kept skidding, spinning to the side and then forward—and crashed into a telephone pole on the other side of the road.

The impact jolted me in my seat, the hood crumpling in toward me. In the same moment, the airbag burst out with a *bang*, smacking into my face, chest, and the arm I'd flung across the wheel to turn it. Pain radiated through my hand and the side of my torso, and my eyes stung. A chalky powder prickled down my throat.

I blinked hard, and the stinging sensation only deepened into a sharper burning. Even as the airbag deflated, the world around me looked blurred. Involuntary tears flushed the chemicals from my eyes, but I still couldn't see for shit.

Damn it. I had to get out of here—grab my things, run for it, find another car or a bus I could jump onto.

I groped for the tote bag, and another jab of pain shot through my wrist. I could hardly move it without gritting my teeth. Fucking hell. The crash had hurt that too.

I twisted at the waist to reach for my bag with my other hand and winced at the ache that spread through my side. My ribs had gotten in on the game as well. From the feel of them, they were only bruised, but I'd broken enough of them in the past that they were way too sensitive to getting bumped around.

Hazards of the job.

Clenching my jaw against the various pains, I snatched the handle of the tote bag and shoved open the driver's side door. The world outside swam before my still-blurry eyes, but I had to keep going. I took a deep breath and pushed my way out of the car, trying to do most of the work with my left arm.

It didn't work as well as I'd hoped, and I staggered out of the car, my legs wobbling and a fresh rush of pain penetrating my chest. The rain drenched me in an instant. It also flushed my eyes, alleviating a bit of the sting but not clearing my vision particularly well. I couldn't tell how much of the blurring was because of the water and how much from the airbag's chemicals now.

"Hey," a deep voice said from behind me. "Are you all right?"

I whirled, and my legs swayed again, still shaky from the crash. I stumbled right into the chest of a large, muscle-bound man. He caught my elbows, and I jerked away instinctively.

Who the hell was he? What did he want with me?

"Hold on," he said. My hazy vision made out a broad-shouldered form nearly a foot taller than me, the square-jawed face topped with dark hair. It was hard to make out what expression he was even making or anything else beyond that.

He held up his hands in a gesture of surrender. "I'm just trying to help you. That was a hell of a crash."

Oh. That did kind of make sense, didn't it? Good Samaritans or whatever. Probably just looking for the ego boost of saying he'd come to someone's rescue, but nothing necessarily nefarious.

It wasn't just him, though. Three more figures gathered around us, all male, all with at least half a foot and fifty pounds on my well-toned but trim frame. Where had they all come from?

Where was the car I'd thought was tailing me? Had these guys come out of it? If they had, what were they planning on doing to me?

I tugged the tote bag's strap over my shoulder instinctively so I'd have my hands free to fight, not that one of those hands felt up to engaging in combat at the moment. At the same time, a slimmer figure with a face framed by light red hair leaned toward me. "Is she okay?"

"I'm fine," I lied automatically, taking a step back and dodging another man who'd come up beside me. "Really, thank you for your concern, but—"

I turned, and banged my hip on a newspaper box I hadn't seen between the darkness and my blurred eyes. My right hand shot out automatically to help me catch my balance, and agony lanced through my wrist. I couldn't stop myself from hissing at the pain.

"You don't seem okay," the first guy said, swiping rain from his face. "That wrist might be broken. We should call an ambulance."

Another of the men who'd approached us jerked around as if to stare at the one who'd spoken. All I could make out of this one was a sharp chin and blond hair plastered to his skull. "Julius," he said in a voice that had an edge to it.

Julius. The name seemed to fit the imposing masculinity that radiated off of every inch of the first man's frame.

I didn't want to stay here with him and whoever these other guys were, and I didn't want to be taken to any hospital. If the people who'd slaughtered the household were looking for me, I couldn't afford to leave any kind of paper trail.

That was one of Noelle's first rules. Never, *ever* let anyone make a permanent record of your presence.

"I'm fine," I said again, taking another step back. My legs were getting steadier, at least. I blinked, unsuccessfully willing my vision to clear more, and restrained a shiver at the chill of my soaked clothes and hair. "No need for an ambulance. I was almost home anyway. I can make it there on my own."

No need to follow me. Just let me leave.

"I can't let you go walking around when you could be battered up more than you realize," the man named Julius said. "Here, if you don't want an ambulance, I've got some basic medical training. Let me look you over quickly, and if I don't see any reason to worry, then you can be on your way."

He made the suggestion sound perfectly reasonable. His firm baritone was the kind of voice used to making commands and having them followed. But that only made me balk even more.

I didn't take orders from him or any other random guy. I didn't want him or his friends getting any closer to me than they already had.

He'd accepted my refusal of proper medical attention awfully easily, hadn't he? Was that normal, or did it mean *he* hadn't really wanted to bring anyone else onto the scene either?

"You really don't need to go to that much trouble," I said. That sounded decently normal, right? "If I start feeling worse, I have my own doctor I can call. I'd be more comfortable with that than a stranger, obviously."

The men shifted on their feet around me. I had trouble keeping track of them all in the hazy darkness. I started to swivel to keep all of them in view, and the blond guy grabbed my elbow, more gently than I'd have expected given the tone of his voice earlier. "You've obviously hurt your wrist," he said with a new air of concern. "And it looks like you've got blood on your shirt. Did something happen before the accident?"

My gaze jerked down and made out a blotch of red on the blue T-shirt now plastered to my body. It had to be Anna's blood, from when I'd caught her in the doorway. My pulse stuttered. "I—I must have gotten scratched up a bit in the crash. It's nothing serious. Really, I'd rather just go home. On my own."

"We can't leave you alone in the rain when you're injured and defenseless," Julius said.

I had to hold in a laugh at the word "defenseless." He didn't have a clue. Even injured, I had little doubt I'd be able to hold my own against one of them, maybe even two. I could have broken the hand the blond guy still had on me if I'd really wanted to, if I wasn't trying to play normal in case they were ordinary bystanders after all.

Instead, I just tugged my arm away from him, and to my relief, he let me go.

"Look, I'd rather be on my own than surrounded by strangers," I said. "I'm just a little bruised up. I've got to deal with the car and the rest of this mess, but I can handle that. You can all go back to whatever you were doing."

The blond guy's head cocked. He stepped back with a shrug. "Fine, if that's what you really want."

"It is," I said, turning toward the sidewalk—and a sharp pinch bit into my lower spine.

The last thing I was aware of was the give of my knees as blackness swam up over my vision and completely blanked my mind.

FOUR

Talon

JULIUS CAUGHT the woman before she'd quite hit the ground. She lolled in his arms, obviously dead to the world. I pocketed the syringe I'd used to knock her unconscious and glanced at the crashed car, swiping the raindrops that were finally starting to let up off my smooth scalp. "Do we want to do anything about the vehicle?"

Julius considered it. "I don't think going to that kind of trouble is necessary. It wasn't hers to begin with, so there's nothing to tie it to her or us. Check inside for blood or anything she might have left behind, though."

She'd never gotten around to closing the driver's side door. As Julius carried her back to our car, I peered into the darkened interior. I couldn't see any bodily fluids on the seats, even after I flicked on my phone's flashlight to be sure. I plucked one dark hair off the leather surface.

There was a coffee cup that must have belonged to the car's owner, since this woman hadn't had a chance to stop for a drink. A shard of glass and a dinner knife lay on the passenger seat. None of the windows had shattered, so the glass hadn't come from there. Odd but not really useful. I tucked them into my pocket alongside the syringe anyway.

I made it to our car just as Julius lowered the woman into the trunk. My gaze lingered on the smooth planes of her face. She was young, no more than her early twenties, but she didn't look scruffy or like any kind of punk.

What had driven her to steal that car? What had she been doing by the mansion?

Garrison had grabbed the bag she'd been carrying. He tossed it into the trunk with her and stalked to the door to get out of the rain. Julius closed the lid of the trunk, and the rest of us piled into the car afterward. I took the driver's seat again, but I didn't start the engine, waiting for Julius's cue.

"What the fuck are we going to do with her now?" Garrison asked. He'd put on a softer front briefly with the woman when he'd been trying to cajole a little information out of her, but now he was back to his usual snarky self. "Not take her home like a stray puppy, I assume."

"If she's from the mansion, we should probably kill her," I said. I didn't relish the thought—killing in the middle of a job, where everything was orchestrated and certain, felt very different from murdering a random woman we'd picked off the street—but I wouldn't balk either. If that was what needed to happen, then so be it. She was nothing to us.

Julius had gotten in beside me. He rubbed the bridge of his nose, more pensive than decisive at the moment. That didn't seem like a good sign. Pensive was for planning a job. Once it was underway, Julius kept everything running with brutal efficiency. It was one of the reasons I trusted him with my life.

"We still don't know if she has anything to do with the job," he said. "We don't know anything about her."

Blaze spoke up from behind me. "She was pretty cagey. Most people wouldn't argue about getting help after a crash like that. But she might have been nervous about the whole stolen car thing or whatever made her steal the car."

He glanced at Garrison. The two might squabble in their bantering way a lot, but Blaze knew as well as the rest of us that the youngest member of our crew was the best at reading people. That was one of the reasons we'd brought him on.

"She definitely didn't want anything to do with us," Garrison said, slouching back in his seat and shaking some of the rain off his pale shaggy hair. "She was nervous, avoiding questions, and more worried about getting away from us than her injuries. But none of that tells us anything for sure." He paused. "Why don't we turn her over to the client and let *him* sort out this shit?"

"If it turns out we missed something important

regarding her, dropping her in the client's lap isn't going to look good for our reputation," Julius pointed out. "We need to understand exactly how she fits into this situation before we can handle her properly. And she *wasn't* on the manifest. Whatever else she's gotten mixed up in, we wouldn't want to turn her over to the kind of people who'd hire us if she's got no connection to the mansion after all."

He frowned, lapsing into silence for another moment, and then said, "We'll take her to one of the safe houses and question her when she wakes up. She doesn't look like she'd pose much of a threat. Garrison, you can get just about anything out of anyone, and she'll be shaken up anyway. It shouldn't take long to drag the story out of her. Then we decide whether we need to end her or cut her loose."

Garrison opened his mouth and shut it again. I could tell he was both pleased with the praise, which Julius doled out sparingly, and annoyed at the diversion from our plan. "Fine," he said finally. "I'll get her talking, no problem."

Blaze had perked up. "When we've got proper lighting, I can take a picture of her face and send it through my app. Run any IDs she's got on her too." *He* never shied away from the opportunity to put his skills to use.

A prickle of uneasiness ran through my gut. This woman was an unknown variable—who knew how she might disrupt our carefully constructed operations? But that was the only emotion I felt about the situation—about as much emotion as I ever felt. I didn't react to things with the same energy other people seemed to, which meant I never totally trusted my own judgment when it came to dealing with other people, unless I was simply judging the most ideal way to kill those people.

Julius and I had been in this since the beginning, but there was a reason he was in charge and I was his right-hand man. Following his orders had never led me astray.

"Sounds like a plan," I said, starting the engine. "The nearest safe house is over on Grant St."

Julius shook his head. "That's not quite soundproofed. We don't want anyone hearing her if she starts making a racket. Let's go with the one on Carmichael Blvd."

I pulled away from the curb without another word. He was right about that too. The Carmichael safe house was a basement apartment beneath a house we periodically used for short-term rentals to make it look inhabited. There was no one in it now, and the basement was outfitted with plenty of insulation. Not even a scream would make its way outside.

———

When we reached the apartment, Julius carried the woman straight to the smallest of the three bedrooms. I understood immediately. As a basement, all of the windows were narrow, but our captive was pretty slim. None of us would have stood a hope in hell of squeezing through any of them except the main one in the living room, but she might have managed the slightly larger ones in the bigger bedrooms. This one was too small even for her.

The air in the place smelled stale, unused—which made sense, since we hadn't come by in a while. I was pretty sure I had a change of clothes stashed here somewhere, though. I could get out of the damp shirt and jeans when we were done with our initial inspection.

Julius flicked on the light and laid the woman on the twin bed, which was made up with sheets and a thin blanket on the off-chance that we needed to crash here some night. If we were sticking around until she woke up, I guessed one of us was taking the sofa.

Garrison patted down her wet clothes quickly, which was his usual role in the middle of a job, since he didn't generally get involved in the killing part. He let out a hum and pulled a few jewel-laden necklaces from one pocket, which looked expensive even to my inexperienced eyes. From her other pants pocket, he produced a wad of cash. He unfurled it and fanned it out. "There's at least three grand here. And those necklaces are worth maybe twice that much."

"Could be stolen like the car," Blaze suggested, shifting his weight eagerly on his feet. "No wallet or anything?"

Garrison grimaced. "This is it. Unless there's something in her bag."

Julius upended the tote bag onto the chair in the corner. Several more pieces of jewelry tumbled out, along with a small heap of clothing… and a worn stuffed tiger that looked as if it'd seen better days.

Garrison raised an eyebrow at that. "Cash, stuff that can be pawned for more cash, clothes, and a personal belonging. That paints a pretty clear picture. She was running away—from someone or something."

"Without any ID on her?" Blaze said, obviously frustrated that he couldn't work his computer magic on it.

"Could be whoever she was running from had it under lock and key," Julius said. "Take your photo of her face. You can still use that."

As Blaze got out his phone, Julius turned the woman so she faced the ceiling, her black hair fanning out across the thin pillow. Her face had come out of the crash relatively undamaged, only a faint bruise forming at one corner of her jaw.

Blaze tipped his head to the side with a skeptical look. "Not sure how much we'll get with this. People's faces take on a different shape when they're slack like that, and without her eyes open—but I'll see what I can turn up."

When he'd snapped his picture and started tapping away on his phone to set up whatever he needed to do in that app of his, Julius bent over the woman and started to ease aside her outer clothes with an analytical precision. "Let's see if anything else about her appearance can tell us a story."

As he uncovered her torso from waist to collarbone, baring everything except her breasts in their modest sports bra, Garrison sucked in a breath. I went still, staring.

Her abdomen was lean and strong with an array of muscles I could tell came from regular, intense workouts. But more unusual were the scars marking it: dozens of them, long and short, some cuts and some burns, darker or fainter depending on how long it'd been since the wounds had been dealt.

The largest one covered a section of skin about as long and wide as my thumb next to her belly button. A thinner but longer line cut across her shoulder, disappearing beneath her bra and showing on the other side where it crossed her ribs. The others dappled her skin all across her torso, many no bigger than a tiny nick.

Garrison let out a low whistle. "I could come up with a few theories now about *why* she'd have needed to run away."

Blaze glanced over, and his eyes widened. "Someone was messing with her on a regular basis."

"Or maybe she was messing with other people," I said, raising my chin toward her sculpted abs. "That kind of musculature would have taken years of hard, rigorous exercise to build. She isn't any wimp."

It took my body two years to become a mold of pure power and strength, with a lot of effort every day to maintain it. The girl before us could have been my smaller, feminine twin.

"She doesn't have any fresh wounds," Julius observed. "The blood on her shirt didn't come from her."

"Turn her over," Garrison suggested.

Julius did, and we all noted the newly forming bruises

that covered her right side where she'd taken the worst of the airbag impact. He was careful not to press on those and to move her injured wrist gently. Was he worried about her? It was hard to wrap my head around that kind of compassion when nothing like it stirred in me.

But then, you didn't need to feel sympathy to know avoiding further injury of someone who wasn't your enemy—yet—was the just thing to do. And if Julius followed any kind of code, it was for justice.

The woman's back was mottled with the same sorts of scars. I spotted at least one that looked as if it'd been from a wound so deep it must have taken weeks to recover from it.

What the hell had she been doing to take a blow like that? Or had she not been doing anything, just enduring abuse from some other party while she trained to get ready for her escape?

The form in front of me looked like both an opponent and a victim. I didn't know how to fit those clashing elements together in my understanding of her.

"Hey, look." Garrison leaned forward and swept her hair to the side of her neck, revealing a tattoo on the base of her skull just above her hairline.

We all bent over, examining the small shape. It was hard to make out much with it embedded under her hair. Garrison's attempt at uncovering it had still left it looking like little more than a blotch, vaguely circular with a couple of bumps protruding on either side at a diagonal. I didn't recognize the shape as anything meaningful.

"That's not any gang symbol I'm familiar with, as far as I can tell," Blaze said, "but I'll see if I can dig up anything on that too."

Julius tugged her shirt back down and rolled her onto her back again. We gazed at her in silence for a long moment.

Blaze lowered his phone, a sly smile crossing his lips. "If nobody else is going to say it, I will. She's fucking hot."

Julius rolled his eyes. "Not exactly a productive observation. Get on with your computer work."

Garrison stepped back too, but I thought I caught a glint of approval in his eyes when he looked her up and down one last time.

I hadn't let myself think about it while she'd been exposed, since we'd been focused on the business of unraveling the mystery she presented, but now, studying her leanly muscled form with Blaze's comment ringing in my ears, a twinge of arousal woke up in my groin. It would be something to fuck a woman that physically capable. To feel that strength moving against me in tandem with my own. Her face with its straight, sloping nose and high cheekbones was hardly difficult to look at either.

Not that I expected to have a chance to indulge that kind of urge with her. I only fucked women I didn't have to see again, who were completely separate from every other part of my life. This one had already gotten more entangled with my work and my crew than seemed safe.

Hell, we might still have to kill her. Anyway, I doubted

she'd be in the mood to be thinking about getting it on with anyone when she woke up and found out she was a prisoner here.

Julius motioned us all out of the room. "Go get some sleep while she does. I'll check over her injuries more closely and then do the same. We'll see what she can tell us when she wakes up to fill in all the blanks."

FIVE

Decima

THE AIR around me was clammy and chilly. Without opening my eyes, I reached for the covers at my side—covers that I must have kicked off while I slept.

As I moved my arm, a painful ache in my side worked its way into my consciousness. Then a jab of pain shot through my wrist. Why was I hurt?

A flash of Anna's bloody, pain-marred face passed through my mind, and my eyes snapped open. They stung for a moment until I blinked the tinge of discomfort away and focused my vision on the ceiling.

The paneled ceiling. The ceiling above my head in the household had been smooth and white—not *paneled.*

The previous night floated up through my memory—the attack on the household, my hurried departure, that oh so wonderful drive through the rain… and the crash. The men who'd supposedly come to my aid.

And then I'd blacked out.

But where had I ended up after that? This wasn't a hospital. No tang of antiseptic cleaner and sterilized surfaces hung in the air. It smelled of dust and stale coffee with a hint of masculinity.

I turned my head slowly, taking in the small, cement-floored room that contained nothing but a bed, a wooden chair, and a large rug. At least I could see properly now, the chemicals finally wiped from my eyes. Still, fear trickled through my chest. I squared my shoulders against it.

Fear was weakness. Fear would be the reason I got killed. There were plenty of other emotions—powerful emotions—to choose from, so I needed to pick wisely. Rage and vengeance were my top two options, but I chose the third, the one that had served me well many times in the past.

A cool, focused calm.

I pressed my left arm into the mattress and pushed myself upright, trying to avoid clenching the muscles that I knew would bring a deeper ache into my ribs. Even so, a groan slipped from my lips. I examined my right arm, which had been placed in a firm plastic brace as I slept.

Otherwise I was dressed exactly the same as when I'd left the household. I didn't look or feel as if anyone had violated my body. A quiver ran down my spine at the thought, but I dismissed it. No point in worrying about what *might* happen, only what was actually happening right now.

I released a long breath, my bruised ribs throbbing with the deep exhale. My gaze lifted to the door. My instincts urged me to run for it, but the trained part of my mind knew I had to play this smarter. Whoever had brought me here would be waiting outside that door, and escaping that way might be impossible, especially with a sprained wrist and bruised ribs.

Instead, I allowed my eyes to flick toward the window. It was set high in the wall, which confirmed what I'd already suspected from the smell and the floor: I was in a basement. A stream of sunlight seeped through the glass, offering a thin yet cheery light, but my heart sank.

There was no way I was squeezing my shoulders or hips through that tiny rectangle. I'd had enough practice at wriggling through small openings to judge it at a glance.

Shit.

I needed another strategy, and I needed it quickly. Did I have anything like a weapon on me?

I patted my pockets, thinking of the dinner knife and the shard of glass. My stomach clenched for a different reason. My pockets were totally empty. Not just of weapons, but of the rolls of cash and the jewelry I'd grabbed to fund my self-assigned mission.

How the hell was I going to track down the murderers who'd killed Anna, Noelle, and the others if I didn't have anything to pay my way?

I glanced around the room, but the tote bag I'd stuffed

the rest of my belongings and more jewelry into was nowhere in sight. My pulse hiccupped.

No, no, no. I had no money, no weapons, and injuries that'd slow me down in a fight. I had no one to turn to for help. I had nothing. Nobody.

Gritting my teeth, I took a deep breath to steel myself. I was Decima, protector of the household, and I'd get through this. I'd see my mission through.

But the first step in doing that was figuring out where I was and who'd brought me here. I wasn't tracking down any murderers while I was stuck in this room anyway.

Whoever had taken me, they'd stolen the loot *I'd* rightfully stolen. And it hadn't even really been stealing when I'd done it, since I was the sole remaining survivor of the household—everything left in the house might as well have been mine. Of course, what did I expect from the kind of person who'd haul an unconscious woman into a strange room somewhere?

I considered the window again, scooting to the edge of the bed. I should be able to reach it if I pulled the chair over—my ribs were going to just love that move. But even if I couldn't escape through that opening, I might be able to catch the attention of some passerby…

A click caught my attention. My head jerked toward the door. The previously locked door, judging by the rasp of a deadbolt shifting with the turn of a key. All my senses went on even higher alert. I tensed where I sat, preparing to fight for my life if I had to.

The door swung open to reveal a man.

A *massive* man. He stood several inches over six feet and ducked through the low doorway, a habit he'd likely developed after hitting his head a handful of times in the past. His dark brown hair, short and methodically cut, matched the scruff that covered his jaw and neck. Beneath the neckline of his tight-fit shirt, there were various places where tattoos peeked out from his brawny chest, though I couldn't tell what they were.

From the lines just starting to form at the corners of his eyes and mouth, I estimated he was in his late thirties. And he hadn't had the easiest of lives. The bottom of his left ear was ragged with missing flesh. I couldn't tell from this far away what'd done it, but it'd obviously been an unpleasant situation.

"How are you feeling?" he asked, his voice just as deep and gruff as I'd expected from his appearance. It was a familiar voice.

"You were at the crash," I said. The big guy who'd reached me first, who'd offered his medical training. I hadn't been able to make him out well enough between my blurred vision and the rain to recognize him on sight, but that commanding voice was unmistakable.

He nodded, taking a slow step forward. "That's why I'm asking how you're feeling. You collapsed on us, and we weren't sure what to do, since you were pretty insistent on not going to the hospital. I hope you can forgive me for not being willing to leave you lying in the road. We brought you back here, and I've patched you up." He nodded to my wrist. "It's just sprained, not broken."

"Fantastic," I said tersely. The sarcasm wasn't polite, but I didn't see any need to put on a friendly front with this guy. He was making it sound as if I'd fainted, but I hadn't *felt* dizzy beforehand. Had the crash caught up with me suddenly… or had he and his friends messed with me somehow?

But as long as he was playing the good guy, I could play along a little too. "To answer your question, I'm a bit sore but otherwise fine."

"That's good to hear. There wasn't much I could do for your ribs." His gaze traveled over my chest, but without any trace of a leer, and then back to my face. "I'm sorry— you must be pretty confused. If you didn't catch my name last night, I'm Julius."

The nickname I most often went by when dealing with anyone outside the household fell from my mouth automatically. "Dess." Sometimes I had other aliases for a specific mission, but Dess was my all-purpose public name, just a shorter version of Decima. Noelle said it was always best to have one you could respond to easily, naturally.

Julius moved another step closer, and it took every ounce of my willpower not to shoot forward and knock him to his knees so I could dash past him. If I even could knock him over. He was bigger and probably stronger than me, all my training aside, and I was in pain. I still didn't know what exactly he was up to.

"Dess," he said, testing the name—weighing it for who knows what. As he said it, he cocked his head to the side, and a flicker of deeper recognition sparked inside me.

Maybe it was the tone of his voice or the way the light hit the chiseled planes of his handsome face at that angle, but I had the abrupt sense that I'd seen him before. And not in a bad way. The tug of emotion inside me felt almost reassured by his presence and his authoritative stance.

What the fuck? I must have been more shaken up by the crash than I realized. I mentally shook myself and studied him surreptitiously. The sense of familiarity remained, but I couldn't place him.

It didn't matter. What mattered was figuring out his motivations: had he and his friends really been playing hero, or had they knocked me out and dragged me here for some nefarious reason? And if the latter, did that reason have anything to do with the massacre in my home?

"What were you doing there last night?" I asked abruptly.

Julius blinked and gave me a quizzical look. "We were heading back here after a party at a friend's house, and we saw you hit that telephone pole. We're not the types to just keep driving when someone's obviously in trouble." He paused and reached behind him to pick up something he'd left by the door. My tote bag.

My gaze tracked it as he held it up, my fingers itching to grab it. It looked as full as it'd been when I'd left, but that didn't mean it had anything except my clothes and that stupid stuffed tiger in it.

"We were actually wondering if you were in more

trouble than just the crash," Julius said, his voice dipping lower. Something about the assured baritone sent a whisper of heat over my skin that I almost... liked?

Focus, Decima.

Julius was still talking. "When we checked you over for ID to try to find out who to call to let them know where you were, we didn't find any, but we did notice this stuff." He pulled out one of the necklaces and then waggled a roll of cash. "And you've got blood on your shirt even though you don't have any cuts on you. What happened to you before you got into that car?"

"I don't really see how that's your business," I said, like a regular person who had nothing to hide but wanted their privacy would. Right? I didn't have enough practice at being a normal person to be sure, but the response felt reasonable. "Thank you for stopping and helping me, but I don't know you, and I'd really like to get out of here now."

Julius contemplated me, his gaze curious but penetrating. I met it, narrowing my eyes and daring him to question me further.

The way he effortlessly held my gaze drew up another unexpected feeling in my stomach that fluttered and multiplied. The strength that he exuded, both literally and with his mere presence, called to a part of me that had long remained dormant. This was a man who got things done.

But what was he going to do with me?

The question didn't unnerve me as much as it should. Julius folded his arms over his chest, and the movement brought up his sleeve to reveal a pointed shape that was part of one of his tattoos creeping over his bicep.

Were we playing some kind of game of cat-and-mouse where neither of us was showing all our cards? I still couldn't tell what his intentions were, and that made me hesitate to make any aggressive moves.

If this was a game, he probably figured *he* was the cat in it. Ha. I doubted he could possibly imagine how many men like him I'd taken down in the past several years.

Julius offered a casual shrug. "I just want to be sure we're not sending you out there into some kind of danger. It's hard not to worry, considering the state we found you in. Or maybe we should be worried about whoever you got this hoard from."

Oh, it wasn't me who was in danger. It was the people who'd massacred the household and made the grave mistake of leaving me alive, and when I figured out who they were, they wouldn't know what hit them. Every feeling I'd experienced as I held Julius's gaze faded, replaced with the same steady rage that would continue driving me until I completed this mission successfully.

If he wanted a story, I'd give him a story.

I blew out a breath as if I was frustrated with the situation. "Fine. If you insist on knowing—my boyfriend won that crap in some stupid poker game. He was so drunk he passed out, and I saw my chance to get away, and I just —I grabbed it and ran for it. Things haven't been so great between us for a while."

I swiped my hand across my face and looked down at

my shirt. At the bloodstain the rain hadn't quite washed out where a spurt of Anna's blood had hit the fabric. My mind leapt to the next explanation. "I get nose bleeds when I'm stressed sometimes. It must have happened while I was leaving without me even noticing it, and some got on my shirt. I don't know what else I can tell you."

Julius nodded, but his wary expression didn't change. Something I'd said wasn't lining up with his assumptions, and I didn't know how to fix it. Had I shown the wrong emotions for the story I'd given? I'd never had a boyfriend before, let alone an awful one. I didn't know what it was like to be someone desperate enough to take off on that boyfriend in the middle of the night. Maybe I should have tried crying? But tears didn't come easily to me.

I hadn't even cried for Anna, not really.

Julius didn't argue with me, though. He set my tote bag down on the chair. "We didn't find a phone on you. I'm guessing you don't want to check in with this boyfriend, but is there a friend or relative you were heading to that you'd want us to get in touch with? If someone was expecting you, they must be panicking by now."

I shook my head quickly. "I don't have a phone—he broke my last one a few days ago. No one knew I was coming. I didn't even know where I was going yet."

That last part was true enough that a twinge of loss ran through my chest and into my voice. Something shifted in Julius's expression.

He motioned to the bag. "Well, you can take that with you when you leave. I don't want to get in the middle of some domestic dispute. And by the sounds of things, you'll need that stuff."

Seriously? I resisted the impulse to snatch the bag up right this moment and kept my voice carefully neutral. "So I can go, then? The question period is over?"

"This isn't a prison," Julius said. "I *do* have first aid training from my time in the military, and in my opinion, especially if you don't have anywhere specific to go, it'd be better if you stayed here another day or two to make sure there aren't any lingering effects from the crash. Unless you're more comfortable with the idea of going to the hospital now?"

Would he actually take me to one—out of this room, into a place where I could much more easily escape him and his friends? I wet my lips and decided to call his bluff.

"You know, I was panicking last night and obviously not thinking clearly. I probably should get a doctor to check me out."

Julius stepped back toward the doorway without any sign of apprehension. "I'll take you right over there, then." He motioned for me to join him.

That easy, huh? Still wary, I stood up and reached for the chair to take my bag.

The moment I took a few steps, a wave of dizziness crashed over me. My head spun. I stumbled and banged my knees on the edge of the chair, grasping it with my good hand just before I fell all the way to the ground.

"Whoa, there," Julius said. He gripped my other arm just above my elbow and guided me back to the bed. My vision swam, my thoughts still jumbling with dizziness. "I think you'd better get a little more rest before you try to go anywhere. I'll get you something to eat—maybe that'll help you get your strength back."

He sat me down on the bed and walked right out of the room, closing the door behind him.

I pressed the heel of my hand to my forehead, but now I just felt exhausted. Whatever had happened to me during or after the crash, it was definitely worse than it'd seemed before I started trying to move around.

Didn't that mean Julius really should get me to a hospital fast? Should I insist he call an ambulance?

I couldn't focus well enough to decide what the smartest course of action was. One clear thought pierced through the jumble alongside a sinking sensation in my gut.

No matter what Julius had said, this room was essentially a prison, and if he decided he didn't want me leaving, I was stuck in it with no clear way out.

I'd rest all right. I'd rest and heal, as quickly as I could, and then I'd show these assholes that no one kept me caged for long.

SIX

Decima

I TRIED a few times to stand and approach the door, but when I nearly crashed to the floor on my third attempt, I waited until the dizziness in my head had faded. The last thing I needed was to approach Julius weakened and unable to defend myself if it became necessary.

It wasn't until the daylight outside beamed with the full brightness of mid-day that I managed to take several experimental steps around the room without wobbling. I tested my newfound strength by changing from my blood smeared clothes which were stiff from drying on me after getting drenched by the rain, into a fresh pair of sweatpants and a T-shirt from my tote bag.

When I felt confident enough in my ability to stay steady, I walked to the door. I clutched the handle with more confidence. Sure, my ribs hurt, and my wrist ached, but all of that was manageable pain.

Whatever needed to be done so I could get out of here, I'd make it happen.

I twisted the knob. It turned easily, no longer locked. Every nerve on the alert, I eased the door open.

The walls in this place must have been thick, because I'd only caught faint murmurs through them before, nothing I'd been able to decipher as words. The moment I peered into the wider room outside, a rush of sound washed over me.

It was an open-concept space, nothing but a kitchen island separating any part of it into specific zones. To my right, in the kitchen area, Julius was standing by a slim man with pale red hair who was talking animatedly while spinning his fork in a plate of spaghetti.

"But the size of that thing! It's not just a snake, it's a fucking green anaconda. Seventeen feet long! It'd eat you and a hundred snakes for breakfast."

"You've got to stop watching those documentaries," muttered another man who was standing beyond them by the stove. "Or at least quit it with the random fact regurgitation." His pale, shaggy hair sparked a sense of recognition—he must be the one who'd talked to me last night at the crash scene after Julius.

At the same time, a dull thudding reverberated from the other side of the room, catching my attention next. A fourth man, his shaved head gleaming under the recessed lights and lean muscles flexing over every inch of his body, was slamming his fists into a dangling punching bag in rapid succession. He stepped back, bouncing on his toes, before going back in for the metaphorical kill. His technique impressed even me, and I'd been practicing all forms of combat my entire life.

His lean, sculpted physique spoke of years of training too. Not just strength but discipline. The sweat dampening his shirt emphasized those planes even more, and an errant thought slipped through my mind: What would it be like to run my fingers over those muscles?

A flicker of heat tingled over my skin, and I yanked myself back to reality. What was it about these guys that kept pulling my head in ridiculous directions? I had a job to do, and as far as I knew, all four of them stood in my way.

I stepped over the threshold, and the door I was still holding squeaked. The room fell silent in an instant. The three men in the kitchen turned toward me, even the redhead pausing with his spaghetti-laden fork halfway to his mouth. The man at the punching bag lowered his arms and turned my way with studied precision. For a second, I found myself pinned by his icy blue eyes, even from ten feet away.

"Dess," Julius said, and my attention snapped to him. I kept tabs on the guy with the shaved head from the corner of my eye. Turning my back on any of these men felt like a dangerous game.

Julius smiled, subdued but warm, as if we were all

friends here. Yeah, right. "How are you feeling now?" he asked.

"Better," I admitted. That much would be obvious, considering I'd made it this far without tripping over my feet.

Should I ask to leave again? Apprehension held my tongue. They'd been careful about it, but it'd seemed pretty clear these guys didn't really want to take me anywhere. Were they just run-of-the-mill pricks, or did they know something about me and maybe even the massacre at the household after all? I had no idea how much of the story Julius had given me I should believe.

If I acted like I was in a hurry to get out of here, they'd go on the defensive. Better for me to study them a little and get a better sense of what I was up against before I made my escape, especially when I had injuries slowing me down.

"It's good to see you on your feet," the redhead said with a grin, recovering his previous exuberance. "Dess is an interesting name. I don't suppose you've got a last name too?"

I wasn't sure why that mattered, but I had my alias all lined up anyway. "Parker," I said briskly, and glanced around the room, the back of my neck prickling with the sense of having all four pairs of eyes still fixed on me. "You all know my name now, but I only know one of yours."

Julius raised his eyebrows at the others. The first to speak was the man by the stove. He flicked on the burner under a kettle and turned toward me. "Garrison," he said, raising a hand in greeting. Yes, that was definitely the voice I'd heard with the blond guy last night.

There was something unsettlingly perfect about his smile, as if he'd picked the exact right angle of his lips to convey friendly warmth. Maybe it was because the warmth he seemed to be conveying didn't match the irritated tone he'd spoken to the redhead with just a minute ago. He'd made a similar switch in attitude last night, hadn't he?

He looked to be the youngest of the bunch, early to mid-twenties if I had to guess, but there was something older in the steadiness of his gaze.

The redhead smiled too, but his grin was a little crooked and overwide, which made it feel more genuine. I figured he was in his twenties too, though closer to the other end. He glanced around at his companions. "I like her." Then he met my eyes, his own dark ones sparkling with curiosity. "I'm Blaze, and he's Talon," he said, gesturing to the man who had been pounding the punching bag moments ago, who let out a grunt of acknowledgment.

Blaze. That'd be easy to remember with that hair, which fell past his ears, nearly long enough that he could have pulled it into a ponytail. And Talon... I couldn't think of a name more fitting for a man who looked built for mowing people down.

Julius had mentioned time in the army. The younger guys didn't look military-fit, but Talon was. Had he and Julius served together, maybe? The shaved head made it harder to tell, but I thought they were about the same age.

I didn't have a whole lot of experience with the lives of regular people, but it was a little odd for all four of them to be here in this apartment together, wasn't it? I took another careful step forward, putting on a smile of my own as if I was relaxing into their company. If I seemed to let down my guard, they'd be more likely to let down theirs.

"Julius mentioned that you're all friends," I said. "And roommates too, I guess? Or are you family or something?"

I doubted the latter, considering how different they all were in coloring and build, but it was a way to frame the question without outright asking, *Who the fuck are you and is this an attempted kidnapping?*

Well, maybe not just attempted considering I was here in their apartment with no definite way out. My gaze flicked briefly over to the windows. The one near the punching bag and another in the kitchen area were as high as the one in my bedroom, but big enough that I thought I could leap through one pretty easily... if I got the chance.

"We're kind of both," Blaze said, still grinning. "And we work together too."

Huh. "What kind of work?" I asked in a getting-to-know-you sort of tone.

"Landscaping," Julius said smoothly, and Blaze snorted as if something about that answer was funny.

"We're very good at it too," Garrison said, giving Blaze's stool a teasing kick. "Every place we work on we leave looking much better than before we got there."

I took in the amusement now dancing in Blaze's eyes and the other men's impenetrable expressions and wondered what the joke was. But at the same time, I couldn't help noticing how easily they interacted, building off each other's responses, even Talon nodding at Julius's statement. I didn't see that kind of camaraderie often.

I wasn't sure I'd ever felt it with another person myself. Even with Noelle, who I'd spent way more time with than anyone else, I'd always been tense around her, driven by the need to meet her expectations and the wariness of what would happen if I didn't.

No, she and I had never been *friends*. I'd trusted her with my life, but I'd still had my guard up, presenting myself the way I knew she'd want.

Would I ever get a chance to work with a team like this now that everyone who'd had a hand in raising me was gone?

An unexpected twinge ran through my gut. I swallowed hard, willing the bloody memories of the carnage away.

"I hope that taking care of me hasn't interfered with your work," I said, putting out another feeler to test their reaction. "I wouldn't want my stupid accident getting in the way of your job."

Julius waved his hand dismissively with the same assurance he'd had from the first moment I'd smacked into him. "It's no problem. We're on our weekend right now."

He was obviously the leader. The others followed his cues.

I tapped my lips. "Right. That's why you were out last night when you saw me get that fender bender. Where were you going?" Julius had already told me there'd been a party, but I wanted to see if his story would stay straight.

Talon moved closer with controlled strides that were closer to a prowl. He frowned as he reached me, his shoulders squaring and his cool eyes flashing. It was obvious what *his* role in the group was: the intimidator.

"I'd like to know what *you* were doing in that part of town," he said.

If he thought I was going to cower in the face of his flex of power, he had the wrong woman. I raised my chin and stared straight back at him. "I'm pretty sure I asked you that question first."

His voice lowered into something closer to a growl. "A lot of shady shit happens in that neighborhood. You're in *our* apartment—I think we have a right to know what we've dragged in here, even if you needed the help."

I bit back a snappy retort about how I hadn't asked for their help, and in fact I'd told them to leave me the hell alone. If they didn't know why I'd been driving that way, did that mean they didn't know where I'd come from either? Was it the cash and the jewelry they'd spotted on me that'd made them bring me here, and nothing more than that?

Julius had seemed to indicate that he was accepting my story. Maybe he would let me walk out of here if I said I wanted to.

Before I could decide on my response, Garrison walked over almost close enough to touch me, bringing a whiff of cinnamon and musk with him. "Okay, enough badgering her, Talon. She's been through some shit. Cut her a break." He turned to me. "Don't mind him. He gets a little overprotective of our space. I'm making hot chocolate—would you like some?"

Hot chocolate? An eager jolt ran through me so abruptly that it took all my effort to suppress my outward reaction. My mouth was watering in an instant.

I'd actually never tasted the beverage before, but my favorite part of every birthday was the chocolate bar that Anna would bring alongside my dinner. That was the only time Noelle had approved of the treat, saying it was all empty calories. And these guys had it lying around their apartment, just casually downing a cup of it here and there like it was no big deal.

"I would," I said, schooling my voice into a neutral tone. Might as well get one benefit out of this crazy situation. "Thank you."

Garrison went back to the stove. He set out a second mug, sprinkled a packet of powder into it, and poured boiling water from the kettle to prepare my liquid gold. Blaze beckoned me over to the stool across from him, which wasn't especially close to any of them and should allow me to keep all of them in sight.

I hesitated for a second and then walked over to take it. Better there than staying beside Talon the guard dog.

Even if that guard dog came with the most impressive set of muscles I'd ever laid eyes on.

I told that part of my mind to shut up and perched on the stool. Garrison poured a dollop of cream into both mugs and then set them on the island, one a little closer to me. He raised his to his lips, watching me through the rising steam. "It's just instant stuff, nothing fancy, but I like this brand."

As if I cared about fancy. It was *chocolate*—I was already sold.

It took all of my self-control not to shoot forward and chug the scolding liquid. Instead, with purposeful control, I curled my fingers around the handle and raised the mug as slowly as Garrison had.

My first sip nipped my tongue with a burning sensation, but the rich, nutty sweetness smoothed out the pain in an instant. Fucking hell, it tasted like heaven.

"Is it good?" Garrison asked with a glint in his hazel eyes that suggested he could already tell just how much I was enjoying it.

"It's great," I said, restraining my enthusiasm, and allowed myself a larger swallow. Some small piece of me asked in a very tiny voice whether it would really be so bad to hang out with these guys a while longer, especially if I could talk them into sharing several more mugs like this with me, and I told it to shut up too.

Talon ambled over, his gaze shooting daggers at Garrison. "Now that you have some fucking hot chocolate, do you plan on answering some of our questions?"

I narrowed my eyes at him, watching for his reaction. "I never asked you to bring me here. I don't think I owe you anything."

He scowled. "I think you owe us a little more of an explanation after we saved your ass."

Garrison clucked his tongue chidingly and shot me a conspiratorial smile. My hackles automatically went up again. Did he think he'd won me over just because I was enjoying what he'd poured in this mug?

"What I think my friend here *meant* to say," he drawled in a teasing tone, "is that we want to make sure *you're* not in any danger right now. Julius says your stash of money and jewelry came from a boyfriend? Is he likely to be out there searching for you?"

My non-existent boyfriend would probably have run screaming at the sight of just Talon's glare, but I wasn't going to prop up the guy's ego by saying so. I sipped my hot chocolate, distracted by a momentary swoon. A weakness, maybe. Delicious? Absolutely.

"Nah," I said, putting on a shudder as if remembering something that bothered me. "He liked to push me around when I was there, but he's probably too high to get much past the front door." I cut my gaze to Talon. "Yes, it's a bad fucking neighborhood. I grew up there. Is that a crime now?"

Often with assholes the best way to get what you wanted was to put them on the defensive. They weren't used to it. And the truth was, I felt more at ease talking to Talon with his body carved out of muscle and snarling face than Garrison with his kindness I couldn't help being suspicious of. At least with the guard dog, I knew where I stood.

"It's pretty strange that you don't have anyone at all you need us to call," Talon said, seeming unfazed. "No family? No job? All you've got is this man of yours?"

I bit my lip. I might not have any experience with romantic relationships, but I had plenty of grief and horror to draw on thanks to last night's events. "That's all he let me have," I said in a small voice, as if ashamed.

"You really need to let up on her," Garrison said to Talon, swatting at him, and turned back to me with a gentler expression. "The guy sounds like a total prick. Is it because of him that you've got all those scars?"

All those scars. A shiver traveled down my spine. "How do you know I have scars?"

I already knew the answer. They must have looked me over—including under my clothes—while I was unconscious. Had they *touched* me?

But somehow Garrison managed to look even more horrified than I felt. "Oh, God, don't get the wrong idea! While we were carrying you in, your shirt rode up a little, that's all. It was hard not to notice them."

For real? I couldn't put my finger on anything, but something about his demeanor kept rubbing me just a smidge the wrong way.

"Just answer the question," Talon snapped.

"Why?" I asked with the sudden sense I was being interrogated. The questions were starting to go beyond what anyone would be concerned about with a stranger who'd theoretically be walking out of their lives any minute now. "I already told you that you don't have anything to worry about. It's not like anyone even knows I'm here."

Which was the point, wasn't it? Why were all of them so intent on questioning me in their own ways? Sure, they may have been concerned about who they brought into their home, but if they'd actually been worried, they could have kicked me out right now. They could have dropped me at the hospital despite my original protests.

Unless they thought I'd done something worse than steal some crap from an abusive boyfriend. The massacre at the household must be all over the news by now. Had they realized I'd been coming from that direction, wondered about the blood on my shirt and my loot because of that?

Did they think *I'd* committed the murders?

SEVEN

Garrison

I WATCHED Dess cradle her hot chocolate. She seemed totally unaffected by Talon's relentless front of hostility. I'd seen people crumble under one of Talon's mere stares. This woman was a mystery, that was for sure.

I cut in again, tired of participating in a game that she seemed all too good at playing. The only reason we continued this good cop, bad cop routine was her reaction to *me*. Talon's threatening accusations didn't seem to get under her skin, but my gentle questioning did. I could see the way I unsettled her.

It was easier to get a read on how honest a person was being if their emotions were off kilter. I still couldn't quite pick apart how much of her story was true. I thought I'd caught flickers of genuine distress and shame in her expression, but was it a fraction of a larger trauma she was trying to suppress or a sign that she wasn't really all that affected?

"Where do you live in that neighborhood?" I asked. "One of us could go to your house and gather some belongings for you. If your boyfriend is as useless as it sounds like, I'm sure Talon or Julius could handle him just fine."

Dess scoffed, revealing nothing but mild distrust behind her storm gray eyes. Right now, they resembled steel—sharp and clear.

I had to cut through that steel in whatever way I could —subtle but penetrating, the way I always worked a job.

"You think I'd give away my address to four total strangers?" she asked, looking around and meeting everyone's eyes before turning her gaze back on me. Cold. Detached. Unreadable. Blaze shifted in his seat across from us but kept his mouth shut. He knew not to interrupt a gambit once it was in progress.

Talon stepped forward with the air of menace he gave off so easily, but I put out my arm, stopping him in his path. "Enough." I stepped around the island closer to Dess, my body language poised to be open and inviting. "We just want to help you, really. Even that lout does. But if you're still not comfortable, I totally get it. I'm not going to push."

Reverse psychology was absolutely a thing. In my experience, most people who'd balk at a direct question found themselves spilling the beans as soon as you told them they didn't have to answer after all, as long as you framed it right. Especially women, who were so often programmed to please.

Not Dess.

She stayed silent, her muscles stiffening as she turned her mug of hot chocolate in her hands and then took another sip. I couldn't suppress the twitch of my cock as I watched her savor the liquid, her tongue darting out to swipe the last traces from her lips, her expression briefly relaxing with apparent delight. She looked so damn sexy relishing the offering I'd made for her.

I shut down that twinge of attraction, just as she flipped the script.

"How about you explain why you brought me to your apartment instead of the hospital," she said, arching an eyebrow.

I didn't allow anything to show on my face. "Were we not allowed to be concerned?"

"I'm pretty sure a normal concerned person would have taken me to the emergency room."

Talon smacked his hand down on the island. "Now you're complaining about being here? You made it pretty fucking clear that you wanted nothing to do with any hospital."

"I think I also made it clear I wanted to be left alone," Dess shot back.

I held up my hands. "You can't expect us to leave a woman who's fainted from her injuries lying at the edge of the road. We're not some kind of psychopaths. Whenever you need to leave, the door's open to you.

Hell, we can take you to the hospital after all if you want."

Years of practice allowed me to smooth out the edge that wanted to creep into my voice. What kind of game was she playing with *us*? It was starting to feel like one, and I didn't like that at all. I was supposed to be the one who ran the games around here.

How the fuck would this look to Julius and the other guys if I fell on my face in the one job they'd given me today?

Dess adjusted her stance on her stool again, and I noted the drooping of her eyelids. I'd slipped a sleeping pill into her mug—she'd blame her growing exhaustion on the accident. The more physically helpless we could keep her, the easier it'd be to hold her here while we figured out what she was really up to without giving away that we wouldn't actually let her walk out the front door.

As soon as she figured out she'd essentially been kidnapped, most of my usual strategies would become useless. You needed to generate a certain amount of good will to con a person.

"I'm still thinking about it," Dess muttered. It'd clearly taken some effort for her to speak clearly. The pill was kicking in fast now.

I cocked my head with a sympathetic vibe. "You're looking a little wiped. You *are* still healing from that crash. If you need to—"

"I'm fine," she insisted.

I raised my arms in a gesture of surrender. "Again,

what you say goes. You know yourself way better than the rest of us do."

The line of bullshit I spoon-fed her didn't seem to loosen her guard in the slightest. The good cop, bad cop routine had gotten us nowhere. The kindness that I tried to show her hadn't had any effect on her.

For the first time in nearly a decade, I had no idea how to get a true read on a mark. She admitted nothing with her words or glances, other than a few tiny details that would give us no advantage.

The question ran through my mind again. Who the hell was this chick?

And why wasn't she pushing harder to get away from us? I'd been prepared for that, and she obviously didn't trust us any more than we trusted her... but she hadn't come out of the room demanding to leave immediately. She hadn't even taken me up on my supposed offer that she could walk away right now, although maybe that was because she could tell she wasn't in any state to make it very far on her own.

She took another deep swig of her drink, likely in an attempt to jar her into alertness. If anything, it'd have the opposite effect.

Her body started to sway, and her spine went even more rigid. She was definitely noticing that she wasn't at her best. I could read that much in her posture.

After taking one last gulp from the mug, Dess pushed herself to her feet. She held her legs tensed, managing to keep her balance despite the toll the sleeping pill must have been taking on her senses. "You know, maybe I do need to get some more rest. Thank you again for the hot chocolate."

"Get as much sleep as you need," I said, and Julius nodded.

She strode stiffly but quickly back to the bedroom where we'd set her up, just barely keeping it together. I still caught her teeter just as she reached the doorway. She kicked the door shut behind her.

I'd bet she'd flopped right down on the bed the second we couldn't see her. She'd been trying to keep up a front of being in control, but she'd be out like a light in a matter of minutes. Those pills were potent stuff.

Blaze started tapping away on his phone. Talon sighed, shaking the tension out of his stance and looking more like the imposing but not outright murderous guy he normally was—when we weren't out murdering people, at least.

Julius waited a few minutes and then went to the bedroom door. He opened it a crack. "Dess?"

No answer. He stepped inside, and I heard the rustle as he must have given her a shake. He came back out, shutting the door again, and rejoined us. "She's dead to the world. What did you make of her?"

My stomach sank before I answered. "I got next to nothing," I had to admit. "She's intimidated by kindness more than hostility, which might make sense if the abusive boyfriend story is true, but I couldn't even tell for sure about that. She didn't respond in a typical way to just about anything, but it was all in different atypical ways." I raked my fingers through my hair in frustration.

"Fuck." Julius rubbed his hand over his face, looking equally annoyed. And there was no one to blame but me. "Do you think she was lying about everything?"

"I don't know. If she lied, she's a *great* liar, but she didn't say anything in a way that screams 'truth,' either. It could have all been a lie."

"Or it could have all been the truth," Blaze put in.

"Yeah, that too."

Talon didn't seem to react to the news, which was par for the course, but both Blaze and Julius looked uneasy.

"At least we know her full name now," Blaze said, turning back to his phone. "Here we go. Dess Parker. It's pretty uncommon, I think—yeah, there's her driver's license photo."

He showed us the image on his screen, which was unmistakably the woman currently sleeping in the other room, maybe a year or two younger. I was hit by a jolt of surprise. Somehow I'd assumed she'd given us a fake name.

"Twenty-two years old," Blaze said, flicking through the various files he'd brought up. "No criminal record. Brief stint working for a clothing store downtown. Has a credit card that's always been paid off on time. Went to elementary and high school in the city but no sign of a college education." He frowned. "This is... this is weird."

"What's so weird about any of that?" I demanded.

"Lots of us aren't brainiacs who jizz at the idea of sitting through years of boring lectures."

Blaze rolled his eyes at me and waved his phone, his leg swinging in his usual fidgety way. "That's the thing. There's *nothing* remotely weird in here. It's all very basic, very typical... I don't know. It just feels too clean to me."

"Are you suggesting she's got an entire history of false documentation set up?" Julius asked with a tone of disbelief.

Blaze held up his hands in surrender. "I don't know. Nothing about any of this looks faked either. Usually I can spot a clue or two. I guess if she's been under a boyfriend's thumb for most of her adult years, she just might not have been interacting with the outside world much."

Was it really possible that we'd kidnapped an abused woman fleeing a monster, a victim who'd just happened to end up in the wrong place at the really wrong time?

Before that question could sink in, my phone buzzed. I pulled it out of my pocket and checked the ID. My back drew a little straighter. This might be a problem too, but it was a problem in my usual wheelhouse.

"It's the client," I said. "I'll take this outside."

Julius motioned me onward. He knew as well as I did that we didn't want to take any chance at all of Dess overhearing this conversation.

I went out the door and up the steps to the scruffy enclosed backyard. Julius and Talon had built an arching greenhouse-like roof over it which I appreciated year-round for the privacy it offered, though especially during the colder winter months. During the summer, we kept a couple of panels propped open and a fan going to circulate the air. The yard was still a bit sweltering.

As soon as I'd stepped outside, I cleared my throat, deciding on what persona I'd use for this call. I always dealt with the clients, and I never used the same voice or demeanor more than once. The less our clients knew about us, how many people we had working for us, and who those people might be, the safer we stayed. We couldn't work in the shadows if they knew much more about us than our group name.

I forced my voice up an octave. "You've reached the Chaos Crew."

"Put me on with the man I spoke to last time," the man on the other end demanded.

I suppressed a laugh at his stupidity. It had always been me. I could have transitioned back into the deeper, more masculine voice I'd used before, but he didn't have control over this conversation. I did. "I'm representing the Chaos Crew today."

"I don't give a fuck who's representing them. They didn't complete their job," he spat into the phone, and I stiffened. "Something is missing from the house that should have been there."

"The Crew killed every person inside that house, per the manifest, and they didn't take anything with them," I assured him. "It was a successful job with no hiccups."

"Did they find any hidden areas in the house that weren't mentioned in the manifest?"

"Are you implying that the brief you provided was faulty?" I asked. "I certainly hope you didn't put the Crew in danger by leaving out information."

The man remained quiet for a moment, giving me the answer that I needed. There *had* been information he hadn't included in the job details they'd passed on. It didn't matter what words he spewed to deny the claim after that telling pause.

After dealing with Dess, it was almost a relief to be able to spot the lie so easily.

"I gave you all the necessary information to ensure the job was completed successfully," he snapped. "But clearly you screwed up somewhere."

I wished I had chosen a more intimidating persona, maybe channeling Talon. Too late now. "Are you going to tell me *what* exactly was missing?" I asked. My thoughts darted to all that jewelry Dess had been carrying.

But what were the chances she was a thief who'd broken into a home, found a vicious massacre there, and decided to continue with her robbery like it was nothing? And why would the client be so worked up about some pieces of jewelry anyway? It'd been expensive stuff, sure, but he'd placed more money in escrow for the job than the whole lot would have come close to being worth.

"That isn't your business," the client said. "What matters is that it's gone, and you're the only people who've left the house in the timeframe."

Jackass. How did he expect us to help him if he wouldn't even explain what the problem was?

I let my voice get clipped. *"We deliver expertly orchestrated chaos.* Our motto doesn't lie. Your instructions were to kill everyone inside the place, and I guarantee that the inside of that house was a chaotic bloodbath when the crew was finished. Nobody escaped. Those were the terms, and they were met to anyone's satisfaction. And now you're accusing us of *stealing*?"

The man hesitated. "I'm not accusing your team of anything. But something *was* taken from that house, and we will be doing a close investigation to determine who was responsible. If we find that the Chaos Crew interfered in any way that was not outlined in the contract, there will be severe consequences. For the sake of your crew, I hope that you have nothing to do with this. We aren't playing Candy Land here."

I had a snarky remark at the tip of my tongue, but he ended the call before I had a chance to launch it.

I looked down at my phone, my forehead furrowing. We hadn't taken anything from the mansion. Hell, we hadn't even *touched* anything in the place other than our bullets and blades severing all those bodies—and me patting them down for weapons and phones after. As always, we'd followed each clause in the contract, and we'd completed the task with no hitches. Julius wouldn't tolerate anything less.

Well, there'd been almost no hitches. What could we call Dess?

EIGHT

Decima

IF THE FOUR men who'd taken me into their home were at all offended that I insisted on making my own plate at dinner—acting as if I didn't want to impose on them any more than I already was—none of them called me on it. I didn't intend to let any of them touch my food or drink again.

I didn't know what had made me so tired earlier today. It could have been an aftereffect from the crash. Or it could have been something funny about the hot chocolate Garrison had given me. He might have used its deliciousness to cover up something much more ominous.

I'd only woken up just before dinner, the smell of frying chicken and garlic making my mouth water. It seemed reasonable to eat when I could to get my energy up for my escape. I was increasingly sure that as soon as I pushed the issue, it'd come to a fight. I had to be totally ready for that fight, or I'd end up even worse off than I was now.

When I ducked into my bedroom after dinner, I tucked bills from the rolls of cash into my pants pockets, my bra, and even the waist of my panties—as much as I could carry without my cargo being noticeable through my clothes. I didn't want the men to have any clue I intended to make a break for it until the last second. The jewelry I'd have to leave behind, but it'd have been a hassle to pawn it anyway. Cash was simple and straightforward, like any good mission should be.

I lingered for a moment over my tote bag. Leaving behind my other change of clothes was no big deal—I could buy or steal more—but a strange sadness prodded my chest when I thought of abandoning the stuffed tiger.

Ridiculous. It wasn't as if I could stuff *that* in my bra and have no one notice. A fuzzy toy wasn't exactly necessary to any of my plans.

I pushed the unexpected ache deep down inside me like the other random emotions that rose up now and then and ambled back into the living area, acting as casual as I could.

Four pairs of eyes tracked my movements the moment I emerged. I wasn't getting away with much at this exact moment. I'd need to examine the door and the windows more closely and position myself when I asked about leaving so I could spring for my best escape route as soon as they showed their hand.

For the time being, I sat down on the sofa in front of the TV and groped around for the remote. There *had* to be information about the murders on the news, right? Maybe I'd hear something that would help my mission, like potential suspects or evidence police had uncovered.

I turned the TV on and flipped through the channels, watching for a newscast. I hadn't actually watched the news often. The broadcasts never showed up on my TV in the household, and whenever I'd been in the middle of an assignment and had access to a TV, channel surfing had felt like an unprofessional distraction.

Even now, as my finger tapped the button, Noelle's voice echoed in the back of my head. *When you're on a mission, nothing matters but that mission. Keep your eyes on the prize.*

The muscles in my hand twitched, and I almost put the remote down. But looking for news *was* part of my current mission, even if Noelle hadn't assigned it to me. I wasn't getting to the prize of destroying the people who'd slaughtered the household until I knew more about them.

Blaze plopped down on the sofa a couple of feet across from me. "Planning to watch anything in particular?"

"I feel like I've been out of touch for days," I said. "I figured I'd check the news and see if I missed anything important."

"Ah, you want channel 26, then. All news, all the time." He grinned.

I tapped in the numbers, and the screen immediately flashed to a view of some kind of political press release room. The newscaster's voice droned over the visual. "The surprising outcome of Bill 401 is sweeping through the nation. Damien Malik, with the tie-breaking vote, sent this historic bill into effect. Now, we as a nation must ask ourselves: What does this mean for us? We can expect—"

We could expect me not to give a shit. I leaned back, waiting for the story to switch.

Over the next half hour, the reporters covered a business merger, an overseas military operation, some storefront vandalism, and a rabid raccoon. Apparently all of those things were more pressing than a dozen people brutally slaughtered in their home. I frowned at the TV. They *were* going to get to the household eventually, weren't they?

"If you're looking for something specific, you could borrow my laptop," Blaze offered, gesturing to the computer on the coffee table.

I eyed the device and then glanced at the man beside me. I'd rarely had unrestricted access to a private computer, but I knew that one internet search could bring up thousands of results. But should I be suspicious of his motives?

"If you wouldn't mind," I said.

He snatched it up before I could reach for it myself and handed it over with one of his wide smiles. "Anything for a pretty lady."

A prickle ran down my spine at the flirty compliment, but he didn't move any closer, and his tone was more playful than… than the low, sweet tones in my memory that made my hackles come up. I smiled back mildly, containing my adverse reaction, and opened the laptop.

Sliding over on the sofa, I tucked myself into the corner and surreptitiously angled the screen so none of the men in the room should be able to see it. Then I quickly typed in the city name and the word "massacre."

Nothing came up except a couple of results about a short story competition years earlier where one of the winners included that word in the title. Was I being too poetic about it? I switched to the more basic "murders."

That got me a bunch more articles, but none of them were from the past couple of days. Knitting my brow, I found the option to sort by date, but that didn't help either.

What the hell? How could no one have reported on this yet? Had nobody noticed the carnage after a whole day?

I guessed it was possible. I had no idea how much the people in the household normally interacted with anyone outside, who might have come by in the past twenty-four hours and discovered the bodies. But still...

An apprehensive twang ran through my nerves. It didn't feel *right*. And my instincts were honed by years upon years of experience with dangerous situations.

"If you're having trouble finding something, I'm happy to lend a hand," Blaze said in the same light tone. "Not to brag, but I can track down just about anything on the internet. And it'd be a pleasure to be of service." He winked at me.

Another unwelcome shiver shot down my spine. Where was he trying to take this?

"That's all right," I said. "I can manage."

I'd braced for another overture, but he just shrugged, still smiling and got out his phone. He might have liked attempting to flirt, but he didn't seem to be all that committed. My pulse stopped thumping quite so fast.

It was fine. He wasn't like—like the one who'd—

I shoved that thought aside before my gut could completely clench up and studied the screen again. Maybe if I modified by region? Tried a different word like "killings" or "slaughter"? I even added "household" to the string, as if the people who'd trained me were likely to use that term with anyone outside our home.

Nothing relevant popped up for any of that. I sucked my lower lip under my teeth, just barely restraining myself from giving in to the urge to nibble at it—a bad habit Noelle had badgered me about for years. I hadn't hidden my reaction quite well enough, though.

Garrison sauntered over to the sofa, stopping behind Blaze but watching me. "You look awfully bothered by what you're seeing, Dess."

He had more snark in his tone than concern. I contemplated him as my fingers moved over the keys through the processes I'd learned to clear my search history. As perfect as his kindness earlier had been, it'd vanished in the time I'd been asleep, so I had to assume he'd been faking that reassuring persona. I couldn't tell if this was the real him or some other front he was putting on, though.

Well, if he liked to snark, let's see how he reacted to having it thrown right back at him.

"What, your face?" I retorted, looking him over. "I imagine you get that reaction a lot."

That couldn't be less of the truth, and he probably knew it. The sandy blond hair that fell in tousled waves gave him a beachboy vibe, and the rest of him—broad shoulders with an understated strength that wasn't as spectacular as Julius's brawn or Talon's sculpted form but more impressive than the average guy—wasn't exactly hard on the eyes either.

And when his lips curled with a hint of a smirk, a flicker of adrenaline shot through my system that wasn't entirely unpleasant.

"You'll be comforted knowing that my face has never been called bothersome before," he said.

I raised my eyebrows as if in disbelief. "I guess your company hasn't been very honest with you, then."

Blaze cut into our conversation, leaning forward and reaching for the laptop. "What *are* you looking up?"

"Nothing now." I tossed it back to him and got up, stretching my arms as if I was bored with the conversation but taking the opportunity to meander a little closer to the door.

The second Blaze flipped open the laptop, my gaze darted to him. He aimed one of those bright grins at me as if he was enjoying showing off. "Easy enough to find out for myself."

Wait. He couldn't—

But he was tapping away on the keys, his gaze sharpening into an intentness I'd only witnessed briefly before. Cold fingers clamped around my stomach. All at once, I was sure he could dig up my searches no matter how thoroughly I thought I'd erased them.

If he found them, he'd know where I'd really been last night. Or at least that I'd been involved in something much more horrifying than a spat with a cruel boyfriend.

Whether these men knew more about the massacre than they'd let on or not, I was screwed. If they *did* know about them, I was super screwed.

I backed up a step, my pulse racing twice as fast as before. This wasn't how I'd meant things to go.

"Here we are," Blaze said cheerfully, and then his eyebrows drew together. His gaze leapt to me with a look that was unmistakably startled—and far too knowing.

Shit.

Pure instinct, driven by panic and self-preservation, sent me bolting toward the front door. A shout went up behind me. Talon charged after me. He reached me before I made it there, snatching my arm and spinning me around.

Thankfully, he'd grabbed my injured side, leaving my fully functional arm free. My well-honed body leaned into the momentum and jabbed my opposite elbow into his face. He dodged that blow only to step straight into the path of my ramming knee.

I caught him in just the right spot that pain spasmed in his expression and his grip on my arm loosened. Not much, but enough that I could yank free.

Julius had already moved to block my way to the door. With a fresh burst of adrenaline thrumming through my veins, my gaze locked on the nearest window, in the kitchen area. I hurtled toward it, ignoring the throbbing that was already spreading through my bruised ribs at the exertion.

I leapt onto the counter without breaking stride and flipped over to slam both my heels into the glass. It didn't budge. *Come on.* I whipped my feet toward it even harder, and with a cracking sound, a line formed down the middle of the pane.

Before I could shatter the glass completely, two pairs of hands clamped on my body and dragged me off the counter.

I flailed out with my good hand, my elbows, my knees, and my feet, all seeking the most vulnerable spots I could strike. The throbbing in my side expanded into a piercing agony that made my breath catch, but I couldn't afford to stop. In my line of work, stopping usually meant dying.

My knuckles caught Talon in the throat. One of my knees clocked Julius across the cheek so hard he grunted, and his hands shifted. I tried to squirm free, intent on making it back to the window and the small hope of freedom it offered.

But the stomp of my foot into Talon's calf, hard enough to fracture bone on a good day, landed weaker because of the pain searing through my torso. I had an opening when I could have gotten a stranglehold on Julius and maybe even broken his neck—but on my bad side, where my wrist screamed the second I swung it into action.

I let out a grunt of my own, my focus wavering, and Talon slammed his taut arms around me from behind. He pinned both of my arms to my sides in an iron grip. I pushed and flailed against him, but he managed to hold me so my heels only clipped his legs without doing any real damage while my ribs felt as if they were stabbing right into my lungs.

"Nice try," he grumbled in my ear, "but you're not going anywhere."

He swiveled me to the side just as Garrison shoved a wooden chair with wide arms into place next to us. Talon shoved me into it, using his knee to hold my legs down, bracing my forearms against the arms of the chair. All I could move was my head, and his was too far away for me to butt it, as much as I'd have liked to right now.

He wasn't just strong. This asshole knew how to fight —*really* fight. But if I hadn't been injured...

I met his eyes with a glare, and he gazed back at me with no sign of anger or even irritation. Suddenly I was sure even his supposed frustration with me this morning had been as much an act as Garrison's kindness. His pale blue irises held nothing but cool indifference, like this was just a job to him rather than a matter of survival like it was for me.

I should have been chilled, but the sight woke up something else inside me. I was abruptly hyperaware of the flexing of his hands against the bare skin of my arms, of all the power emanating from his pose over me. Of how close he was leaning—not close enough for me to launch another attack, no, but enough that his breath grazed my face with each exhale.

He was breathing a little raggedly. As strong as he was, I'd given him a challenge even with my injuries. And he'd given me a hell of a challenge too.

An unexpected heat pooled between my legs, a sensation I'd never felt before except when I touched myself there. The image passed through my mind of him leaning even closer, pressing all of that sculpted power right against me, and I didn't shy away from it. If anything, my body welcomed the idea.

I'd never wanted a man before. Except maybe that one —for the short time before I'd realized the poison that lay behind his sweet words. Talon wasn't like that at all. He was pure, brutal strength, on display without excuses or any kind of veneer, and something about that called to the deepest part of me.

As Talon stared down at me, I thought something shifted in his gaze—a flash of what I almost imagined was his own arousal. Then Julius strode into view, holding several plastic ties in his hands, and I jolted back to my horrifying reality. I was a captive here, way more so than I'd been a few minutes ago.

The leader of the group wrapped the ties around my wrists and then my ankles, binding me to the chair. He tugged the plastic strands tight enough that they bit into my skin—or in the case of my wrist in the brace, enough to make the sprain ache. He wasn't going easy on me, that was for sure.

As soon as the restraints were in place, Talon stepped back—and pulled out a pistol. I hadn't even been able to tell he was wearing one. He pointed it at me, aimed straight at my forehead, his expression back to its impervious blankness.

No matter what other feelings I might have briefly stirred in him, I had no doubt that he'd put a bullet in my brain without a second's hesitation.

Garrison stood next to him, his arms folded over his chest. Blaze came up at Talon's other side, his laptop still open, clutched in his hands, carrying the evidence I'd inadvertently provided him with.

Julius stepped back from the chair, swiping his hand across his cheek. A bruise was already purpling the skin there. I held in a smile of satisfaction. If I was going to go down, at least I'd left a mark on these pricks.

When he spoke, Julius's voice was hard and unrelenting. "It's time that you tell us exactly what you were doing last night."

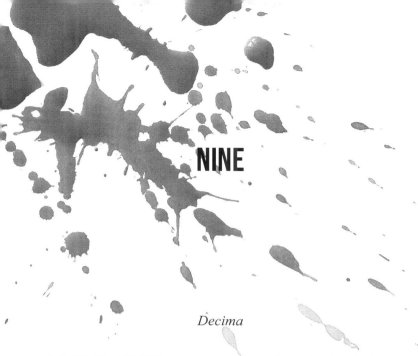

NINE

Decima

AS THE FOUR guys stood around me in the kitchen, their silence ate away at my confidence. Talon had a gun, Julius and Garrison both looked ready to kill me first and ask questions later, and Blaze... well, Blaze looked excited, bouncing his weight from foot to foot.

I should have strategized or, at the very least, taken a moment or two to *think* rather than making a kneejerk response. Noelle preached to always act, never react. Maybe I could have come up with some excuse to buy me more time to make a proper run for it. Maybe I should have known not to use the laptop at all, realizing Blaze would be savvy enough to crack the typical protections.

My jaw tightened as my frustration with myself and the situation I'd gotten myself into grew. I'd made too many poor decisions within the span of a few minutes, and those decisions could have deadly consequences.

"Are you going to say anything?" Julius asked, his voice taking on an even more commanding tone.

Would they torture me? I couldn't tell how far these men would go for the information they wanted. I cleared my throat and allowed my lower lip to tremble.

"Don't you fucking dare," Garrison said sharply, and my eyes shot up to meet his. "We're not going to fall for waterworks."

I couldn't suppress the feeling that my entire life—everything I'd ever been trained to do—had been for nothing. It didn't matter now. I was tied to a chair, a gun pointed at my head, and I might never get my chance to avenge the household.

Garrison might not be buying the innocent act, but that didn't mean the others wouldn't be swayed. In my experience, few men were totally unaffected by a woman in tears, one way or another.

"I don't know why you have me here," I said, willing a quaver into my voice. "Please."

"How did you know about the murders?" Blaze asked, pointing to the laptop's screen.

"I don't—"

"Don't fucking lie to us." Julius leaned over my chair, bracing his hands next to my elbows. His tone refused any argument, deadly serious. "There's no way in hell some regular woman off the street knows how to fight like you just did. So don't try to pretend that's what you are."

His aura of authority wafted over me, and a tingle ran across my skin. I had the ridiculous urge to rise up to meet him, to soak up all that commanding confidence. I couldn't remember ever being in the presence of a man who wielded more control than he could with just a few sentences.

But I couldn't let him control me, even if some stupid part of my brain was swooning.

His eyes, blue like Talon's but a much deeper shade, held mine unwaveringly. I had the unnerving sensation that he could read what was going on inside my skull. That he might even be able to sense the way my panties had just dampened, damn them.

I sure as hell hoped not.

"You don't have anything to say for yourself?" he asked.

Since silence wasn't working, I tried turning his cool confidence back on him. "I don't owe you answers any more than I did before," I replied, hardening my expression. "Even less now, really. Am I supposed to trust you after you tied me to a fucking chair? Dream on."

Blaze let out a low whistle, and Garrison shot a glare at him.

To my surprise, Julius straightened up. His expression shifted from menacing to contemplative.

"You make a fair point," he said. "We're asking a lot from you. So maybe it's only fair that we explain a little more about why we're asking these questions at all. But what I'm going to tell you could put our jobs and our lives at stake. Once I've told you, we can't let you leave until we're sure of *you*."

Interesting. I arched my eyebrows at him. "Since it doesn't look like you have any intention of letting me leave anyway, I'll take that deal."

The corner of his mouth twitched—with the start of a smile or a frown? I couldn't tell, he smoothed it out so quickly. The man had iron control over himself as well as everyone around him.

"All right then." He tipped his head toward the other men. "It's possible you've already guessed that we're not actually landscapers. We're cops, and right now we're investigating a horrific murder spree that took place in a house not that far from where you had your accident last night. Actually, we saw you while we were on the way to the scene of the crime after a neighbor called in a report of hearing gunshots fired."

A little of the tension in my chest loosened. "You're with the police?" That fit a lot of what I'd observed about them that hadn't made total sense before. And if it was true, it also meant that I was a little safer than if they'd been mass murderers or some other kinds of psychopaths themselves. Cops could still push people around, and from what I'd learned in my training, you couldn't trust any of them not to be dirty, but there were limits on how violent they were likely to get.

They might happily toss me in jail and throw away the key, of course. My situation was still pretty freaking shitty.

"Undercover detectives," Julius clarified. "We caught

you speeding away from the scene of what turned out to be a major crime, with blood on your shirt and what looked like stolen goods on you. And when we ran the plates on that car and contacted the owner, it turned out it'd been stolen—from someone you've never mentioned in your stories. Understandably, we couldn't let you just wander off."

They'd known about the massacre and the stolen car the entire time I'd been here. Somehow I wasn't surprised. I did have to point out, "I'm pretty sure kidnapping is still illegal no matter how many badges you have."

Garrison didn't look quite so peeved anymore. His lips curved into a cocky smile. "When you're undercover, you don't have to follow the rules quite so closely."

I drew my gaze back to Julius, since he was the one in charge. "Why didn't you tell me all this to begin with? Why make up all those other stories?"

"A lot of people in trouble freeze up when they're around cops," Julius said. "We wanted to see if you'd let anything slip when you weren't on your guard. Obviously that hasn't worked out so well. So here we are." He paused. "We have reason to believe that the perpetrators of those murders are still on a rampage, looking for something they expected to find in the house but didn't. Seeing as you had all that fancy jewelry on you, you might be not just connected but another target as well."

I kept my expression impassive, but inside I itched with confusion. If the murderers had been looking for the jewelry I'd grabbed, why wouldn't they have taken the stuff before they'd left? They'd been gone by the time I did my search of the house. It wasn't as if the stuff I'd taken had been hard to find.

But then, just because these guys were cops didn't mean they had everything right. He might have completely made up that part in the hopes of intimidating me into spilling my guts.

"You obviously have *some* connection to the murders," Blaze piped up, his usual energy almost subdued as he studied me. "Your searches prove it. You were trying to find news on a massacre that happened in this city in the past twenty-four hours. There haven't been any other murders in the past three days, and this situation hasn't been publicized yet."

"Yeah," Garrison said, raising his chin. "There's no way you could know about it unless you had an inside scoop. So why don't you get on with explaining yourself, now that Julius has laid everything out for you?"

I wet my lips, absorbing all the new information *they'd* given me. I couldn't tell them the truth—that was out of the question. But I had to tell them something they'd believe. Something that wouldn't set me up for jail time.

I could easily retract some lies and replace them with new ones. Now that so much more was out in the open, I could concoct a ruse that better fit the circumstances—one that nobody would suspect.

And now that I knew who they were, maybe I shouldn't be trying to leave. They were cops with access to police resources—things like running plates, which I couldn't have done on my own. And they'd already made progress toward identifying the murderers. If I stayed with them, I'd get information that I wouldn't be able to find on my own.

It'd be awfully useful to have two strong fighters, a tech genius, and a skilled manipulator doing a bunch of my legwork for me. Noelle always taught me to utilize every available advantage. This could be a *huge* advantage. They might lead me right to the perps, and then I could deal out my own brand of justice.

"Will I go to jail for stealing?" I asked, letting myself nibble at my bottom lip so I'd appear anxious.

Julius shook his head, pulling a second chair in front of me and sitting with his legs spread wide. "We handle bigger matters. We don't give a shit about petty crimes."

"You won't report it?"

"We won't."

I didn't necessarily believe them, but if they tried to prosecute me later, I could deny this conversation had ever happened. I nodded slowly, compiling a story out of details I'd used on various jobs in the past, tweaking it to fit the unique situation.

"I did go to the house where the murders happened," I whispered. "Looking back, I wish I hadn't, but I can't change it now. One of my friends lives—*lived*—there, and she said I could come and stay whenever I needed somewhere to go."

"Why did you want to stay?" Julius asked.

I forced a pained look into my eyes. "I know you saw

some of my scars. I didn't lie about having a boyfriend with a temper."

Julius motioned for me to continue. "So you went to the house to escape him?"

I dipped my head, a piece of hair falling into my face. "Yes. I'd finally worked up the courage—I was going to hide out there until I figured out how to get my own place where he wouldn't find me—but I didn't know what had happened there until I got inside. My friend's parents didn't like me, so I always snuck in by going over the wall and through the back door. I slipped inside last night, and that's when I found… that's when—"

The sadness that filled my voice as I envisioned Anna gasping for air was no act. I cut myself off, my throat constricting. My mind flashed to the faceless woman who could have been Noelle, and the sense of loss deepened.

"Your friend's name?"

"Anna," I said, because it was easier to sell a lie when you mixed some truth into it. "She—she was dead with the rest of them."

Julius's brow furrowed, his gaze unrelenting. "Your friend offered you a place to stay, so you went to her house, found her dead, and decided to rob her and her family?"

When he put it like that…

I ducked my head as if I was ashamed of myself. "I had nowhere to go. No money, and nothing but a bag of clothes. I didn't have a *choice*. My friend would have wanted to help me in any way she could, but she died.

What use would a few things have been to a dead person, anyway? I saw all that blood, all the bodies—and I just panicked. I hardly even realized what I was doing. I don't know what else to tell you."

"Then you stole a car," Garrison pushed.

"My boyfriend taught me how so I could help with some of the crap he was mixed up in," I said in a small voice. "I'm not saying I made great choices that night. I was in so much shock—but that's no excuse. I'm sorry I didn't explain all of this earlier, but I had no idea what you guys wanted with me. I wish I'd stuck around and called the police when I found them. If there's anything I can do now to help catch the psychos who did that, I'll do it. Anna and the rest of them—they deserve justice."

The men looked at one another, their expressions unreadable as they silently communicated amongst themselves. I could lie about my history and backstory all day long, but the truths I'd incorporated—the way I genuinely cared for Anna and Noelle, my determination to avenge their deaths—should have helped sell the story.

"It sounds like you've endured a lot," Blaze said before anyone else had the chance to speak, and a flicker of relief passed through my chest. He sounded convinced.

I only nodded weakly in response.

Julius was still frowning. "How did you fight us so well?"

Good point. Even held back by my injuries, it had to be clear that I was well-trained to men who'd done plenty of training themselves.

"Mixed martial arts starting when I was ten years old," I said with a shrug. "Competitive MMA when I turned twelve, added karate to the mix when I turned fifteen."

"Then how did your boyfriend manage to beat the shit out of you?" Garrison asked.

His insensitivity made my anger flare. "You're an insensitive prick, aren't you?" I snapped at him, the way I thought a woman in my circumstances might. "I got into training because I thought it'd help me—my father used to —" I shuddered. "But I guess it backfired on me. That's how I met my boyfriend—he was one of my instructors. He was always a little better, a little stronger than me."

The one benefit to my injuries was that I could hope these men hadn't been able to tell just how unlikely that'd be when I was at my full capacity.

"All right," Julius said. He didn't look particularly affected by my sob story, but he wasn't trying to pick it apart anymore either. I'd call that a win. He took a step closer, looming as he peered down at me. "We can't let you just wander off. Like I told you, we can't risk you compromising our covers. You could be a key component in our investigation—and it's possible the murderers are out for your blood too. You'll be safer with us anyway."

I glanced down at my wrists and tested my luck. "Are you going to keep me tied up the whole time?"

Julius did offer a hint of a smile then. "I think we can give you that much freedom. Just be aware that if you try to make a break for it again, we will intervene."

Something in his words cued Talon to put his gun back

in his concealed holster. Julius reached for the ties, pulling a knife from his pocket. I held myself totally still as the gleaming blade sliced through the plastic.

When my first wrist released, I swiveled my hand, loosening the stiff muscles. How much could I convince them to loop me in on their progress with the case? I had to work this advantage in every way I could while I had the opportunity.

"I might be able to help your investigation," I suggested as the tie around my wrist brace fell away and Julius bent down to tackle my ankles.

He glanced up at me, no less commanding when he was lower down. "How do you expect to do that?"

I groped for a reasonable proposition. "It was dark when I got to the house, and obviously I didn't stick around to pay a lot of attention to the place. Maybe if I could look around the property in the daylight, I'll see something that you all missed. I've been there enough times to have a pretty good memory of how it should be."

Julius let out a thoughtful hum. "We'll see. We've definitely had enough excitement today. Talon, take her back to her room for the night."

Talon moved forward to escort me. I leapt up from the chair and to the side before he could outright grab me. "I can walk on my own." I turned to look at Julius again. "And I *could* help you. I want the bastards responsible to rot in hell."

Julius didn't respond as Talon motioned me toward my bedroom. He might not be aiming his gun at me, but we both knew he had it on him. The other three were probably armed similarly. Gritting my teeth, I strode back to the bedroom one step ahead of him.

The second I walked inside, Talon closed the door behind me. Then came the unmistakable sound of the lock clicking into place.

They didn't trust me all that much, not yet. I'd just have to find a way to change that.

TEN

Blaze

EVEN FIRST THING in the morning at this time of year, the roofed backyard was hot enough to send sweat trickling down my back. I wanted to pace to let out my restless energy, but walking around only made the heat more uncomfortable.

Nothing was as uncomfortable as the tension between the four of us, though. I couldn't remember the last time that the Chaos Crew had been so divided in our opinions, but a pretty girl and an angry client seemed to bring out our different moral compasses.

"Toss her to the client, and let him handle the little thief. Wiping our hands of her will be the best thing we could do," Garrison said, shaking his head. "What's she worth to us anyway?"

"It doesn't matter what she's *worth,*" Julius said

evenly. "It's a question of what's justified. If we believe her story, then she barely had anything to do with the job. It might look worse for us to admit someone got past our surveillance to see the scene of the crime. And whoever hired us for the job, they're not likely to want witnesses walking around."

Despite what he was saying, I could hear the doubt in his words. Dess could be a threat to us as much as to the client, depending on how much exactly she'd seen. Julius put the security of the crew above all else.

"*If* we believe her," Garrison said in a scoffing tone.

"She hasn't acted as if she knows we had anything to do with it," I had to point out. Dess hadn't exactly warmed up to us in the past day, but we hadn't given her much of a chance to. She hadn't seemed scared of any of us—the opposite, really. I'd rarely seen anyone *less* nervous when faced with Talon's physical prowess and icy gaze.

Garrison grimaced at me, which meant he couldn't argue against that specific statement. That fact didn't stop him from going on, though. "You heard her. She stole from her friend after finding her dead. Do we really want a chick like that sticking around?" He took a swig from his morning mug of hot cocoa.

I didn't know how he didn't end up as wired as I was with all the sugar and caffeine he put in his system. The guy downed the stuff like an insomniac chugs coffee.

Talon grunted. "It didn't sound like she had another option. Desperate people do desperate things. But that applies to how she might act with us too. She's unpredictable."

Talon would go along with whatever Julius decided in the end, but he'd want to come to that decision quickly. The guy always preferred to deal with potential threats as swiftly as possible.

"Exactly," Garrison said. "And the client is breathing down our necks. If it's those necklaces and the cash he's after for whatever reason and he finds out we kept them from him, it'll be our heads on a platter. We're just seeing the job through."

What he said made logical sense. I couldn't deny that. But something in me balked at his suggestion anyway. The same something clenched up when I saw how pensive Julius looked as he rubbed his jaw, as if he was seriously considering Garrison's suggestion.

Dess had a quality to her that I couldn't quite put my finger on, but it intrigued me—maybe *because* I couldn't identify it. She wasn't like any other woman I'd ever come across, and I'd made the acquaintance of quite a few in my time.

I wasn't thinking just with my dick, though. She might have been mysterious, but I didn't think she was an enemy. She'd done what any of us would have done when trapped: fought to escape. Her story was tragic but understandable.

If we threw her to the client, he'd almost definitely kill her. How would we be any better than the asshole boyfriend she'd finally escaped?

I cleared my throat. "We all know what'll happen to

her if we hand her over. She's going to end up dead, and possibly tortured plenty before then. All because she ended up in the wrong place at the wrong time? I thought we only hurt people who deserve it."

"It wouldn't be *us* hurting her," Garrison said with a twitch of his jaw that indicated he wasn't as indifferent to Dess's fate as he was pretending. "Would you rather we handed ourselves over instead?"

The sneer in his voice would have raised most people's hackles. I knew it was just Garrison being his usual arrogant asshole self.

"Well, personally, I'm confident that I can defend myself if the client tries to pick a fight," I replied evenly, deliberately poking at him with the words. The implication was, of course, that *he* wasn't so sure of himself.

Garrison's eyes flashed, and his jaw tightened even more. "Why would we put ourselves in danger if we can avoid it?"

I shrugged. "What part of our code makes using an innocent girl as a shield an acceptable approach? Or are you in favor of throwing out the whole code now, just because she made you feel incompetent?"

"We *think* she's innocent," Garrison retorted. "Do we really know her?" At the edge that came into his voice, I knew I'd hit another solid blow.

It was way too easy heckling Garrison. He'd never drop his mask completely, but he couldn't put on a total front with us. We might not know all of each other's dirty secrets, but we knew the biggest one that mattered right now, the one we were all mixed up in. It was good for him to remember that.

Besides, Julius was listening. I was mostly talking for his benefit.

I shot Garrison a wide smile. "I think I know her better than I know you."

His mouth snapped shut. It only took him a few seconds to loosen up his posture, taking a deep breath and regaining his composure. "Then I'm doing the job Julius hired me for well."

"Enough," Julius ordered, raising his hands. We both fell silent, our attention turning to him. He frowned, and then tipped his head toward us. "We don't know how true her current story is. We also don't know if those necklaces are even what the client was worried about. Acting without information—or with the wrong information—is what screws people over. We'll take her to the mansion today and see how she reacts to the crime scene."

Talon frowned. "The client could have eyes on the place now."

"The client doesn't know who we are or what we look like," Julius said. "We can play it cool, just walking by. We won't stick our necks out too far, but we'll see what she gives us. If she puts one *toe* out of line, she's gone."

Garrison sighed but nodded. Talon rubbed his hands together as if he was ready to get going immediately. Relief coursed through me. I didn't know what'd happen to Dess after today, but I'd convinced Julius for now.

Which meant I had a little more time to figure out that intriguing part of her.

"Do we have any leftover pasta from dinner last night?" I asked, springing to my feet. My stomach had been growling for the last half hour, and I couldn't wait any longer. Carbs were the fuel for the energy I couldn't help expending even when I was sitting still—well, relatively still.

Julius's mouth curved into an amused grin. He gestured me toward the door. "It's in the fridge. We all know better than to get between you and your noodles."

I snorted and trotted down the steps to the safe-house apartment. When I reached the fridge, I paused, the door to the bedroom we'd stuck Dess in drawing my gaze.

Our guest deserved some breakfast too, didn't she? Although somehow I suspected pasta first thing in the morning wouldn't be to her tastes.

I strolled to her door and knocked, turning the lock in sync.

"What?" she said, sounding alert enough to reassure me that I hadn't woken her up.

I peeked inside. She hadn't turned on the overhead light, so the only illumination came from the small window at the top of the wall. Dess sat on the bed at the edge of the stream of sunlight, one leg crossed and the other pulled up next to it, providing her chin a place to rest. She considered me with obvious wariness. Her long black waves cascaded down her arms and brushed her raised leg, where her toned muscles showed through the fitted sweats.

With legs that looked like that, I'd fight for her to stay here forever.

"Good morning," I said. "I thought you might like some breakfast. Come out whenever you're ready."

Leaving the door open, I ambled back to the kitchen, dumped the garlic chicken linguine onto a plate, and shoved it into the microwave. By the time I'd finished tapping on the controls, Dess had emerged into the main room of the apartment.

She glanced at the other guys, who'd just come back in, and then at me. "I wouldn't mind breakfast. What are you offering?"

I'd already looked through the cupboards. Steffie updated our safe-house stashes on a quarterly rotation, so while we didn't have much of anything fresh on hand, there were plenty of non-perishable options. "Since I'm assuming you're not a weirdo like me who would eat pasta ten times a day if I could, there's pancake mix, frozen waffles, and a couple different kinds of cereal." We'd thawed the freezer milk for the latter yesterday.

Dess cocked her head. "Cereal sounds fine. Point me to it, and I'll get it out."

She'd learned to be cautious. Did she realize that we'd drugged her before, or was it force of habit? She'd still been shaken up by the accident when she'd accepted that mug of cocoa from Garrison yesterday.

I appreciated her sense of self-preservation even if it

worked counter to our goals. As the microwave beeped, I made a quick motion. "On top of the fridge. Bowls are in the cupboard beside it. Help yourself."

I grabbed my linguine, sat on a stool at the far end of the island, and started shoveling down my fuel, pausing to savor the first bite. I might eat it mainly for the energy boost, but I enjoyed a well-prepared plate all the same.

As Dess contemplated the two boxes of cereal and tentatively poured herself some of the nut-laced, not-so-sugary kind Julius favored, Julius and Talon drifted over. Julius took the cereal box after Dess finished with it, and Talon grabbed a smoothie he'd mixed earlier out of the fridge. Watching him chug it, I held back a grimace. I'd seen what he put in those things, and I'd sooner have licked the lawn out back.

Garrison sat on the sofa, watching us as he nursed the rest of his cocoa. Sometimes that was all he put in his stomach until lunch.

Dess perched on the stool a few feet over from me, braced toward the edge as if she thought she might have to spring off it at any second. I didn't need Garrison's skills with body language to pick up on the signs that she'd needed to be on guard a lot in her life before now.

She ate a couple of spoonfuls, chewing slowly and thoroughly. Her gaze dropped to my leg, which was doing its typical bounce against the rung of the stool.

"Do you ever sit still?" she asked, not with the snarky tone Garrison would have used but like she was genuinely trying to understand.

I'd spent my entire childhood being chastised for my restlessness, but I wasn't that kid anymore. I had better things to worry about.

I flashed her a smile. "Rarely. It helps me focus. All the energy I need to power this brain ends up filtering down into my body too, and I've got to let it out somehow."

She cocked her head again as she chewed. I liked the hint of playfulness that came into her face at that angle. "I guess that makes some kind of sense."

"About as much as Blaze ever does," Garrison had to remark. We both ignored him.

"I find many good ways to put it to use," I said, letting a teasing note come into my voice. I wasn't going to turn all my charm on a woman who'd just fled an abusive relationship, but a little light flirting couldn't hurt. Maybe it'd make her feel better knowing at least one man could appreciate her without beating up on her at the same time.

"Feeling better today?" I added. I took another bite of pasta and motioned to her wrist.

Dess let out a soft chuckle. "I feel kind of like I was hit by a small train."

Her tussle with Julius and Talon yesterday wouldn't have helped her healing, but she didn't sound upset about it.

"Not a large one?" I joked.

"A large one would have finished the job," she said dryly.

A laugh I didn't have to force tumbled out of me. Dess

didn't strike me as a woman who put much stock in being funny. She seemed like she lived a serious life with serious problems, but she obviously didn't let it get her down too much. I liked that about her too.

"Well, I'm definitely glad you didn't meet one of those, then," I said.

"No? It seems like I've messed with your job quite a bit."

"Aw, totally worth it to have a pretty face like yours around instead of only having these lugs in sight." I winked at her and gulped the rest of my pasta. Even a heaping plate always seemed to vanish so quickly.

Dess's posture tensed. Maybe I'd said something that'd reminded her of her boyfriend's comments. I chucked my plate and fork in the dishwasher and came back to lean against the island a little closer but not *too* close to her. "But hey, having a new voice with new thoughts in the mix is an excellent addition to the crew too."

She relaxed enough for a sly glint to come into her eyes. "Does that mean you've considered my offer to check out the crime scene and see if I can help?"

"That's Julius's call. I'll let him talk to you about that. But I can promise you that *I* have no doubt I'd enjoy your company."

She gave me a bemused look as if she wasn't sure how seriously to take me. "You hardly know me."

The words echoed Garrison's point—made with much darker intentions—so well that I had to counter it. "Well, everything I know, I like."

Just then, a strand of her hair slipped from behind her ear to drift across her face. I reached automatically to tuck it back, my fingers just grazing her cheek—

Dess moved so suddenly I didn't have time to so much as catch my breath. One instant I was touching her face, the next she'd lunged forward to shove me against the edge of the island, one forearm smacking the center of my chest and the other hand at my throat. There was no humor at all in her eyes now, only fury and... and something behind it that looked more like panic. The faintest tremor ran through her limbs against my body.

"Keep your hands off me," she snarled, her voice somehow soft and yet full of the promise of death at the same time. My pulse stuttered. All at once I was sure she *could* kill me in the space of a second if she'd really wanted to.

"Get *your* hands off Blaze, or you won't be around to have any opinions on what he does with his," Julius said with just as clear a threat in his tone. He'd whipped up his gun from where he'd taken a seat at the corner of the island, and he aimed it at Dess. Talon had drawn his as well. I couldn't see Garrison in my current position, but the click of a safety from several feet behind me told me that for all his snark, he'd leapt to my defense as well.

Dess jerked her hands back to her sides, with a wince as her braced wrist brushed her side. I stared at her for a moment before yanking my gaze away. The other guys gradually lowered their guns.

"I don't want him touching me, or any of the rest of

you either," Dess said tightly, her gray eyes smoldering like embers. Then she sat back down on her stool and picked up her spoon as if she hadn't just pinned me against the countertop like I was a fifty-pound child.

My throat didn't even hurt, but my pulse was still racing. Someone had definitely hurt Dess before—bad. But she had more capacity to deal out hurt than I'd given her credit for too. I swallowed hard and stepped away.

I'd spoken up for her. I really hoped that hadn't been the wrong call.

ELEVEN

Decima

IN THE MOVIES I'd watched that involved the police, they pulled up at crime scenes, flashed their badges, and strutted all over the place. But those were uniformed cops, not undercover detectives. It made sense that the men who'd essentially taken me prisoner would operate differently to avoid blowing their cover.

We circled the block in their car, with me wedged in the back between Talon, who didn't appear to care, and Garrison, who I caught flashes of irritation from, though he mostly kept quiet. They seemed to think it was better that I wasn't squashed too closely against Blaze after my demonstration of my feelings on personal space this morning.

It'd been an involuntary reaction. I was probably lucky none of them had shot me in the heat of the moment. I hadn't wanted to hurt him, not really; I'd only wanted to make sure he never touched me like that, with all those wheedling compliments and admiring glances, ever again. That he never stirred up the memories of a time when I *hadn't* been able to enforce those boundaries, and everything... everything had been horrible.

A ghost of that old pain trailed over my thighs, and I willed it away. It'd been years. It shouldn't have still affected me. Or maybe it made sense that it did, when it was the only real experience I had with getting close to a man when I hadn't been focused on how to kill him or someone around him.

Still, I could tell my reaction this morning had been an error from a strategic perspective. Blaze had been by far the friendliest out of the four men who were holding me captive. He was probably my best shot of getting the information I needed and getting away from them when the time came—if I hadn't just blown that shot.

He was sitting in the front passenger seat now, monitoring video footage of nearby streets on his laptop. From the little bit he'd said out loud to the others, I'd gathered he'd been able to hack into the city's street cams.

Whatever he saw on them, he seemed satisfied with it. "We're good to go," he announced without looking back. He hadn't met my eyes since breakfast, as if he thought I might get just as pissed off about his gaze being on me as his hands.

Julius parked a couple of blocks away. We all got out onto the sidewalk, Garrison scooting after Talon and me rather than going out the door on his side, I guessed to keep me consistently surrounded. Lovely.

The man in charge had already given us the drill before we'd arrived. We were going to walk past the mansion's front gate and around the corner to check out one of the side walls. Any more of a circuit around the place, and we'd look suspicious. We were all wearing sunglasses and baseball caps in a variety of styles to obscure our faces, not that anyone could see much of me while I had four men who were all several inches taller than me around me.

With the June sunlight searing down over us, the dark glasses only cut down the glare, helping my ability to make out details rather than hindering my vision. As we reached the edge of the household's property, I scanned the stone wall, the vines that clung to it here and there, and the street around us.

It looked like a totally different place from the shadowy estate I'd fled across two nights ago, but my stomach clenched as we came up beside it anyway. Images from the massacre flickered through my mind, and I closed my eyes. Julius turned to look at me when I slowed, and I almost shook myself out of it, but caught myself just in time. I was playing the part of a grieving friend. He'd be more suspicious if I *didn't* seem affected.

"Sorry," I said quietly. "It's just hard, being back here, remembering what happened…"

"If she's not up to the job—" Garrison started.

Julius cut him off with a sharp tone. "We're here now." He nodded to me. "If you see anything that sticks out to you, say the word. If not, we're no worse off than when we started."

I had a feeling he'd still be annoyed that they'd taken the risk of hanging out around a crime scene they were trying to keep on the down low if I didn't come up with anything. I *needed* to show them I was a valuable asset so they'd share enough with me that I could use them too.

I got my first break as we came up on the gate. My gaze caught on a small, dark shape on the pole just outside the entrance, tucked against the fixture for the electric wires.

"There's a camera there," I said, tipping my head as subtly as I could. "I never noticed that before. It's on city property, so it couldn't have been put there by Anna's family, but it wouldn't make any sense for the city to want a view of their front drive. Maybe the murderers put it there."

"Why would they do that?" Julius asked.

I braced myself for a snide expression, but his face showed genuine curiosity. Perfect. I shrugged. "I don't know. If it was important to them to kill everyone in the house, maybe they'd want to monitor the entrance to be sure no one got away?" I shot another surreptitious glance at the camera as we walked right past the pole. "It looks new, too. No bird crap on it like there is on the post around it."

Julius checked it out for as long as he could before we'd ambled by, equally careful with the angle of his head. "You have a point there. Good work. Keep going."

I couldn't tell whether they'd been aware of the cameras already or I'd pointed out something new, but the praise sounded as genuine as his earlier curiosity. Garrison was studying me from the corner of his eyes a little more assessingly, as if he was realizing he might have underestimated me. Yeah, I'd call that good work.

The perps had been good with their work too, but then, I'd already known that. After we rounded the corner, I almost missed the subtle telltale signs. When my attention snagged on them as I studied the wall, I peered closer for a few beats and then dropped down as if I needed to tighten the shoelace on my sneakers.

"What are you doing?" Garrison asked, but without quite as much snark as before. He couldn't help being curious too.

I suppressed a smile. "I just wanted to give you a chance to look too without it being too obvious why we're stopping. This works, right? I think this might be the spot where the murderers got onto the property. You can see a couple of places where the vine's pulled off just a little— that happens sometimes when I'm climbing over, but I was on the other side last night. And there's kind of a scrape mark on one of the stones near the top, just a small one."

"What makes you think that had anything to do with the murderers?" Blaze asked from behind me. I couldn't see his face, but he didn't sound as tense as I'd have expected speaking to me.

I straightened up, and we started walking again. "I could be wrong. It just seems pretty high up for it to have been someone simply bumping into it. And the vines would have grown back unless they were disturbed pretty recently. I don't think people were climbing into the property very often."

The scuff had also shown the faintest hint of the tread of a shoe, but showing *that* much perceptiveness might make these guys suspicious rather than impressed.

And they did seem to be impressed. A trace of a smile had touched Julius's lips. Talon let out a low chuckle. Garrison kept his mouth shut, which at this point I counted as a win. Blaze was tapping something into his phone behind me at a pace that sounded eager.

"You've got keen eyes," Julius said. "Where'd you pick up observational skills like that?"

Okay, so maybe he was impressed *and* suspicious. An answer leapt to my tongue. "I guess all the physical training I did taught me to think on my feet. It's a lot more than just strength and fitness, the instructors always liked to say. You have to anticipate your opponents' moves in advance as much as you can." That wasn't even a lie.

I hesitated as if embarrassed to admit the rest, which was totally made-up. "And, you know, living with my dad and then my boyfriend... I had to stay on my toes, keep alert to their moods and any clues about what they were getting up to so I knew how to avoid trouble as much as possible. Not that it helped me all that much in the long run." I ducked my head and rubbed my elbow.

The tapping behind me stopped momentarily. "You got away from them in the end," Blaze said softly, and it hit me that I'd been forgiven. At least by him. The knowledge sent a weird flutter through my chest.

Julius didn't argue with my story. I couldn't help pressing my advantage. I'd coughed up some intel for them—now they owed me.

"So," I said as we meandered on along the long stretch of the side wall, "do you have any idea *why* this happened? I mean, some of the people Anna lived with could be jerks, but—I can't imagine—for someone to kill them all like that... *She* never hurt anybody."

Garrison made a scoffing sound, his usual attitude returning. "I don't think you knew your 'friend' all that well."

"What do you mean?"

"All those people definitely weren't a family," he said in an almost gleeful tone, as if he enjoyed the possibility that he'd horrify me with his revelation. "And they were mixed up in all kinds of shady shit. Human trafficking would be at the top of the list."

"Garrison," Julius said with a warning in his voice, and the younger guy had the decency to look chagrinned.

I was too busy reeling from his comment to appreciate seeing him chided. Human trafficking? The household? In all the work I'd done for them and with my trainers, I'd never seen any hint of that kind of activity.

"That's ridiculous," I couldn't help saying. It must have been stories made up by our enemies, the ones we'd been working so hard to protect ourselves against. Maybe even the same pricks who'd ended up slaughtering everyone else in the house.

Garrison just grunted. I'd cut off the information supply instead of opening it up. I had to turn the momentum of the conversation around quick.

"If you think that, you must have found out a bunch about them and who they supposedly worked with or whatever, right?" I said. They'd said someone was sniffing around about missing items from the house. "You must have an idea already of who did it."

"Not something we can share with a bystander," Julius said, his tone firm. "That sort of information is classified."

They definitely had suspects. "I'm hardly just a bystander anymore," I pointed out. "I might not have known much about what went on around Anna, but I talked with her pretty often. Sometimes she mentioned people who'd come around. If you give me a description or a—"

"What part of 'it's not happening' do you not understand?" Garrison snapped.

I was pretty sure he was just sore about the fact that Julius had laid down the law. "I'm *trying* to help."

"And we'll let you know if you can offer more assistance than you already have," Julius insisted.

We were getting close to the corner of the property. "This is the spot," Talon remarked in his cool, deep voice, the first time he'd spoken since we'd left the car. Maybe even since we'd gotten into it. I was way too aware of his muscular frame just inches from my own body. His voice wasn't as commanding as Julius's, but it drew my attention all the same. My mind kept tripping back to the startling hunger he'd stirred low in my belly when he'd leaned over me in the chair.

"The spot for what?" I asked, refusing to let his presence distract me.

As we kept walking, our pace slowing just a little, Julius fished a plastic bag out of the leather messenger bag he was carrying. "I know you were in a tough spot, but you have plenty of cash. I don't think you need the jewelry you grabbed. My suggestion is that you leave it here so that there's no chance of the murderers tracking you down. If they are looking for those items, you're better off without them."

My hackles rose. "You went through my things again?"

"Only to give them back to you." He handed the plastic bag to me. "I don't see any cameras right here. No one but us would know how the jewelry ended up in the yard. It's your decision, but I recommend you take my advice. It'll also mean we have no evidence we could bring against you in court."

He'd promised they wouldn't arrest me for robbery—but of course I couldn't trust a promise from cops, especially ones who played as fast and loose with the law as this bunch did.

My fingers tightened around the plastic. But the necklaces inside meant nothing to me. I didn't even know who they all belonged to. I did still have the cash, currently tucked into my pockets.

And that point about no evidence against me was pretty compelling.

We'd almost reached the corner. I met Julius's eyes, and could see plainly in them that I had to do this if I ever hoped to get them on my side.

Let this gesture buy me a sliver of trust.

I lowered my hand and swung my arm upward at just the right angle to send the bag sailing over the wall without the gesture being too obvious. Because maybe there were cameras even *I* hadn't spotted. My loot thumped to the ground on the other side.

"There," I said, picking up my stride and forcing the men to walk a little faster around me. "Now let's catch the assholes who killed my friend."

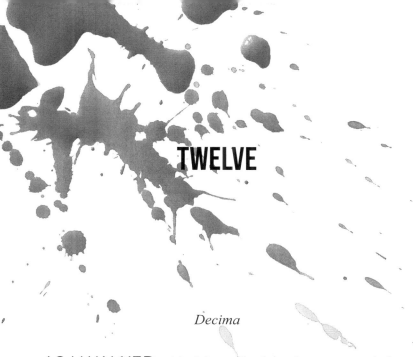

TWELVE

Decima

AS I WALKED with the men back to the car, my mind spun through the possibilities. I couldn't tell whether I'd gained any real trust by abandoning my stash of stolen jewelry. Julius was stonewalling any attempt I made to find out more about their potential suspects, which to be fair was probably what his job required. I'd hoped he'd be more flexible on that policy like he had with certain others, but it'd hardly been a guarantee.

For now, I also had a little more freedom than when I was shut up in their basement apartment, which was where I had to assume we'd head right back to if I didn't come up with another idea quick.

What would I want to do with this freedom? Where would I want to go?

My thoughts drifted to the few contacts Noelle had

introduced me to during various assignments—people she'd told me I could turn to for supplies or a little assistance, though she'd warned me never to reveal too much to them. The main ones weren't located anywhere near this suburb, and I couldn't see any easy excuses that might let me get to them without drawing too much attention from the cops around me. But there was one about a half hour's walk from here.

If I couldn't drag any information out of the guys, I might as well turn to my own sources. I might have gone to this one in the first place if it hadn't been the middle of the night. I only knew where to find him when he was at work.

It was mid-afternoon now. I could make this work. I'd *better* make it work, or what the fuck had all my training been for?

I rubbed my mouth as if I was thinking hard and then spoke up. "I don't know if what I saw around the house was helpful, but if it was at all, we could try retracing the route I took to get to the house the other night. Maybe something else will jump out at me that could be connected."

Garrison's head whipped toward me. "Awfully confident already, aren't you? We didn't sign up for a walking tour. What are you going to want next—your own badge?"

I narrowed my eyes at him. It was obvious that out of the four men, this one was going to be the *least* likely to ever warm up to me.

"A little less snark from you would be great," I replied.

Garrison let out a huff. "It comes with the package, sweetheart."

Julius had tipped his head to the side, considering. "We're already out here," he said. "I don't see how it could hurt. We wouldn't want to leave any stone unturned, would we, Garrison?" He shot the younger guy a pointed look over the top of his sunglasses.

Garrison grumbled under his breath, but Blaze piped up from behind me too. "It might also be good to know where Dess was coming from, in case the murderers figure out she was involved and try to track her down."

There was something odd about his tone even though he was technically supporting me, but I couldn't put my finger on it. And it didn't really matter, because Talon nodded, and Garrison shut up with a resigned sigh.

"You're at the wheel," Julius said to me.

"Okay, take the next right."

We wandered along the sidewalks, turning here and there, with me making a show of stopping to "remember" which way I'd come or to examine an occasional signpost or front yard. After several blocks, Julius deemed it safe enough for me to step right into the lead, relying only on my cap and my sunglasses to hide me. I hadn't spotted any more illicit cameras since we'd left the mansion behind, so I wasn't particularly worried.

If we ran into the murderers, I'd be happy to show them just how sorry they should be.

When the stretch of small shops I'd been watching for

came into sight up ahead, I slowed down. I stopped a few doors down from my intended destination and looked around with my hands on my hips, blowing out a frustrated breath.

"No luck, huh?" Garrison just had to say.

"I'm sorry," I said, biting back the sharper words I'd have liked to aim at him. "I really thought there might be a chance... but then maybe the pricks responsible never came anywhere near here."

"This is where you live?" Blaze asked, coming up beside me. His thumb kept flicking over the screen of his phone even while he was gazing at the buildings around us.

"Not quite. I figured if I haven't seen anything yet, we're out of luck. I don't want to get *too* close in case my boyfriend—if he saw me—" I hugged myself, hating playing a wimp but knowing it'd work in my favor.

"We'd make short work of *that* prick," Talon muttered in an unexpected show of protectiveness.

"I'd still rather not have to deal with him." I winced and looked around, pretending to notice the bakery for the first time. "I could try to make it up to you for wasting your time. Moe's has the best cookies. I don't know about you, but I could really use a pick-me-up right now."

The guys exchanged a glance. "We don't need anything," Julius said, "but you can grab something for yourself. You're not going alone, of course, so if you were thinking about making a run for it—we're sticking with you until we know exactly what and who we're dealing with."

I rolled my eyes as if it didn't matter to me. "You made that clear already. Fine, come in and enjoy the heavenly sweetness. No skin off my back. You can protect me from any murderous psychos who might be lurking between the donut racks."

Blaze snorted and ignored Garrison's glare.

We ambled over to where we could see through the bakery's window. It was a popular spot, with several customers already squeezed into the small space.

Julius motioned to Talon. "Watch the back door. I'll go in with her. You two loiter outside like you do so well." He aimed a slightly wry look at the two younger men and then moved to open the bakery door for me.

When we were inside, he stationed himself next to the entrance. Perfect. He thought he had to worry about me taking off—it'd never occurred to him that I might be looking for something inside this place.

The smell really was heavenly, a mix of buttery pastry and dusted sugar. I licked my lips automatically. Weaving through the browsing shoppers, I scanned the area behind the counter and display cases for a familiar bearded face.

My heart sank. I'd just assumed he'd be here today, but of course he didn't work *every* shift. The only employee behind the counter was a heavy-set woman I'd never met.

Well, I still had to put on a show of going through with my story for being here. I got into the line of people who were ready to place their orders, tapping my pocket with its roll of cash. I didn't really want to waste any of my limited money on cookies if I *wasn't* getting a meeting with the contact out of it, but I might be able to spin this at least a little to my advantage. Noelle had let me get a cookie here the few times we'd stopped by—to keep up our appearance as customers—and I hadn't been lying about them being damn good. The only thing better was pure chocolate.

As the woman right in front of me paid for her order, another figure strode out of the back, carrying a large tray of fresh cookies. Relief washed over me at the sight of his round face with its scruffy beard. He was here after all.

I restrained a smile that would have given away that I was pleased about more than the baked goods and stepped to the side as if I wanted to check out the cookie offerings more closely.

The guy glanced up and froze at the sight of me. He looked as if he nearly dropped the cookie tray. Setting it down behind the display case quickly, he shook his head as if to clear it and met my eyes again.

The tag on his uniform said *Jay*, but I'd be willing to bet that was at least as much of an alias as *Dess* was, if not totally separate from his real identity. People who worked on the underground side of things had to be careful.

"Hey, Jay," I said quietly, leaning against the glass. "Those are some great looking cookies there."

"Let me know what you'd like, and I'll box them up for you," he said in a professional tone, and then dropped his voice so no one would hear it through the chatter of the store except me. "Are you okay? I heard—I wasn't sure if you—it's awful. I'm so sorry."

The condolences made my stomach wobble in a strange way. He was the first person I'd talked to in almost forty-eight hours who had some idea of who I was and what I'd really gone through. But I couldn't afford to get emotional with Julius watching over me.

For an instant, I wanted to blurt out everything—Anna dying in my arms, the crash, the cops. Maybe Jay could help me get away from Julius and the others. But as soon as the impulse rose up, I had to quash it.

What were the chances that this guy, who was barely out of his teens, could fend off four highly skilled cops? I'd only be getting him in deep shit. I had to stick to what I'd come for—and maybe I'd still get something more out of the undercover detectives if I had some patience. If I blew their cover right now, I could be screwing myself over too.

Jay's comments told me that even if the cops were keeping the murders quiet, news had already spread through underground channels. I dipped my head in acknowledgment and held up my arm with the wrist brace. "Thank you. I got out, but it was... Let's not talk about it." I pointed at the chocolate chip cookies with their blobs of cocoa-y goodness. "Five of those. Pack them slow. Have you heard anything about who was responsible? I didn't see them."

Jay grabbed a fresh pair of gloves and tugged one and then the other over his hands to buy time. "No idea. Sorry about that too. People are talking about how bad it was, but no one's mentioned anyone taking credit so far."

Damn it. I guessed that'd been a lot to hope for. "Does anyone seem particularly happy about all those people being gone, even if they're not claiming responsibility."

"Not that I've noticed." He paused as he folded the box he was going to put the cookies in. "I did hear through the grapevine that someone's looking for you."

My spine stiffened. "Me? Who's looking?"

"I mean, they didn't give your name. Or theirs." He cut a sly glance my way. *He* didn't know any of my names either. "But word went out through one of the more private channels that if anyone ran into you, they should pass on a message."

My heartbeat sped up. Now we were getting somewhere. "And what was that message?"

He made a face as he stacked the cookies in the box. "It didn't make a lot of sense to me. The whole thing was that 'the woman with the red polka dots wants Noelle's black-winged sparrow to visit her.' I knew that had to mean you." He nodded to my dark hair.

The woman with the red polka dots. My spirits lifted alongside my thumping pulse. I knew who that was—one of the other contacts Noelle had introduced me to. *She* must know something.

Now I'd just need to figure out a way to get to her that my current jailors would accept.

"Thank you," I said to Jay again, and moved to the cash register for him to check me out. The exhilaration of the progress I'd made took away any sting out of handing over the money.

I strode out of the shop without glancing at Julius, figuring he wouldn't necessarily want people knowing we were together anyway. Outside, I quickly ambled several feet from the bakery so Jay wouldn't be able to see my companions through the window. I didn't want *him* passing on strange stories about the new company I was keeping.

If I'd had any dreams about breaking for freedom, the cops would have banished them in a snap. Julius came up right behind me, Blaze and Garrison converging on me in the same second. Talon prowled out of the alley to round out the squad that was either my protective duty or my captors, depending on how you looked at it.

"There," I said breezily. "We all survived, didn't we? And I bought cookies for all of you anyway. You really do need to try them. I promise you'll thank me."

I popped open the box as if I wanted nothing more than to share my treat. My buoyant attitude came easily with the news I'd just gotten, even if I didn't know how I was going to take my next steps yet.

I wasn't surprised that Blaze grabbed his cookie first. He sank his teeth into it, and his eyes widened. "That's fucking fantastic! I think the walking tour was worth it."

Garrison picked up his and sniffed it before looking at it skeptically. "It smells like a goddamned waste of time to me."

"If you don't want it, I'm happy to have two," I said,

holding out my hand, but he jerked it back and took a bite, if only just to spite me.

When I held out the box toward Talon, he hesitated, looking almost startled by the tiny gesture of kindness. He picked one up gingerly and looked from me to the cookie and back. Not the same as Garrison's skepticism, but a wariness nonetheless. Something about it made my gut twist despite my good mood.

Julius accepted his without any sign of how he felt about it, which I guessed was better than a refusal. I picked up the last cookie and pushed the edge into my mouth.

The buttery, chewy dough flooded my mouth alongside a punch of chocolate. A satisfied hum escaped me, maybe close to a moan. When I opened my eyes, Talon was still studying me, though the flash of heat I caught in his gaze stirred my emotions for a totally different reason.

"It's just a cookie," Garrison muttered, but I noticed he'd already polished his off and was trying to surreptitiously lick the crumbs off his fingers. Ha.

I didn't have many tools to work with here, but I'd milk what I had for as much as I could. Who knew? Maybe a little literal sweetness would soften these jaded cops enough to give me the opening I needed.

THIRTEEN

Decima

I SAT in the basement apartment with only Talon and his silent stare to keep me company.

Had it been the cookies that'd convinced the four men that I was now safe with just one guard, or maybe my willingness to throw the jewelry back to its rightful place? Whatever the case, they'd left right after dinner, and I felt three times less suffocated by masculinity as I leaned back on the well-worn sofa.

Unfortunately, their loosened security didn't get me closer to my goal. I needed to go and see the contact who'd sent out a message to me, and it wasn't like I could slip past Talon's penetrating gaze.

She must know something important, or she wouldn't have reached out like that. But I needed to go *alone*. No way were the cops letting up on my supposed protective detail completely.

Sitting for long periods had always made me irritable and impatient. Being watched by a brooding man with icy blue eyes—eyes that matched his cool demeanor and impervious personality—only amplified my restlessness. I couldn't find the people who'd murdered the household while I was stuck in here. All I could do was wait until I got an opportunity to escape that I was sure I could take advantage of in my injured state.

My eyes caught on the punching bag across the room that I'd seen Talon working over to impressive effect. If I couldn't go anywhere, I could at least put my body in motion. I shouldn't let my body go soft while I lounged around here.

I only gave myself a moment to contemplate my injuries before standing. After grabbing an elastic from my bag in the bedroom to tie back my hair, I walked over to the bag. I ran my fingers down the leather surface, finding it just as heavy and sturdy as the punching bag I'd used for years in the household.

All the pent-up feelings that I'd held inside myself for the last few days were close to erupting, and this was the only way I'd be able to lessen the strain. Working out had always been a way for me to focus, to feel in control. With my bruised ribs and a sprained wrist, my exercise would be limited, but I could still make the best of it.

I turned my back on Talon, refusing to let his

unwavering gaze influence me as I worked out my frustrations. No doubt he watched me as I stretched in place, my ribs protesting. I pushed through the pain, knowing that it wasn't as important as my need to feel in control of *something* in this apartment. The ache centered me and reminded me of my strength.

I did three rounds of floor work, eyeing the bag with each crunch. I had to improvise on some routines, unable to do a full sit-up with the rib pain that stabbed through me when I tried. My pushups, usually flawlessly executed, had to be one-handed, so I could only do half my usual reps. Every move was a fight through discomfort, but once I'd completed the first stage of the workout, I gave myself a satisfied smile. I'd won the battle.

Standing, I faced the punching bag. I closed my left fist in the way I'd been trained for years to do. My other wrist throbbed when I tried to flex it beneath the brace.

No problem. Noelle had seen that I was well-trained on both sides.

I threw my first punch.

My ribs protested as I shifted my body into the strike, but it felt *good.* A sliver of tension fell from my neck and shoulders. I mocked a right punch, stopping before my fist collided with the bag, and twisted left, allowing my full force to fall behind the blow.

I lost myself to the flow of my punches, allowing my breath to flow in sync with them. As my breathing accelerated, so did my fists. I allowed the memories of the previous days to sweep through me and strengthen my blows. The anger. The denial. All of the emotions swelled within me until my strikes became the only thing keeping me grounded. The feeling of entrapment became a song for my fists to use as guidance.

I switched to a few kicks, and Anna's pain-stricken face drove my next strikes. When I returned to punching, a small part of me expected my fist to go all the way through the bag, destroying it with the frustration and grief tangled inside me.

A touch on the small of my back jarred me from my trance. I whirled with my fists up, one already flying out for a knockout blow.

Talon caught my left hand with his much larger fingers, guiding the momentum of it to the side of his face and forcing me to stumble to the side with the sheer force of the attempted blow.

I shook myself as I caught my balance, gritting my teeth in anticipation of a mocking criticism. To my surprise, I got the opposite.

"You've got good form," Talon said, without showing a hint of emotion.

I raised my eyebrows at him. "I thought you'd already figured that out."

He gave a subtle shrug. "You weren't exactly focused on technique the one time I've seen you fight."

Fair. I cocked my head. "Can I keep going?"

He nodded to my hands. "Your footwork is more suited for a dominant right hand."

That came as no surprise. I might have strengthened my left side for the sake of practicality, but my right side had always been my strongest.

"Yes," I said. "I imagine it is, considering I'm right-handed." A little impressive that he'd been able to tell just by watching me for a while, though.

He considered the brace holding my stronger wrist captive. If only he knew the things that I'd done with my left hand alone. The guns I'd used to take lives. The knives I'd wielded against my opponents.

I was *proficient* with my left hand. That was all I needed.

"I can show you a couple of adjustments that would help you switch over," he offered. "If you want."

He may not have been expressive, but I caught the undercurrent of interest in his voice now. He was impressed. Maybe only as if I were a toy he could play with to see what it could do, but I'd caught his attention enough for him to give some kind of a damn.

Was that a good thing or a bad thing?

Having seen *him* in action, I could tell he might have a few tips that would actually be useful. That was why I was still here, right? To use these men however I could?

I gave Talon a single nod. As he kneeled in front of me, I forced myself to hold still. He nudged one of my feet and then the other, adjusting their placement and angle just an inch here and there. His fingers brushed my calf before he straightened up, and even with the fabric of my sweatpants between his skin and mine, a quiver of heat shot up my leg.

When he stood, I lifted my fists and tested a punch. I felt the way my body moved in line, allowing just a little more power to fall behind the blow. I smiled and met his eyes. "Thanks."

"Can I join you?" he asked, and I froze in place, not prepared for that question. He went on into my startled silence. "I have some punching mitts for practice. We can use those."

I opened my mouth, closed it again, and shrugged. It'd be a welcome change from the punching bag—a new challenge. "Sure, why not?"

He grabbed the punching mitts out of a trunk against the wall near the punching bag and tugged them over his hands. Before he was fully prepared, I threw a punch, testing my form. The strike hit the padding over his hand with a loud thud.

Talon let out a grunt that might have been approving. "Good one," he said, holding both mitts up between us.

I gave him a satisfied smile. "It should be."

The breath that escaped his mouth could have almost been mistaken for a laugh. Almost. "You're very sure of yourself when it comes to certain things, aren't you?"

Right, I couldn't forget that I was playing the role of Dess the abused daughter and girlfriend. But that Dess had still trained her ass off; she'd escaped the villains in her life.

I let my lips curve slyly. "This is the whole reason I'm still alive." He had no idea how true that was.

Then I struck.

Talon was ready. He met my left-handed strikes with the gloves, and when I lifted my knee in an attempt to get an advantage, he whipped his hand down to stop the blow before it made contact with his gut.

He did leave a small opening with the gesture, though. With my free right elbow, I twisted and caught him in the ribs. A woosh of air left him as he bowed at the waist slightly.

I tried to press my advantage by getting in a jab to his jaw, but Talon had already recovered. He fended off each of my strikes with a precision I'd only seen before from people with a military background. That only strengthened my suspicion that he and Julius might have that background in common. I guessed it wasn't so unusual for former soldiers to end up joining the police force. Similar lines of work, just different in scale.

Abruptly, Talon shook off the mitts and took a swing at me. My reflexes were well-honed enough that even in my surprise, I jerked out of the way. His fist narrowly avoided colliding with my face.

I sucked in a breath and took a step back, raising my arms defensively. Adrenaline thrummed through my veins, much more pleasant than the frustration that'd gripped me before.

"Oh, you think you can take me?" I taunted, wiping a

bead of sweat from my brow and jumping from foot to foot.

"I know I can," Talon said.

He lashed out again, so fast I had to duck beneath his arm, my ribs groaning in protest at the maneuver. He might not have been quite as bulky with muscle as Julius was, but that allowed him more speed—and he was fucking fast.

While squatting, I jabbed him in the stomach with a fist and then stood, aiming for his face. Talon batted my hand aside. He came at me with his full body weight and flying punches, and the only option I had was to run away —which wasn't an option I was interested in taking—or to meet them head-on.

I blocked with my uninjured arm and kicked out at his thigh to create distance between us. It'd have been easier with two fully functional arms, but I'd make do with what I had.

I hadn't gotten to spar like this in years. Even Noelle hadn't been this much of a challenge recently. It was *amazing*. I could feel myself stretching, pushing harder to match my opponent, like I hadn't since I was a teenager.

When I aimed another kick, Talon grabbed my ankle, twisting so viciously that I nearly lost my balance. He yanked me toward him and whipped me around before I could recover. One of his arms wrapped across my waist, pinning both arms to my side like he'd done when he'd caught me trying to break the window, and the other rested against my collarbone, too close to my throat for comfort.

My breathing shallowed as I recognized the danger. What did I know about Talon, really? He was in law enforcement and insistent on keeping me "safe," but who knew how much of that was just a front? Maybe that was all Julius's idea, and he'd rather get me out of the way so they could focus on their real work.

I jerked my body to break his hold, but his grip tightened. "Dess," he said, my name a faint whisper of breath against my ear, "you might be more skilled than most, but you're not better than me."

It should have been fear that froze me to the spot, but I felt something else much more unexpected. The feel of his body pressed against mine sent a sudden flare of heat to my core.

With Blaze's touchy flirting and gentle advances, I'd felt nothing more than annoyance and a jolt of panic at the associations that came with that kind of come-on. Talon's dominating presence provoked a completely different sensation, something that made me want to grind against him in an embarrassing way.

I reined in that ridiculous urge and turned my head to the side, allowing my lips to hover a mere breath from his as I spoke. "What a testament to your skills: fighting and winning against an injured opponent. You must be *so* proud of yourself."

All at once I was aware of his pulse thumping through his body against me, picking up in tempo. He wet his lips. How *would* it feel if he pressed that mouth against mine? Would they be as strong and firm as the lean muscles that pressed into my body, or would they be cold and sharp like his icy eyes and terse responses? What would it be like to have a man like this work over my body as skillfully for pleasure as he did in combat?

Would it be so awful to find out, if it was what I wanted and not something being forced on me?

My pussy outright throbbed. Talon's gaze seared into mine, no longer so icy after all. In that instant, I thought I might actually *get* to find out.

Then his arms shifted around me, and his elbow tapped the most painful spot on my ribs. My head jerked down, a hiss of pain escaping me.

Talon let me go immediately. "Sorry." He stood tall, the artificial light gleaming off his shaved scalp and chiseled features. Another flicker of heat flashed in his eyes before fading away.

It seemed like whatever had happened between us in that brief moment hadn't only gotten to me.

I cleared my throat. "I'd like to try that again when I'm fully healed. I always appreciate a challenge." I knew I could take him when I wasn't held back by unwanted handicaps. He moved quickly and swiftly, but so did I.

"It won't make a difference," Talon replied.

"Who's confident now?" I said, grinning.

But he didn't reply, just picked the mitts off the floor and tossed them back into the trunk. Apparently sparring practice was over.

I eyed the punching bag, but I was bored with it now—

and maybe I'd made some headway with Talon that would get me something else I wanted.

I set my hands on my hips. "So where did everyone else go while they left you to babysit?"

Talon didn't look at me. "It's official business."

"Yes, I realize that. They're still working on tracking down those pricks who murdered Anna and her family, right?"

He turned to face me then, his eyes narrowing. "Official. Business."

"Buzzkill," I said, rolling my eyes. "I might be able to help."

"Stop," he demanded.

"Are they looking at the crime scene again? I could check out the house itself, put on a more thorough disguise if you're so worried. Maybe I'd—"

"I'm not talking to you about an ongoing investigation or making any decisions about your involvement," he said, slowly and firmly. My heart sank. Every word felt like a new, sturdier wall he was erecting between us.

I thought I'd gotten somewhere with him, that he was starting to respect me.

"You can't really think I'm incapable of contributing after the things I spotted around the property today," I insisted.

He sighed and motioned toward the bedroom I'd been using. "I think it's time you went to bed."

I gaped at him and folded my arms over my chest. "Excuse me?"

"Go to bed," he repeated forcefully.

"That's what I thought you said." I took a step toward him, staring him down. "I don't care if you're a cop, a military man, or a damn alien. You will not order me around like that. I am *not* a child."

His gaze darted down over my body, lingering for just a second on the curves of my breasts and hips. When he met my eyes again, my skin tingled with more unsettling heat.

"I'm well aware of that fact," he said, in a tone that drew my eyes back to his mouth with the thought of the other uses it could be put to. Then it pressed flat before he said, "But I'm still telling you it's time to turn in for the night. Our apartment, our say goes."

I scoffed at him. "You and your whole damn team are insufferable." But I didn't really want to be out here with him if he was going to be such a prick about it. I spun on my heel and marched into the bedroom. The door closed with a kick and a thud.

I sank down on the bed. My gaze fell on the tote bag on the chair, and all at once my fingers itched to dig inside it for the stuffed tiger, to hug it to my chest as I curled up on the bed. As if I really *were* a kid again, trying to drift to sleep in my lonely rooms in the household.

But I wasn't that kid anymore. What was wrong with me?

I lay down on the firm mattress with my back to the chair, but a ghostly impression of the toy tickled my arms as I tucked them in front of me. Some small part of me, one I squashed deep inside but that I couldn't totally ignore, did feel like a little kid again. A confused, lonely kid far from home...

Even though this was the first time I'd been away from the household without knowing exactly where I was and what I was meant to be doing, something about that sensation was so familiar. How could that be?

FOURTEEN

Decima

"WE'RE TAKING YOU SOMEWHERE," Julius announced, and took a swig of his morning coffee.

I considered him from my perch at the kitchen island, where I'd just finished a bowl of cereal I'd again insisted on pouring myself. His expression gave nothing away, but then, it never did.

The fact that I might be getting another opportunity to see something beyond the confines of this apartment had to be a good thing. "Where?" I asked, picking the imaginary lint from my shirt as if his answer didn't matter to me all that much.

Garrison arched his eyebrows at me from where he was sitting on the other side of the island, savoring a typical mug of hot chocolate. It was just close enough for a trace of its creamy scent to reach my nose, and I started salivating even though my stomach was perfectly full.

"Do you really think you have a choice, sweetheart?" the younger guy asked. "This isn't a city tour, even if you tried to treat it like one yesterday."

I ignored him, fixing my attention back on the man in charge.

Julius gazed back at me evenly. "Do you want to help with the case or not?"

I made a face at him. "I'd kind of like to know where we're going first, that's all. Is that so much to ask after you've basically taken me prisoner?"

Julius frowned. "You're not a *prisoner*."

"Really? Then what would you call it?"

"You know you're here for your own protection. We're keeping you safe."

I shrugged and carried my bowl over to the sink. "And protecting *your* covers. I haven't seen any reason yet that proves I need this level of protection." *Tell me more about what you're up against, what kind of people you think I should be scared of. Give me some details.*

Julius looked at the ceiling as if he needed a moment to regain his composure. It wasn't my fault. I tried to ask the necessary questions to get right to the point, but he and the others repeatedly deflected. I didn't *want* to play a game of back and forth with the guys, but I didn't have another choice if I wanted to get anything out of them.

"You could just tell me where you want to take me," I suggested. "How hard is that?"

I could tell that he'd decided to appease me before he opened his mouth. He took a deep breath, but before the first word came out, the window above the kitchen counter burst inward with a crash of shattering glass.

As I spun around with a lurch of my heart, two smoke grenades careened inside and thumped on the floor. A dense fog billowed through the room, prickling into my eyes and obscuring everything around me from view. All I could rely on were my ears—which picked up the screech of the front door's hinges being slammed apart by some massive force and another crash of glass from the living room.

Footfalls thudded from all three directions. Gunshots boomed. I dropped to the ground, my pulse still racing but falling into a familiar rhythm that steadied me.

This was the kind of moment I was made for. Every instinct quivered on the alert. All my attention narrowed down to the simple goal of staying alive—and taking down anyone who wanted me to be otherwise.

More shots were ringing out. Was it enemy fire or the cops shooting back? There was no possible way to distinguish friend from foe with the suffocating smoke.

I pulled my shirt over my nose and mouth, gaining little relief, although my lungs were now prickling along with my eyes. At least the smoke didn't taste like it'd contained anything outright toxic. I'd experienced pretty much every awful hand weapon known to humankind over my years of training, and there were plenty worse than this.

Of course, most of those were only used in the middle of a warzone. What the fuck was going on here? Who would have wanted to attack a bunch of men most people shouldn't even know were cops?

Did it have anything to do with the massacre at the household?

The shots had fallen away into grunts and the fleshy smack of fists landing blows. They must have realized only a fool would fire into a room where they couldn't tell whether they'd hit an enemy or an ally. The sounds didn't tell me how many attackers we were facing, but from my initial impressions, two or three had come in through each access point, maybe a couple more than that through the front door. We were outnumbered as much as twice over.

We? What was I even thinking? I didn't owe the cops anything, and I wasn't in any position to take on as many as a dozen attackers whether they were related to the household's murders or not. It was the cops' job to handle these assholes. I'd seen how capable they were at that job. They didn't need me anyway.

This was the perfect opportunity to escape and never look back.

I army-crawled in the direction of the door, careful to make no noise as I went. Here and there I had to adjust my course to squeeze around a piece of furniture or dodge stomping feet. More punches and kicks thudded around me; a bone cracked. Someone groaned.

It sounded vaguely like Julius.

I hesitated next to the sofa. I had to keep going, didn't

I? It was a tough world, and I wouldn't risk entering a fight that had nothing to do with me.

Or did it have *everything* to do with me?

Julius had claimed that they were protecting me, and while I'd assumed it was an unnecessary precaution, maybe I'd been overly skeptical. What if this attack wasn't an attempt to capture or kill them, but to do those things to *me*?

A sharp cry of pain split through the air. Was that Blaze?

Logic told me to continue forward, but my body balked. Even highly skilled fighters could be overwhelmed when they were greatly outnumbered and taken by surprise. I might be able to make a break for it, but the four men who'd brought me here wouldn't necessarily survive this attack.

They'd held me here, refused to let me leave... but they'd also helped me after the car crash. Patched me up. Made sure I was reasonably comfortable and well-fed. They'd even catered to my request to walk around the mansion and then go buy those damn cookies yesterday.

It might be because of me that whoever was attacking them had even identified this apartment as theirs.

I hadn't been able to save anyone in the household. I hadn't even known the massacre was happening until every single one of them was dead or as good as it. This time, it wasn't too late to step in.

I didn't have to let another group of people die around me. I could save someone.

My chest clenched around a sudden rush of determination. I didn't second-guess the emotion. *This* was what I'd trained for. This was the one way I knew I could make a difference in the world, and I wasn't going to fail again.

Springing to my feet, I took in the room. As I swiveled, I made out thinning patches in the smoke.

There—that guy with the ski mask was one of our enemies.

I dove at him, reaching for his head. He didn't even see me coming. My fingers dug into his jaw, and I wrenched his face around so sharply his neck snapped even as he made his first movement to buck me off.

As he crumpled to the ground, Garrison scrambled up from where he'd been knocked down at the attacker's feet. He stared at me, but I didn't have time to worry about what he thought of my kill. There were more sounds of fighting all around me.

Another masked man hurtled out of a thicker patch of smoke. I struck first, knowing that my advantage would come from the man's shock.

He swung at me with a knife. I ducked and snatched his wrist with my left hand to prevent him from using the blade. At the same time, I swung my brace around, pummeling his temple with its stiff surface. The throb of the impact ricocheted up my arm, and my ribs groaned with the effort, but the man stumbled to the side, slightly stunned.

He lashed out at me again, but I had already moved,

yanking his body off balance. I squeezed his wrist, twirling it around his back in a maneuver that I knew would jerk his shoulder out of its socket. A pop sounded through the room, and a groan spilled from his mouth.

"The fuck," he screamed, the knife dropping from his twitching fingers. I kicked the back of his knees, and he collapsed forward, a strange sobbing gasp coming from his lips.

In an instant, the knife was in my hand. I plunged it straight into his back, angled perfectly to ram between his ribs and into his heart.

I knew I'd hit home when the body beneath me sagged.

The smoke was clearing more, drifting out the shattered windows and the open doorway. A hint of a fresh breeze tingled in my throat.

As I spun around, I noted the three other bodies already on the floor—all of them masked, to my unexpectedly intense relief. One of them was bleeding out from a deep slash across his throat. Another had a bullet wound in his chest. The third might have only been unconscious, but these cops clearly didn't hesitate to fight to the death when their lives were on the line.

Exactly as it should be. Hopefully that'd mean they wouldn't get too judgy about the bodies *I'd* added to the collection of corpses.

On the other side of the sofa, Julius and Talon were fighting side-by-side. For the first time, seeing them from the sidelines rather than as their opponent, I could observe the way they worked in sync. Talon moved with swift but powerful precision, and Julius was the direction to his storm, leading with pure strength and skill as he smashed his knee into one attacker's face and jabbed out his gun hand to put a bullet in another.

Together, they were a force of nature. Outnumbered two-to-one, they still maintained the upper hand in the fight. I'd never seen *anyone* fight quite like that. It was almost beautiful to watch.

But not so beautiful that I didn't notice the man charging at me from the direction of the kitchen, wielding a switchblade in one hand and a butcher knife in the other.

I turned to meet the guy head-on. As I swiveled, I glimpsed Blaze holding his own against another assailant with a skill that I hadn't anticipated from the tech expert, even though his movements were slowed by a wound bleeding on his side. To be a cop, of course he needed to be somewhat physically adept, but it still surprised me.

My attacker was coming too fast for me to completely dodge him. I caught a blow to my shoulder and stepped back from the force of it. Shaking off the impact, I deflected the next one with my bare forearm. Up close, catching sight of my face in a way none of the invaders before had gotten a chance to, he jerked backward with startled eyes. "Who the fuck are *you*?"

It wasn't me they were after, then. They hadn't expected some chick to be fighting alongside the cops, let alone kicking their ass. Too bad for them.

His hesitation was all I needed to swing back and execute a perfect roundhouse kick that rammed into his head. I landed with bent knees, and the man toppled to the ground, unconscious without an ounce of fight remaining in him.

I glanced around the room with a nearly clear view now. All the guys were fending off other assailants, even Garrison, though the motions of his right arm looked awkward, as if he'd been injured too.

When I looked at Julius and Talon, I found Julius's motions were slowing. In the time I'd confronted one man, he'd taken down two, and Talon had incapacitated another. But Julius was favoring one side. The bottom of the left leg of his jeans was dark with blood—his.

Shit. Another attacker stepped into view from the dispersing smoke, his gun aimed at Julius, and I leapt toward the masked man without a second thought.

This guy was taller and broader than the others I'd fought. With only one fully usable arm, I knew I had a challenge ahead of me. I didn't allow myself to glance at the bodies that littered the floor. I didn't bother acknowledging anything around me but my opponent.

He might be bigger than me, but I was *born* for this.

I fell into the rhythm of the fight, using my fists and legs brutally and efficiently enough that it didn't feel like I was impaired in any way. In fact, the brace over my wrist acted as a blocking tool rather than a burden. Using the footwork that Talon had adjusted yesterday, I found myself ducking, weaving, and punching with greater intensity— just as rapidly as I would have with my right arm fully functional.

The man's size didn't matter as he succumbed to my attack, careening to the floor with my assault.

The gun spun away from his hand, but he fell within reach of a discarded knife. He noticed it at the precise moment that I did. I stood no chance of reaching it before him.

So when the man jerked forward and snatched up the serrated blade, I did the only thing I could do. I veered right, clutched his wrist with my left hand, and slammed his forearm into my bent knee.

The first time, he didn't release it, though a groan of pain fled from his lips. I turned my back to his body's mass and used my right arm to add more force to the blow this time. The knife finally clattered to the floor. I pushed him away from the blade, and he held my leg like a lifeline, attempting to drag me alongside him.

I caught the cool leather grip of the knife and whipped it around as the man pulled me closer. With a jerk of my hand, I plunged it into his chest.

He slumped, his breathing sputtering and then halting completely, leaving the room just a little quieter.

I glanced toward Talon first, my eyes drawn to him automatically. He still moved like a storm—quick, brutal, and relentless. He left nobody unaffected in his path of skillful strikes. He looked to be enjoying his last opponent —taking his time with him. I saw the way the man tired, and I could tell that Talon was playing with him.

A yearning in the pit of my stomach arose as I watched him move. He was absolutely extraordinary.

But there were only two attackers left, that one and the one Julius was just heaving into the edge of the kitchen island. The cops could handle the situation from here. I'd done my bit, and now I needed to get going.

As I dashed toward the open doorway, Talon cracked his opponent's skull. I still could have made it, but just a few steps from the blasted-up doorframe, Garrison and Blaze stepped from opposite sides to block my way.

My fists jerked up, and in the same instant, Talon strode over to join them. He didn't seem to notice the blood trickling down the side of his face from a scratch on his forehead.

Garrison smirked at me, the effect only slightly weakened by the tensing of his jaw against the pain he was in. "Where do you think you're going, sweetheart?"

Fuck. I'd waited too long. I swiveled in the other direction, just in time to see Julius marching over.

He took in the room as he approached, limping just a little, and I got the sense he could pick out exactly which kills were mine, though that didn't make any sense when several of them had happened when it was too smoky to see where anyone else was. When he came to a stop a couple of paces away from me, he nodded approvingly.

"Thank you. We might have been in a tough spot if you hadn't stepped in." He gave the apartment another glance and sighed. "We can't stay here after this. Maybe it's time we take you home."

FIFTEEN

Julius

AFTER WE'D MARCHED out of hearing range of the car, parked at the other end of the alley with Dess locked inside, Garrison cleared his throat. His voice came out taut. "It was the Cutthroats."

"What?" I'd already been angry about the attack, but it was nothing compared to the surge of rage that hit me at those words. I'd assumed someone associated with one or another past hit must have been out for revenge and managed to locate us. For it to have been a fellow crew…

Garrison nodded, leaning back against the brick wall on one side of the alley and crossing his arms, moving the right one a little stiffly. His eyes flashed. Knowing how cynical he could be, he probably wasn't as surprised as I was, but I doubted he was any less pissed off.

"I managed to get one of the guys who came at me in a

particularly painful position," he said, a mix of triumph and revulsion playing across his features. "He spilled the beans while begging me not to make the pain worse. The Cutthroats hired the bunch of them to take us out. A little less competition for the prime jobs, I guess?"

Blaze snorted, but he was scowling too. "Maybe if they got their acts together, they'd be able to *earn* those jobs instead of having to slaughter the competition."

"Then they'd actually have to put the work in," Talon muttered.

I dragged in a breath, glancing toward the car where Dess was perched in the back seat. I'd set the locks so they wouldn't open from the inside, but I half-expected her to burst through the glass. The woman was full of surprises.

For now, she was sitting there in the middle of the back seat, apparently calm. She'd have had a hard time smashing through those windows anyway. We had all our vehicles specially outfitted.

I turned back to my crew, shifting my weight and suppressing a wince at the lingering pain in my lower leg. One of those hired punks had lucked out and clipped my calf with a bullet in the initial turmoil of the attack. Blaze had taken a knife jab that'd come just shy of piercing his stomach. Our wounds were patched up now, but that didn't mean they were forgiven.

No one messed with my crew and lived to tell the tale.

We'd certainly left no one living in the safe house. That would make a powerful statement. It'd been easy enough to vacate, since we didn't keep anything there that could be traced back to us and the ownership of the place was through a shell company, but I didn't like that we were down a useable property on top of everything else.

"We'll wipe them out," I said firmly. "After we're done dealing with our current client and the loose ends he seems to think we left. Divided attention gets you killed. But we also have to make sure the Cutthroats can't get at us if they're stupid enough to try again." I turned to Blaze. "How do you figure they found the first place?"

"There's no way to connect us to it through the data trail," Blaze said. "There *is* no data trail that connects all the dots."

"We've been coming and going from that particular spot a lot in the past few days," Talon pointed out grimly. "The safe houses are set up for laying low, not regular activity. All it'd take is the wrong person spotting one of us in the area."

I nodded. "And that means we'd have the exact same problem if we tried to take Dess to one of our other safe houses. The only place that's totally secure is the penthouse."

Garrison bristled. "The only reason it's secure is because no one except us and Steffie has any idea it exists. We can't bring *her* there."

Garrison spat the word *her* as if it burned through his mouth. As if the idea of Dess was acidic and dangerous.

She was definitely dangerous. I'd only caught a few glimpses of her in the attack, the smoke hiding most of the fighting around me, but what I had seen—it'd been even more impressive than the way she'd tried to escape. She'd moved with ruthless efficiency, doing what needed to be done to take down the intruders and doing it fast and well.

And she hadn't needed to do it at all. The door had been slammed right off its hinges, the path to freedom wide open.

"I've said it before and I'm saying it again," Garrison said. "We've got to get rid of her, make her the client's problem. As long as she's with us, she's just going to be trouble."

I'd let myself assume that the whole crew would be unanimous on this question after what we'd just been through. I should have remembered never to take anything for granted.

"She fought with us," I said, hardening my voice. "She could have run for it, but instead she stayed and *defended* us. She took down at least a couple of the mercenaries. Early on, the fight was closer than I'd like. I don't know for sure that we'd all have even survived if she hadn't stepped in. She might have saved *your* life. We might not be clear on how she fits into this mess, but the one thing she's proven is that she isn't out to screw us over."

"Yeah," Blaze said. "I saw you get knocked on the ground, and then she jumped in. If she hadn't tackled that guy, you'd be lying there with the rest of the collection of corpses right now. And you really want to repay her by throwing her to the wolves?"

"The client goes by the name Viper, so technically it'd

be throwing her to the snakes," Garrison muttered, as if that was what mattered.

"And that's much better?" Talon asked.

Garrison just glowered at him. I studied his expression and saw nothing but his usual dissociated prickliness. Now more than ever I'd have liked to know what lay behind those walls. Why did he have such a problem with this woman?

"Just because she knocked the knives from our enemies' hands doesn't mean she won't plunge one into our backs given the opportunity," Garrison said finally.

"Nobody said that we're going to trust her fully," I reminded him. "But it couldn't be more obvious that if she wanted us dead, she wouldn't have helped us. She risked her own life to fight with us, even though we've been holding her against her will."

"And I don't know why the fuck she did that, but the penthouse is our space. Crew only. She doesn't belong there."

"Steffie comes all the time," Talon pointed out.

Garrison rolled his eyes. "Steffie's practically crew too. You guys took her on before you even brought me in."

There was more to his defiance, though, wasn't there? I didn't think he only objected to Dess over Steffie because Steffie had been with us longer.

Garrison might never admit it, but I doubted he hated Dess as much as he pretended. I saw the way they bickered, and I'd noticed the light that had danced in his eyes—a genuine enthusiasm that I so rarely saw in him.

Dess wasn't a danger to our lives, but she *was* a danger to the steel walls he'd built to ensure nobody could get past them.

But then, I wasn't being totally honest with the others about my reasons for wanting to keep her with us either.

There'd been a moment toward the end of the fighting when I'd glanced over and caught a glimpse of her face in the middle of grappling with the last man she'd killed. Something about the cool stillness of her expression and the intense focus in her gray eyes had triggered a jolt of recognition. One that had made me want to run over and tear the guy trying to hurt her limb from limb.

It didn't make much sense. I couldn't place her, couldn't say where or when I might have encountered her before. There was no point in putting much stock in the impression. But even now, when I checked on her stance in the car again, that protective urge flickered up in my chest.

I planned my life and our careers according to hard data and strategic thinking, but I'd learned to trust my instincts too. And my instincts insisted that this woman was someone we should defend just as vehemently as she'd defended us.

I turned back to Garrison. "We already have an extra room, so no one's getting put out on the sofa this time. We can set up a cot in the weight room. With Steffie coming by regularly, she'll have an added layer of supervision. We'll have all our equipment right there, everything we need to take care of our work in one place. You can't get simpler than that."

"We can't hand her over to that Viper prick," Blaze added. "And we can't let her go when we still don't know what her real story is. Julius's approach is the only way that covers all the bases."

Garrison turned his glower on the techie. "You just want another chance to put the moves on her. Nearly having your windpipe crushed once wasn't enough?"

Blaze rubbed his throat. "She didn't hit me *that* hard. And I provoked her. She hasn't been remotely aggressive with any of us except in self-defense, has she?"

Talon hesitated as if he still had a few doubts, but then he dipped his head. "She hasn't. There's something more to her than she's said, but I don't think it makes her a threat to us."

Garrison's eyes became narrower. Then a switch flipped inside of him. He stood straighter, loosened his posture, and placed a cold expression on his face. "Fine, but if she kills us all in our sleep, I hope you die knowing that I was right."

"If we die, you will too, so you won't get much satisfaction out of it," Blaze retorted.

Garrison ignored him and stalked back to the car. He whipped the door open and dropped into the front passenger seat without so much as a glance at Dess. She looked at him and then the rest of us approaching, her expression coolly quizzical.

"We're taking you somewhere," I said as I got in on the driver's side.

She cocked her head, a glint of amusement coming into

her pretty eyes. You wouldn't have known looking at her that just an hour ago she'd stabbed at least one man to death. But then, who knew how much shit she'd seen before she fell in with us. We weren't exactly broken up about the violence we'd dealt out either.

"Let me guess," she said dryly. "You're not going to tell me where."

"You're catching on," Garrison muttered.

I gestured to Talon and gave Dess a mildly apologetic smile. "For this trip, you're going to be blindfolded. I don't want you even *seeing* where we're going."

Her body stiffened just slightly, the light in her eyes vanishing as if storm clouds had rolled in. "Blindfolded? What the hell—"

"You'll be able to take it off as soon as we get inside," I said, cutting her off. "It's a precaution for both our security and yours."

I watched as an array of emotions flashed through her gaze, each pushed away until cool indifference was the last thing that remained. "I feel like it should be illegal for cops to blindfold people and take them places."

Blaze's laugh filled the car, and I went on before he could say something stupid. "It's also illegal to kill people, but on some occasions, it's necessary."

"You're not going to arrest me for that, right? Isn't self-defense allowed?"

"It is," I said. "You were our responsibility, and we're responsible for what happened in the safe house too."

She nodded slowly and leaned into her seat. "Fine, but

you're going to take the blindfold off as soon as we get there."

As Talon placed a strip of thick cloth over her eyes, a sense of appreciation rose up inside me. For the trust she'd just shown us that I wasn't sure we'd earned, considering I was still lying through my teeth about who we were. For the way she'd fearlessly fought on behalf of four men she barely knew. Maybe she was some kind of kindred spirit, a piece we hadn't known the crew was missing. She wasn't an enemy—of that, I was completely sure.

But at the same time, I had no doubt that if she became a liability, I would kill her. The crew always came first.

I just couldn't help hoping it wouldn't come to that.

SIXTEEN

Decima

THE COPS HADN'T SAID as much, but I could tell as soon as my blindfold came off that the apartment they'd brought me to this time wasn't any kind of safe house. To them, this was *home*.

Julius insisted on replacing my wrist brace with a new one, considering the old one had cracked in the fighting. Then they backed off, giving me space to explore the place and take in all of the intriguing details.

I hadn't been able to track the route we'd taken, which had mostly been by car but also involved a descent down stairs into cooler air with a metallic scent, the squeak of a couple pairs of hinges, and a distant rumble that'd made me wonder if we were near a subway line. The last part of the trip had been by elevator, though, and the bright light that assaulted my eyes confirmed that this place was no basement.

The open concept of the room resembled the basement safe house, but it was larger and much more welcoming. A plump leather sofa and matching chairs stood in a cluster around a widescreen TV. The island by the kitchen was longer, and the countertops marble. There were three normal looking doors at either end, which I'd gathered led to the men's bedrooms, the bathroom, and a workout room where Talon was currently unfolding a cot for me.

It would have looked normal—just like an everyday if somewhat posh home—if it weren't for a few details.

The windows all along the wall opposite the front door allowed in plenty of light, but they were overlaid with a film that blurred all view of the outside—and presumably any chance of anyone else seeing in. From the time we'd spent in the elevator, I suspected it was a long drop to the ground.

The front door had a lock that took a keycode, and I could tell the deadbolt it activated was very solid from the sound of it thudding into place after they'd let me in. Another door in the far wall was similarly secured. Where did *that* lead? Weapons? Case files?

I'd just have to find out as soon as I had the chance.

One corner of the apartment had a desk with a massive computer and four monitors. I recognized that as Blaze's domain, so I assumed that the dartboard a few feet away was also his. Whenever he'd last been playing, he'd gotten two in the bullseye.

I had no idea who the knitting bag sitting beneath the small coffee table belonged to. The bag was black and as masculine as a bag could get with screen-printed skulls and knives printed on the surface, but there was no mistaking the needles and skeins of wool poking from the top. Interesting.

Beside the TV sat a movie stand, and plenty of familiar titles greeted me. Many were dramas, a few were horror movies, and the vast majority were action. No surprises there.

I glanced over my shoulder when Talon came out of the exercise room. He walked over to join Julius by a small wooden table next to a whiteboard set up like an easel. Julius had taken out a few plastic army figures which must have represented whatever he started talking to Talon about. He moved them on the board with careful precision and pointed something out, but I couldn't tell what he was getting at.

I wandered closer, hoping to catch a snippet of the conversation, but unfortunately that brought me closer to Garrison. He'd gone right to the stove and put on the kettle, and now he was pouring instant cocoa into a mug.

I resisted the urge to lick my lips—and the more insistent urge to ask him for some. I'd lived with chocolate only once a year for my whole life. Better I went without than trust anything he mixed for me.

Julius and Talon fell silent when I came closer, Julius running his hand over the short brown strands of his close-cropped hair. I put on my best show of not even noticing they were nearby, studying the frame around the nearest window instead.

It was actually worthy of examination. Hand-painted thorns and roses wove around the glass pane in an intricate pattern it was hard to imagine had been done by hand. If it weren't for the slight smear in the corner, I would have assumed it was some kind of wallpaper.

I leaned closer, taking a closer look. The thorns in the painting appeared to wind around and trap the vibrant roses, encompassing them and cutting them off from the rest of their brothers and sisters. Some of the petals looked cut and scratched by the same thorns.

For such a beautiful painting, it was vicious. Had one of the men around me done this? It was hard to picture any of them with a paintbrush in his hand, but then I'd say the same about the knitting needles.

I turned back toward the kitchen just as Garrison put away the box he'd taken the cocoa packet from. My eyebrows leapt up. There was an entire shelf stuffed with similar boxes, with different brand names and logos.

"That's quite the collection," I said.

"Some might even call it an addiction," Blaze piped up. He'd plunked down on the sofa with his laptop, which apparently he preferred to his more elaborate workstation.

I should have known better than to try to make any conversation with Garrison. He frowned at me and shut the cupboard with a thunk. "It's a collection I don't want you messing with."

I quirked my lips up into a cocky smile and lifted my

hands in feigned defeat. I wasn't going to admit how much the thought of all that chocolate—so many different kinds! —made me drool. After all, the last time I indulged my own addiction, I could hardly walk back to my room before passing out.

I took in the whole room again, and another thought occurred to me. I hadn't spent much time questioning the men's living situation in the old apartment, which had felt distinctly temporary. This home was well-lived-in. They'd been here for a while.

I knit my brow and asked the room at large, "Is it normal for cops to live together like this? Can't any of you afford your own place?"

"We're married to our work, and that means practically married to each other," Blaze said, shooting me a grin.

"It's easier when we're undercover," Julius clarified.

I guessed that made sense. I didn't know much about the inner workings of law enforcement, other than it was best to steer clear of its agents altogether. You never knew when a pesky law might get in the way of seeing a job through.

I turned my attention back to the window frame. "Who painted the roses?"

The question had barely left my lips when the front door clicked open behind me. I spun around, my pulse skipping, every nerve going on the alert. Were we being attacked again? Did I need to dive for cover—or a weapon?

But the men around me looked totally unconcerned.

And the woman who stepped through the doorway alone didn't exactly give off a threatening vibe. The tension trickled out of me.

"She painted them," Talon said in answer to my question, jerking his thumb toward the woman, which instantly made me focus even more attention on her.

She could have been cut out of a Hallmark card for grandmothers: short, plump, and with hair that was a messy mix of wheat-blond, gray, and white pinned into a bun on the top of her head. Her eyes met mine, soft but thoughtful. Beneath her loose floral dress, she wore white tennis shoes. Another mix: prettiness and practicality.

"What do we have here?" she said, looking me up and down. Her lightly accented voice—Eastern European, I couldn't place the exact country just yet—was brisker and firmer than I'd have expected from her grandmotherly appearance. There was clearly more to her than met the eye.

While we'd been examining each other, Julius had walked up between us. He rested a hand on the woman's shoulder, and she beamed at him—with all the air of a grandmother doting on her favorite grandson, although given that Julius looked to be in his late thirties and I'd have put her around sixty, she was hardly old enough for that to be true. Then she returned her gaze to me with a much more assessing expression.

"Dess," Julius said to me, "this is Steffie, our housekeeper. She comes by regularly to take care of laundry, dishes, and whatever else needs doing around the apartment. She'll be treated with nothing but respect. Understood?"

It surprised me that he felt he needed to say it and that he spoke with such cool but clear forcefulness about a woman who was essentially their servant. That added to my impression that there was something more to this situation. What kind of housekeeper painted the window frames after she was done cleaning, anyway?

Especially with such brutal yet beautiful imagery.

"Understood," I said, reining in my curiosity. I didn't think Julius would consider a barrage of intrusive questions to be very respectful. "It's nice to meet you, Steffie."

"Dess is going to be staying with us for a little while," Julius said to the older woman. "We have some business to sort out with her, and it's important that she stay safe."

It was a very vague explanation, but either Steffie could read more into it than I'd have expected or she wasn't in the habit of questioning her employers, because she nodded without complaint. "You'll barely notice me around," she told me with a twinkle in her eyes, and glanced back at Julius. "The trees are vibrant today. A few leaves fell on the sidewalk by the bank, but the breeze tossed them away. Otherwise, not so much as a rustle in the branches."

Huh? I studied her and then Julius, who nodded as if her comments had sounded totally normal to him. Something clicked in my head.

It was a code. She'd been passing on information she

didn't think he'd want her saying explicitly while I could hear it.

What kind of housekeeper had a secret *code* set up with her clients?

Steffie bustled off without another word and grabbed a broom from the bathroom. As she swept the floor, the men went back to their previous activities. No one seemed all that interested in what I was going to do here.

Well, Julius might not want me badgering Steffie, but I didn't see why I couldn't badger him. He'd dragged me here along with them, after all.

I marched over to the table where he'd just set out another army figure and motioned to the array. "Does this have something to do with the massacre at Anna's house?"

"We work on a lot more cases than that one," Talon said gruffly, which didn't even answer my question.

I set my hands on my hips. "Of course you do. But that one is the most pressing right now, wouldn't you say? Or are mass murders a regular occurrence around here? For all we know, *we* just got almost murdered by the same people."

"They weren't the same people," Julius said in exasperation, and then snapped his mouth shut.

He hadn't meant to reveal that tidbit. They didn't really want to explain anything to me. I caught hold of the stray fact and tucked it away in the back of my mind. I'd already gathered that the intruders hadn't been after me, but if it wasn't related to the massacre at all...

I frowned. "Why would a bunch of guys come at you with guns blazing if—"

"That," Julius said firmly, "is for us to figure out and you not to worry about. There's no chance of anything like that happening in this building. That's why we came here."

I let out my breath in a huff. "I just want to do what I can to help with the investigation—you know, the one that made you think I'm *not* safe, at least anywhere other than with you—so I can get on with some kind of life that involves more things than sitting around watching you whisper to yourselves. Are we going to get a move on solving this case, or are you all just going to sit around knitting sweaters?" I gestured to the bag beneath the coffee table.

Blaze snickered. None of the men around me appeared fazed by my accusation. Steffie outright laughed, the unexpectedly full sound rolling through the room. "You're going to have fun with this one," she said, and went back to her sweeping.

"Look," Julius said, "you're not a cop, and you're not entitled to being part of the investigation. You don't know how this works. So why don't you treat this as a vacation and relax. There are worse spots you could be stuck, aren't there?"

I supposed he was right. But if I couldn't leave this apartment, I couldn't find a chance to slip away and talk to my other contact. How long was this confinement going to go on for?

"It's a very nice place," I said, making a show of

looking around again. "Sorry if I get a little stir-crazy being stuck in the same small space for days on end."

Julius sighed. "Then you'll be happy to know that we're going out tomorrow. All of us, you included."

The clunk of Garrison's mug and his sudden intake of breath suggested *he* hadn't been in on that plan.

I smiled at Julius brightly. "Wonderful. Maybe you'll even tell me where we're going before we get there this time."

Steffie muffled another laugh. Garrison muttered something under his breath, but he didn't overtly protest. I stepped away from the table with a vague sense of triumph.

This would be my last-ditch effort to learn from the cops. If they led me astray one more time, I wouldn't stay with them. I had to find the savages who'd murdered the people in the household, and I would do it with or without their help.

SEVENTEEN

Decima

THE COPS INSISTED on blindfolding me again before we left the apartment. After the elevator stopped at the bottom, I tried to track the path we took, but they led me around half a dozen turns and along the same slightly musty-smelling passage where a rumbling sound passed us by.

The only thing I was reasonably sure of was that we were near a subway station.

We'd been in the car about ten minutes when Talon finally judged it safe to take the blindfold off, or maybe Julius had given him some signal. I blinked at the sudden brightness streaming through the car windows. We were cruising along a busy street, cars all around us and pedestrians bustling along the sidewalks, tall storefronts looming on either side. A cluster of skyscrapers towered over us just a couple of blocks ahead.

We'd come downtown. I was closer to my contact "with the red polka dots" than I'd been before, at least.

I leaned back in the seat where I was wedged between Talon and Blaze today and studied the back of Julius's head. Talon sat as still as always, and Blaze was jiggling his leg like he so often did when the rest of him couldn't be moving, so absorbed in his phone he probably didn't even notice. It was an odd contrast between the two of them, but I found I didn't mind. It beat having Garrison glowering at me for the whole trip.

But it was the leader of this bunch I focused my attention on now.

"Do I get any clues about where we're headed or why?" I asked, giving the back of Julius's seat a playful kick. "Did you want to make it a game of twenty questions?"

"I don't think that'll be necessary," Julius said dryly. "We're taking a look around one of the victim's workplaces. Since you were somewhat familiar with the family and maybe some of the others who were there at the time of the massacre, I figured it couldn't hurt to have your eyes on the scene too. But *no* touching anything. You see something that feels important, you call one of us over."

"Think you can handle that?" Garrison asked, taking a glance back at me. I hadn't completely escaped the dreaded glower.

I returned it with one of my own. "I promise not to

touch anything unless it's a weapon someone's trying to kill us with." My gaze darted back to Julius. "Which victim? What was the job?"

"I'd rather not skew your judgment by giving you any additional information. If you go in cold, you're more likely to be receptive to all possible evidence."

That sounded reasonable enough, if annoying. I frowned at the buildings outside the window. It hadn't occurred to me that the people who worked for the household had careers outside whatever they did *in* the household, but maybe it wasn't even a job for most of them like it was for me. Maybe they'd all gone out to work elsewhere at least some of the time. What kinds of jobs would they have held?

I guessed I was about to find out.

The parking spots along the sidewalk were packed. Julius took the car past a stretch of office buildings and then pulled over in the first empty spot. He nodded back the way we'd come. "It's about two blocks that way."

We all put on our hats and sunglasses and stepped out of the car. The men fell into step around me like before. Still surrounded. Great.

It was a little tricky weaving through the crowded sidewalk in a clump like that, though. People brushed past us on both sides, whiffs of perfume and car exhaust mingling in my nose. The road provided a constant rumble of engines.

Then Blaze jerked to a stop. He motioned to Julius,

who stepped over to join him, and pointed across the street. "Is that him?" he asked under his breath.

Garrison moved away from me to join them too. Talon, in front of me, simply turned his head, but a sense of opportunity washed over me.

This was my opening. Who knew if I was going to get another one? For these few seconds, I was free to step away and bolt, and the hordes of people surrounding us would make it impossible for the cops to find me once I'd melded with the crowd the way I'd been trained to.

I took a slow step back, careful not to appear tense. Any unusual motions would draw their attention back toward me, so I took three more easy paces backward before turning and slipping around a cluster of women in business suits. With a quick swipe, I removed my cap. I let my posture drop, my knees bending slightly and my back rounding so that my head dipped lower, more difficult to see.

The cluster of women headed into a fancy café, and I let them carry me along with them. The second I passed the door, I darted past the tables and the washroom, dashed along the hall past the kitchen so quickly and quietly no one even called out after me, and was out the back door in an instant.

A map of the city unfurled in my mind. I sprinted down an alleyway, loped across roads, turned several corners, and then hailed a taxi that happened to be passing by. There was no sign of the cops anywhere around me, and now I was going to vanish completely.

As I dropped onto the worn leather of the cab's back seat, a twinge of regret ran through my gut. I hadn't managed to find out anything all that useful from their investigation, and they'd obviously known more than I'd been able to drag out of them. But who knew if I'd *ever* have gotten anywhere with them?

My contact had specifically reached out to me. The information she'd offer could trump everything the cops had in their case file.

The address I gave the cabbie was on the other side of downtown from the household. The edges of the city there were pretty much the opposite of the suburban street where I'd lived. Trampled cardboard rested on the sidewalks, and homeless people sat begging on several of the corners we passed, their eyes tracking the movement of everyone who passed by. Trash blew along the curbs. The buildings could use a fresh paint job at best and gutting at worst.

I got out outside the sagging canopy over the entrance to the local mall. Inside, the florescent lights flickered with dying bulbs, and the smell of grease hung in the air as if that was the main ingredient in the food court—which maybe it was. At least the air conditioning was on full blast.

I walked on, leaving the heat of the summer day behind me. My heart started to thump in anticipation.

The storefront for the electronics store was one of the neatest in the place, phone models and the latest cheap gadgets displayed in rows in the display window. A fake potted plant stood next to the doorway to give the space a homier feel. I'd always thought it was kind of ridiculous, but what did I know about retail strategy?

The woman who'd reached out to me was leaning against the counter next to the cash register. She straightened up the second I walked in, a smile flashing across her face but her stance tensing. She was relieved and yet nervous to see me.

I filed away those observations as I came to a stop a couple of feet from the counter, as if I wanted to check out the hard drives and cables tucked away behind the glass underneath. My gaze stayed on her face.

This contact had picked her temporary code name to go with her message well. The first time Noelle had introduced me to her, I hadn't met anyone with so many or such prominent freckles before. I'd asked why she had polka dots on her face. And the red part—well, her fiery curls must have inspired the usual code name she went by too: Scarlett.

"You got my message, then," she said, sounding oddly breathless. "I was a little worried—I thought they might be wrong—well, it doesn't matter."

My body went on the alert. I stepped closer. "Who's 'they,' and what do they have to do with me?"

Scarlett pursed her lips, her eyes darting around the store and then coming back to rest on me. "Someone reached out—I don't know much about it—I don't really ask questions, you know? They passed something on to me that they wanted me to get to you if I could. They seemed sure you were alive, but after everything I heard about what happened..." She shuddered. "Just a second."

I shifted on my feet impatiently as she turned to rifle through a cabinet behind her. "*Who* passed this thing on?"

"I'm sorry, I really don't know," she said. "There wasn't any face-to-face communication. They left the package on the counter while I was in the back. I guess they must have known I had some connection to you, so I'd have a decent chance of getting in touch."

And whoever had gone to her hadn't hoped to find me directly. Hmm.

"Did they say anything else about me or the murders?" I asked.

She shook her head, her curls jiggling around her face, and tugged a padded envelope about the size of a paperback novel out of the cabinet. "Just that if I could get this to you, I should. They were very emphatic about that."

I peered into her pale eyes as she handed the envelope over. Had she been threatened with some kind of violence if she didn't manage to complete the task? Offered a reward if she did? There seemed to be more at stake here than just handing over a package as a favor.

"And you really don't have any idea who brought it?" I pressed. "Don't you have security cameras in this place?"

Her mouth twitched. Fear. I knew that emotion—I'd watched it cross the face of enough of my victims. But I didn't think it was me she was afraid of.

"Whoever it was, they were too careful to get caught

that way," she said, but I wondered if she'd even dared to check.

"If you'd let me have a look—" I started, and she shook her head more vigorously than before.

"It's already been erased," she said without further explanation, only confirming my suspicion that she was terrified of pissing off whoever she thought she was dealing with.

A wave of frustration rushed through me, but I couldn't change what she'd already done or what she'd refused to find out. At least I'd gotten something here.

My fingers tightened around the envelope. "Thank you. I appreciate this."

She dipped her head in acknowledgment. Her jaw worked as if she was debating what to say next. "You'd better go now. After what those people did to your colleagues—who knows if they're looking for you too."

She had a point. I nodded to her and slipped out of the shop as quickly as I'd entered.

I stopped outside a discount clothing store, facing an inflated image of a model in a dress that was much more sophisticated than anything being sold in the dank interior, and tore into the envelope. A small, cheap plastic flip phone slid out into my waiting hand.

What the hell? I looked it over, tapped the power button, and the screen lit up. But there was nothing on it, just a few basic apps like the address book, which was totally empty.

No answers. No information. It felt like another dead end.

Gritting my teeth, I slipped my hand quickly beneath the collar of my shirt, shoving the phone into one place almost guaranteed to avoid detection: in my bra, under the swell of my breasts. It wasn't exactly comfortable, but it shouldn't catch the eye of roving pickpockets or anyone else who might be concerned there. I tossed the envelope in a trash can next to the shop.

I was just turning toward the entrance when I spotted them from the corner of my eye. Three unfamiliar men were sauntering toward me from the direction of the electronics store, just a little too quickly for a casual stroll. Even without looking at them directly, I felt their gazes on me.

My instincts clanged with alarm.

I swiveled and strode into the store, approaching one of the clothes racks farther inside. As I skimmed my fingers over the outfits without really noticing them, I monitored the entrance at the edge of my vision.

The three men came into the store, which was full of dresses and blouses, nothing they looked likely to wear. And they fanned out with casual precision, moving so that they nearly surrounded me.

Oh, they thought they were getting away with that, did they? I didn't know what their problem was, but I wasn't letting myself be cornered.

Grabbing a dress from the rack at random, I walked

over to a clerk near the back of the store. She gave me a stiff customer service smile.

"You want to try it on, hun?" she asked, waving her manicured hand toward the dressing rooms. "You'll look stunning in that dress. Let me know if you need any help with sizes."

She deposited me in the corner dressing room, hidden by a wall from the rest of the store. I closed the door behind me and shoved the latch over.

It was a tight space. I examined the surfaces for any potential advantage before jumping and bracing my feet in the two corners of the room, holding myself well above the floor.

I waited.

When I heard someone's feet scuff the floor on the other side of the door, I held my breath.

"She was just here," a man's low voice growled, just outside. "She couldn't have gotten out."

"Is there another entrance?"

I heard rustling, and then the door handle beside mine jiggled. "They're all locked. Look underneath."

I waited until I heard the telltale sounds of a man crouching down before I struck. I whipped the door open and dove at him in a smooth motion. The man on the ground didn't have time to do more than jerk up his head before I'd tied the dress around his neck and kicked him in the nose.

He groaned and fell forward, and I hooked the other end of the dress on the doorknob, allowing his full weight to fall into the stranglehold of the fabric. As he choked and sputtered, the second man sprang at me.

I caught him in the side of the head with a roundhouse kick and rammed my elbow into the back of his skull for good measure. He collapsed with a groan next to his companion, and I sprinted out of the dressing room alcove.

Now only one man stood between me and the door. "You might want to check on your buddies!" I called to him cheerfully as I hurried toward the mall courtyard.

The guy lunged at me, and I sidestepped just in time to knock his feet out from under him. Then I sprinted to the mall entrance.

If my pursuers were any good, they'd regroup in a matter of minutes. I'd be even more ready for them then. I couldn't have staged an interrogation in the middle of the mall, but one of the grubby alleys in this end of town? No problem.

I loped a block and a half away and stationed myself behind a tree to wait for my chance.

EIGHTEEN

Garrison

"SHE HASN'T LEFT THE MALL," Blaze said from the front passenger seat, eyeing the computer that was never far from his fingertips. "There are street cams that cover any way she'd leave, and my app hasn't pinged."

He'd developed the software a few years ago—a facial recognition program he claimed was more advanced than the ones even the FBI used to catch criminals. Combined with the city-operated security cameras, Blaze could find anyone from anywhere.

I leaned back in my seat, tipping my head against the headrest. "And does anyone find it interesting that the first place she went after ditching us is a hotbed of criminal activity?"

Blaze grunted in reluctant acknowledgment. "At least

three of the stores in that place are money-laundering fronts."

"And the neighborhood's got more robberies per capita than anywhere else in the city," Julius said from his spot behind the steering wheel. "We know. We still don't know what she's doing in there."

Talon stirred on the other side of the back seat from me. "It's a good thing we gave her some rope so we can find out."

I had to admit Julius wasn't being as soft on the woman as I'd been worried about. He'd come up with this idea to get a better sense of her motives and connections. Allowing her to escape had been the most practical way to discover exactly where she aimed to go and what she wanted to do when we were no longer on her tail.

But we'd never really been far away. She'd taken the bait the first second she could, and we'd been tracking her using Blaze's software ever since.

"There." Blaze tapped his laptop's screen. "She just came out the main entrance."

Julius put the car into drive and cruised around the corner toward the shabby mall. "We'll let her get a little more distance so she doesn't know we were following her the whole time, and then we'll pick her up and see what she has to say for herself."

I couldn't stop my gaze from lingering on the lithe figure on Blaze's screen. The way Dess carried herself was unlike anything I'd seen from her yet. As she strode along the sidewalk and across the street, she looked as if she'd just conquered the world. When she joined a small cluster of pedestrians, I narrowed my eyes, impressed by how well her entire demeanor changed. She *became* her surroundings, mimicking the mannerisms of the bodies around her.

It'd taken me *years* to cultivate the subtle art of merging with a crowd like that. You didn't develop it out of the blue. You had to learn it—either because you wanted to, or because it was the only way you could survive.

And we'd let this puzzle of a woman whose fighting skills could rival Talon's and who wore a façade as impenetrable as mine into our home.

"We're not going to bring her back to the penthouse, are we?" I asked.

"It depends on what she says," Julius said smoothly.

Why wasn't he more concerned about what'd just gone down? "You really think she'll tell us anything remotely true?"

"I think we'll learn *something*—and a lot of that is your job, isn't it? If she's part of something larger to do with the job that we weren't aware of, we need to know that. If this is about something totally unrelated, we need to know *that* so we can finally drop her and get on with our lives."

I snorted. As if there was much chance of that. Julius ignored me.

"She stopped," Blaze announced. "Not too far from the

mall. She's just standing there by a tree... Is she waiting for someone?"

Julius parked, still a few blocks away, and frowned at the computer. "You can't tell?"

Blaze shook his head.

My skin crawled with apprehension. I hadn't liked how much uncertainty Dess had brought into our lives and our work from the first moment we'd spotted her outside the mansion.

I leaned forward and gripped Julius's shoulder from behind. "We should cut her loose now. Pretend we never saw her. It'd be easier—"

Julius's head snapped around, giving me a clear view of his right ear with its ravaged earlobe—a gift from a bullet or a piece of shrapnel sometime during his military career. He'd never given the details.

"No," he said, low and firm with a hint of menace that dared me to challenge him.

I pulled back, my mouth twisting. Julius was the boss for a reason, and questioning him was something that few people dared to do. And when he said no... well, that was final.

I nodded, though all of my distrust for Dess whirled through my mind in a frenzy. This was my crew. My brothers in arms, even if we weren't exactly fighting in any war. I'd kill or die for any of them, and no woman would change that. Dess shouldn't have me second-guessing myself and the leadership roles long-established within the Chaos Crew. She wasn't worth it.

We waited a few minutes, and Dess didn't budge. Blaze glanced at Julius. Our leader sighed and then stepped on the gas again. "Let's go get her."

He cruised down the street, and we all made a show of peering through the windows as if we were on the lookout rather than knowing exactly where our target was. When Dess came into view, Julius sped up. He veered up to the sidewalk right in front of her and fixed her with his best "you've got some explaining to do" expression.

Dess leapt backwards, her eyes flashing, but Talon and I had already hopped out and come up on either side of her. Julius got out too, letting his hand rest on the concealed holster at his hip in a subtle threat.

Dess halted in her tracks. "How…" she started, shaking her head. Her gaze darted toward the mall beyond me, and I wondered again about what she'd been waiting for.

"We've looked through half the city for you," Julius said, putting on an impressive show of frustration. He gestured to the street around us. "Do you know the kinds of things that happen on this side of town? It's even less safe than the last place we found you."

I didn't dare to glance away from her face as he spoke, but I found nothing of importance there. She looked calm, though the tightness in her shoulders suggested a hint of anger that she was caught.

If it weren't for Blaze and his software, she wouldn't have been, but we didn't need to reveal all our tools to her.

"You don't need to protect me anymore," Dess said,

backing up another step, but the Chinese restaurant behind her with a foreclosure sign in the dusty window didn't offer any avenue for escape. "I survived the last couple of hours just fine on my own, didn't I?" She placed her hands on her hips, as if she'd proved something with her little escape attempt.

I saw the flicker of mischief in her eyes that nobody else caught. I noticed the way she shifted her weight from her left foot to her right one as Julius spoke to her, and I knew that she was hiding something. I knew better than to believe anything she said.

"You have no idea what you're dealing with," Julius said. "Whoever blasted their way through that mansion would make most of the criminals around here piss their pants. You may think you don't need us—you may even be right. But you're connected to this case, and until we figure out exactly how you're connected, you're not going anywhere. Get in the car."

Dess frowned at him. Then her eyes flicked to the side again, and an unexpected emotion touched her face—disappointment? Regret?

I risked glancing over my shoulder, but I couldn't tell what she'd seen that'd provoked the strange response. When I looked at her again, it was gone anyway. Her shoulders came down a smidge with what I'd have said was resignation, except she still didn't budge.

Julius moved forward with the full heft of his massive frame and grasped her upper arm. Dess tried to jerk away. "I'm not your property."

"That depends on your definition of property," I muttered.

The look she shot me should have killed me on the spot. "I'm pretty sure cops aren't allowed to take people into custody without—what—a warrant or something? Especially if you've got nothing to charge me with."

I let my lip curl into a sneer. "Did you forget so soon? We're not like other cops, sweetheart."

Julius tugged, and finally Dess came without more of a fight. Maybe she could tell that'd only end up worse for her.

Talon slid into the back seat, and Julius propelled Dess after him. I got in by her other side, more amused than I probably should have been by her irritated huff.

Some part of me kind of wanted to know what would happen if she *really* stepped out of line with Julius. He was ruthless and organized, and if something didn't go his way, his temper would ensure that it got back on track *quickly.* How would Dess react to that military-honed authority?

It'd be something to see, that was for sure.

"Let me guess," Dess muttered as Julius started the engine. "When you got your jobs, they added an extra line to your swearing-in." She raised a hand as if pledging allegiance to the police academy that I'd never attended. "I swear to serve, protect, and only illegally hold a civilian if I think it's absolutely necessary."

"Now you're getting the picture." I glanced over at her, doing my best not to pay attention to her lean frame tucked next to mine or how gorgeous her face was amid its frame of dark waves. Trouble shouldn't look that hot.

But as Julius had pointed out, my main job was figuring out the people we encountered on the job. Time to get that over with.

I folded my arms over my chest. "So, what were you up to out here? Just checking in with some friends? Or, wait, your boyfriend never let you have friends, did he?"

Blaze twitched with what might have been a wince, but he couldn't tell me to play nice. Nice hadn't gotten me anywhere with Dess before, and she wouldn't have bought that act now. I needed a reaction, whether because I hit her in the right emotional tender spot or because she got her story tangled trying to keep up with me. Either would work fine.

Dess simply rolled her eyes. "Maybe I was just trying to get as far as I could from the bunch of you. I used to live in this neighborhood. I know it pretty well—including how to avoid the wrong kinds of people." She gave me a pointed look as if to indicate I was one of the wrong kind.

"I guess that didn't work out so well for you, since here you are back with us. And nothing to show for it either."

I'd hoped for some indication that I was wrong, that she *had* accomplished something in her trek across the city, but I didn't get so much as a twitch of a muscle. "Yep," she said. "Right back where I started. Who should be more upset about that, you or me?"

I would have been annoyed, but some perverse part of

me enjoyed how easily she could give back the snark I threw at her. There wasn't anything wrong with enjoying it, was there, as long as I cut to the meat of the matter before too long?

I shot her a smirk. "What makes you think I don't enjoy your luminous company?"

Dess guffawed. "Oh, only the fact that you've been pointing out how little you want me around for about two days now. Too bad your colleagues don't listen to you more."

Her jab cut *me* a little deeper than I liked. Well, if she wanted to play hardball, I could match her hit for hit. "At least I have a job. You've been scrounging off Daddy and then the boyfriend for years. Is that why you came out here —looking for someone new to leach off of?"

"How do you know I didn't already have someone lined up?"

Was she serious about that? I eyed her face and found the same analytical expression I knew that I'd find on my own.

As I opened my mouth with a retort, the car skidded to a halt so sudden it jolted all of us forward. My chest slammed into the seatbelt—

—the image of a shadowy highway flashed behind my eyes, the screech of tires and a shrill scream echoing in my ears—

—and I blinked, my hand clammy where I'd snatched at the seat in front of me, my pulse thudding at double speed. I stared through the windshield, absorbing the view of the guy who'd swerved into our lane, the daylight streaming over his truck and the street around us.

"...the drivers who don't know how to fucking drive," Julius was grumbling, pressing the horn.

I pushed myself back into my seat, willing myself to breathe steadily, to even out the thump of my heart.

It was nothing. Some jackass was in too much of a hurry to notice he'd almost caused a pile-up. No one had died. No one was going to die.

This time.

My involuntary panic reaction couldn't have lasted more than five seconds. I sealed the holes that had cracked in my walls, setting everything back to normal. But when I looked at Dess, she was watching me, and something had softened in her expression.

She'd seen it. She'd caught a glimpse of me that I'd never have wanted *anyone* to see, not even the men I'd worked alongside through life-and-death jobs for five years now. And in her reaction to seeing it, she was revealing something gentle behind the hardened, jaded front she put on too.

I wanted to destroy that softness. It wasn't what I needed from her. I needed to prove that she was a monster who didn't deserve our trust, not an empathetic girl who'd earned it.

"What?" I spat at her with more venom in my tone than I'd intended. Good. Let her hear the venom. Let her hate me. It would make my job a hell of a lot easier.

"You were in a car accident before, weren't you?" she

said, not judging or prodding, just stating it as a fact. As if it was so obvious anyone could have seen it.

Anger flooded me. I'd worked for years so that nothing like this would happen, so that no one would ever dig down into the parts of my life I kept locked away even from myself, and I'd slipped up in front of the worst possible person.

I narrowed my eyes at her. "Maybe you should be worrying about your own troubles, not imaginary ones. You're in a car with four men who you hardly know, and we could do whatever the fuck we want with you. So keep your nose in your own damn business if you don't want to end up like all of your friends."

A flash of surprise crossed her expression, but there was no fear there. If she felt any, she hid it well enough that I couldn't detect even a hint of it. How the fuck could she be so good at seeing through masks and holding up her own?

And why the fuck did I find that talent so intriguing even as it infuriated me?

NINETEEN

Decima

WHEN WE GOT BACK to the apartment, I didn't exactly *sulk*, but I wasn't going to hang out with the guys like we were best buds and everything was cool either. Why the hell did the four of them have to be so determined to keep my ass around? Why'd they have to stumble on me right when I was about to beat some answers out of those losers who'd come after me in the mall?

And what was up with Garrison? I shouldn't have cared, but I knew genuine pain when I saw it. Somewhere deep behind his snarky front, he was hiding a hell of a lot of it.

It resonated inside me more than I liked. Even the anger he'd displayed when defending his weakness had been familiar. He didn't want me to see that side of him—

the part of him that grieved for something he kept even more hidden.

Yeah, I knew a lot about hiding.

But I couldn't spend all my time here hiding away. If the cops were going to insist on having me around, then I'd just have to continue working that to my advantage in any way I could. I had to get somewhere with them eventually.

I'd been on the verge of taking my chances and making a break for it when I'd seen the men from the mall hustling out from the entrance. If I'd made a commotion then, they'd have noticed me right away and I'd have lost any chance of surprising them; if I'd waited until they were out of sight, I'd have lost them completely. And as soon as the cops had screwed up my shot at getting answers there, I'd been left with no further leads.

I had nowhere to go and limited cash. Coming back here with them had been the best of my bad options.

Weirdly, when I'd stepped through the front door with them, I'd been hit by a waft of relief. Like it was good to be "home." This place wasn't *my* home, and I'd sure as hell better not start thinking of it that way. Maybe Stockholm Syndrome was starting to take hold.

Shut away from the rest of them and the comfort of the rest of the apartment, I dug the flip phone out of my bra. It was a good thing I'd tucked it in there, because Julius had done a quick pat down of my pockets and waistline in the elevator.

The screen still offered me nothing. I made sure it was

set to vibrate, no chance of a ringtone giving it away, and wiggled it behind a small equipment trunk in the corner which didn't look as if it'd been moved in years. There was less chance of the men finding it there than in my tote bag, which they'd already searched twice. I couldn't keep it on me without risking one of them noticing the odd shape beneath my breasts if I raised my arms at the wrong angle.

With that taken care of, a little more of the tension in my chest eased. I took off my brace to test the soreness in my wrist and run through some mild stretching exercises designed to speed along recovery. In a few more days, I might be able to take on all four of the men out there, police and military training or not. Smiling to myself and feeling ready to face them again, I tugged the brace back on and stepped out into the main room.

The only ones around were Julius and Talon. Julius was sitting at the small wooden table, currently cleared of army figures, his brow furrowed. A few sketchy lines that I couldn't decipher marked the whiteboard next to him. He had a notebook propped against the edge of the table, and even from across the room, I could see it held a neatly written list. I couldn't read it from so far away, and I knew better now than to try to get him to show it to me willingly. I might be able to take a peek later.

Talon was poised at one end of the leather sofa… with a pair of knitting needles bobbing and weaving between his muscular hands.

I blinked, making sure I wasn't seeing things. But no,

the brutal, skin-headed undercover cop with combat skills that rivaled my own was definitely sitting there, knitting away. From the looks of things, he'd been at his current project for a while. About three feet of mottled red-and-orange scarf dangled beneath the needles and fell across his knees.

He caught my startled gaze and raised his eyebrows at me as if daring me to say something. "Is there a problem?" he asked in his usual cool tone.

I laughed and walked over to the other side of the sofa. "I thought that maybe it was Steffie who left the knitting bag here. If not her, possibly Blaze. Garrison would have been my third guess. You'd have been last."

I expected Talon to brush off the comment or outright ignore it, but the vibe between us had shifted since we'd sparred the other day. I'd earned a little respect somewhere in there... or else he'd decided I was more harmless than he'd thought, so he didn't have to be quite as defensive. I wasn't sure which worked in my favor better, but I'd definitely prefer the former.

"Any particular reason you'd assume that?" he asked, looping the yarn around the right needle before tipping it and sliding a stitch from the left needle. He continued the repetitive motions so smoothly and quickly I could tell this was far from his first project.

I sat down on the arm of the sofa, feeling safer there than on the cushion a foot or more closer to him. "Somehow I don't think it's going to shock you if I point out that you don't look like a knitter."

He chuckled under his breath as he finished a row. Stopping, he plucked a spare needle out of the bag and held it out to me. I eyed it warily before gripping the hard, thin rod.

"Tell me what you feel," he said.

Would we break out the tambourines after and sing "Kumbaya"? I gave him a skeptical look. "It's a knitting needle."

The corner of his mouth twitched slightly upward. I thought that was a smile. What exactly he was amused by was harder to tell.

He nodded toward me. "*Describe* the knitting needle."

I rolled my eyes. "Metal, smooth, pointy." I waggled it in the air.

"And what other things are metal, smooth, and pointy?"

Oh, all right, I saw where he was going with this. "Knives," I said, leaning back on the sofa and spinning the needle between my fingers. "Razors. Swords. But you're not stabbing anyone with these. You're literally knitting a scarf. Or a very skinny sweater."

"True," he said, taking up his stitches again. "But I *could* stab someone with them if I wanted to. If there's me and a knitting needle standing between you and someone who wants to kill you, you'd be a lot more likely to live than if I were holding a paintbrush or a lump of clay. So I'd say it's a very macho craft."

I could think of about a dozen ways to kill someone

with both a paintbrush and some clay, but it seemed wisest not to mention that. Besides, he had a point.

"All right, grandma," I teased. "In that scenario, I'd still feel better if you had a gun."

He shrugged, eyeing the stretch of woven yarn before him wordlessly. I wasn't oblivious to the fact that each of the men did actually have a gun at their hip at all times. I'd bet Talon could do a good amount of damage with that needle too, though.

Curiosity itched at me. I swiveled so that I was facing him, planting my feet on the sofa cushion. "How'd you pick up the hobby? Were you drawn in by the pointy stabbiness and just decided to stick around for the wool accessories?"

I hadn't known if Julius was listening to our conversation, he'd seemed so deep in thought, but he snorted at that remark. Talon shot him a narrow glance over the top of the sofa and then returned his gaze to me. "Why do you want to know?"

"Because it's a mystery and I have a thing for unraveling them."

He tipped his head to the side in consideration and appeared to decide that my answer was acceptable. "It helps me decompress. When we're on the job, we spend a lot of time on edge, ready to act in an instant, needing to be ready for unexpected developments that could put us all in danger. The patterns I work through with the needles are predictable and straightforward. I want to make a scarf, and I get a scarf. It's a welcome change."

That made a fair bit of sense. Hearing him explain it kind of made *me* want to take up knitting. I watched him for another minute, unable to stop myself from admiring how those powerful muscles could move in such small but still incredibly skillful ways to create a product that had nothing to do with broken bones or blood.

Then he added, in case he thought I might forget what he was capable of, "It doesn't hurt to have a few additional weapons around the place either."

I had to grin. "Of course not."

Talon was the complete opposite of Garrison, wasn't he? Garrison held all kinds of fire in tight while putting on a blasé, disaffected front. Talon appeared unaffected... because he really was that way. I didn't sense that he was holding anything back in his answer. When he didn't want to tell you something, he simply didn't say anything rather than making something up.

I could appreciate that kind of straightforwardness too.

But that didn't mean the guy didn't have *any* emotions. He obviously got comfort out of this hobby. He liked to feel prepared, liked the reassurance of knowing the outcome in advance.

And I'd definitely seen sparks of something more heated in him when we'd gotten close during our sparring session.

It wouldn't do me any good to dwell on that. Watching his hands work was already making my skin tingle in odd ways. I latched onto an appropriate change of subject, what a normal person who hadn't focused their whole life on learning to kill might have said. At least, I thought so.

"What do you do with the things you knit?" I glanced around the room, not seeing any vast quantities of hats or mittens or blankets on display—not even one.

"I knit a new scarf for the guys every winter, because Blaze especially is always misplacing them, and the rest I donate to a clothing drive around Christmastime. What else am I going to do with twenty scarves a year?"

Just like that, my perception of him shifted yet again. There was something so... kindhearted about making clothes to keep his partners warm that didn't fit his icy demeanor at all. And donating the rest to charity? I guessed it'd have been a hassle to sell them or something, but still.

Maybe I should throw out the entire idea of categorizing Talon. It didn't matter how big the box was— he would never fit.

Annoyingly, that made him even more appealing.

Before I could figure out how to extricate myself from the conversation that had drawn me in more than I'd intended, the front door banged open. As Garrison and Blaze strode inside, I sat a little straighter.

Garrison smiled with a cool confidence that gnawed at my nerves, his gaze skimming right over me. Apparently I didn't even exist to him now. Fine.

Julius spoke before anyone else had the chance. "We need to talk," he said in that low commanding voice that his colleagues responded to immediately. Talon put away his knitting and got up. Julius walked over to the kitchen area, even farther from me than he already was, and the other three met him there.

I watched as they gathered on the other side of the island. Their conference began with voices too quiet for me to make out. I got up and ambled over as if I thought Julius's order might have applied to me too, even though I was sure it hadn't.

Julius noticed me before I was even halfway there. "This doesn't involve you," he said firmly, which made me even more certain their conversation had something to do with the household murders. If it had nothing to do with me, why would it matter if I heard a stray word or two?

I had the urge to demand they let me in on the discussion, but I'd seen how well that'd gone in the past— or rather, how badly. So I meandered across the room, not getting closer to them but not veering too far away, watching for alternative sources of information from the corners of my eyes as they fell back into their hushed exchange.

Ah ha. Garrison had left the kettle sitting on the dining table after his last mug of cocoa, and its stainless-steel surface reflected the kitchen interior like a slightly warped mirror. I sank down into one of the chairs at the table with my back to the men and reached for an apple out of the fruit bowl, just to give me a reason to be sitting there. As I ran my fingers over the smooth skin, I let my gaze linger on the kettle's shiny surface.

I couldn't see a whole lot more from here than from the

sofa, but I could see it without them knowing I was watching. Their voices stayed low, but their body language relaxed incrementally.

Julius held his notebook up for the others to see. His small, delicate scrawl was indecipherable from here, but the gesture confirmed that he'd written down something important if I could ever get my hands on it. Blaze moved around the group in his usual energetic way, blocking my view of the others every few seconds. I gritted my teeth. If he would stay fucking still for five seconds...

He began murmuring to Garrison, likely heckling him in the way they *always* did with one another. When he stepped to the side, Talon said something with a wave toward Blaze and then his computers. Blaze grinned—and jerked his flattened fingers past his throat in a vicious gesture I only knew to mean one thing.

Death.

It was *Blaze* making the gesture, though, so maybe it was his over-dramatic way of indicating something less bloody that he was going to do with his computer system? Seeing it unsettled me all the same. Should a cop really look that eager about the idea of killing, even metaphorically?

Of course, as Garrison had gleefully pointed out earlier today, these men weren't typical cops.

Julius said a few more things with brisk motions of his hands. Then Garrison jerked out his phone. He was standing at an angle where the screen, which he was holding away from the other guys, showed up almost perfectly on the kettle's reflection. I restrained a satisfied smile as I noted the four-digit passcode he quickly typed in.

Jackpot. I filed the number away in my mind, tying each digit to an image to make sure it'd stick and I'd recall it when necessary later.

There'd been some development in the case that they didn't want me to know about, but that didn't matter. I crossed my feet beneath the table and brought the apple to my mouth. When I sank my teeth in the crisp flesh, its tart juice seeped down my throat, and then I let myself smile.

I didn't need their permission to learn whatever they knew about the case. I only needed to not get caught.

TWENTY

Blaze

I STRODE to the locked door that led to the stairs, typed in the code, and let it swing open, already feeling rejuvenated by the mere idea of meditation. I was just stepping out into the first waft of fresh air when Dess's voice followed me.

"Where are you going?"

When I glanced back, she was leaning over the side of the sofa where she sat beside Talon. She'd been watching the way Talon knitted so attentively that I hadn't thought she would notice me leaving.

The casual way she spoke to me gave me a weird sense of relief despite the way she'd reacted to me the one time I'd gotten particularly close to her. She hadn't shown a single particle of violence toward any of us since then, and obviously I hadn't damaged her trust in me irreparably.

She seemed to have brushed that moment aside as if it'd never happened, and I was happy to let her do that.

I tipped my head toward the stairs. "I'm going up to the rooftop deck. You haven't seen that yet, have you?" I paused and then decided it was safe to ask as long as I remembered to keep my hands to myself, which I didn't think was going to be a problem after the lesson she'd taught me the first time. "Want to come?"

She sprang to her feet with the effortless yet practiced grace I couldn't help admiring. "Get out of this place for a bit? Hell, yes."

I opened the door wider for Dess as she approached, and she gave me a quick smile as she passed me before studying the stairwell on the other side. "These stairs lead to the roof?"

I pointed upward with a nod. "You've got to have some kind of outdoor space, or it's not much of a home, as far as I'm concerned. I try to get up there every day, at least for my ten minutes of meditation."

Dess had already started up the steps. She glanced back at me over her shoulder with an arch of her eyebrows. "You don't strike me as the meditation type. But then, I wouldn't have pegged Talon as a knitter either."

"I aim to surprise," I said in an automatically teasing tone, and caught myself just before I flashed her a flirty smile. I was too much in the habit of turning on the charm, and she made way too appealing a target for it. But she'd made her interest—or lack thereof—*very* clear.

"Julius taught me," I added in a more subdued tone as

we tramped up the stairs, Dess in front of me. "He has a whole yoga routine he does, actually. He showed me all the moves, but the meditation part was the only thing that stuck. It helps me keep my focus for the rest of the day."

Dess hummed to herself but didn't ask anything else. *Her* focus was fixed on the door at the top of the stairs.

That one wasn't locked. There was no point, since no one could get up here anyway—we'd made sure of that.

As we stepped out into the warm summer sunlight, I made a quick scan of our security measures. The entire space was as big as the common room downstairs. The seamless wooden wall that surrounded it stood ten feet tall, and no structure nearby rose high enough to give a view inside. The outer walls of the apartment building itself were sheer and designed to avoid offering enough ledges or footholds for a person to climb up. The only way anyone was getting a peek or a toe onto our deck was by helicopter.

That was also the only way anyone was going to get off it, other than by going back down the stairs. Dess might have had amazing skills, but she couldn't scramble down a fifteen-story building that offered nothing to hold on to. And I didn't think she was going to be summoning any helicopters.

The space was safe both from intruders and from her making another escape attempt.

I rolled my shoulders back, relaxing with the mental confirmation of what I'd already known, and dragged in a deep breath of the warm air. Being up here was *way* better than the stuffy greenhouse-style yard at the safe house we'd left behind.

Dess took in the space with the same calm alertness she seemed to approach almost every situation. She ambled across the patio tiles and sank onto the wicker sofa near the door. After a moment, she tipped her head to the sky with a small smile.

The look suited her. In the full sunlight, she glowed with artless beauty. The light shone across her silky black hair, the faint breeze stirring the waves against her shoulders. Her smooth skin seemed to soak up every ounce of the sun's rays. Had any of the other guys seen her in this light, or was I the only one privileged enough?

It *was* a privilege.

I forced myself to look away, moving toward the center of the sun-warmed deck where I most enjoyed sitting. I settled there with my legs crossed and got started on my meditation.

With each deep breath, I let go of more and more of the thoughts in their constant whirl in my head. Vaguely, I sensed Dess stand up and move around the roof, but I didn't let her draw too much of my attention. A certainty filled me that even if she did pull off an impossible escape, I'd find her. I had before, and I would again.

Even knowing this, she had too much presence for me to completely ignore her, so I allowed my awareness of her to take a fundamental role in my meditation. Stillness had always been my enemy—something I couldn't quite capture—but the movement of the world around me gave my mind an outlet for its frenetic energy. A car honking below, the occasional shouts from the street, Dess's slow circuit of the deck. All of it centered me in a way I couldn't anywhere else.

Keeping myself still yet in tune with the motion around me despite the chaos in my life gave me a sense of calming reassurance. I could process and release all the input, and it grew sharper with each moment I breathed through the meditative exercise. When my mind latched onto a thought, I released it and allowed it to flow back out of me.

I'd missed my sessions here while we were staked out at the safe house, and now that I was back, I already felt more capable of tackling the world. I felt *invincible.*

I concluded with a few final deep breaths, adjusting to the shift in my thoughts and my sense of my body, no longer quite so restless—for now. Then I opened my eyes.

Dess was leaning against the wall near Garrison's telescope, watching me with her brow knit. I didn't acknowledge her expression as I stood and stretched, releasing the last dregs of tension that remained in my body. With a great sigh, I finally met her gaze fully. "That's better."

She gave me a smile that looked a little puzzled, and her gaze shifted to the telescope. She stepped closer, cocking her head. Garrison would have thrown a fit seeing her running a finger down the sleek black surface of his prized possession.

"Are you a stargazer too?" she asked.

I shook my head. "That's Garrison's department."

"Really?" She studied the telescope a little longer and then dropped onto one of the nearby deck chairs.

I followed suit, picking up a Rubix cube I'd left up here one day or another. My fingers fell into place around its surface, twisting one row and then another. It drove Garrison crazy that I didn't care that I never actually "solved" one of these. I just liked seeing the different arrays of colors that ended up appearing.

"Have you ever used one?" I asked, indicating the telescope.

Dess shook her head and looked up at the sky, exposing the sleek line of her throat. "I've never spent much time outside," she admitted. "And I've never even seen one of these in person. You can really make out that many more stars than just with your eyes?"

"Yep," I said. "And planets and moons and that sort of thing too. I've got to admit, I don't really know what Garrison gets out of it. I can find prettier pictures of space on the internet in two seconds flat."

Dess let out a soft laugh. "Of course you can." She turned back to me, watching the swift but aimless flicks of my fingers over the Rubix cube. "So, what is it *you* like about meditation? It looks pretty boring from the outside."

I had to let out a laugh of my own. Her bluntness was as refreshing as the air up here. I could tell she wasn't trying to be insulting, only making an honest observation.

"I'd bet it does," I said. "Have you ever tried meditating?"

"No to that as well. Apparently I've missed out on a lot of things."

I thought about how to best explain it. I could have given her the response that Julius would have used—the one that claimed that yoga and meditation relaxed the body and improved potential. It allowed for cleaner fighting and a clearer mind.

But I didn't use meditation for those reasons.

I set the cube down on my lap. "Well, the *idea* is that it's supposed to ground you. It stills the world around you, and it allows you to simply exist without being affected by thoughts of the past or the future."

She made a sound of acknowledgment, picking up on my framing. "But for you it's different?"

"Yeah. I can't be still, not really. I've never been able to completely slow down. When I meditate, I can focus on the moving world around me, and it feels like it brings a sort of balance inside me. Recognizing that I'm surrounded by as much energy outside as I have inside me helps to still me in a way, I guess."

Dess nodded, giving me a thoughtful look. "You do seem to move around an awful lot."

I glanced down at my foot, which had begun to tap against the tiles, and grinned. "My mom always said I was full of beans. The doctor said I probably had ADHD, but my parents never really pursued that. They figured I should get it under control through self-discipline or whatever. Which is a lot easier to say than do. I pissed off a lot of the other kids at school, always running around, talking their ears off. We won't get into how many times they kicked my ass."

And worse things that I didn't want to think about. I'd moved on from all that.

"That's awful," Dess said, sounding offended enough on my behalf to gratify me.

I shrugged. "Kids being kids. Grown-ups refusing to do their jobs and rein them in. I figured out some things, made use of the skills I developed to put a few people in their places, and now I've put all that behind me. People can judge me as much as they want, but I am who I am. Take it or leave it."

"So, you just...don't care what people think about you?"

"Well, I care about the people who matter, like the guys I work with, in whatever areas are relevant. But otherwise, no. It doesn't matter what anyone thinks. I lived too long trying to be who people wanted me to be and beating myself up for not fitting their preferences. It was miserable—I won't go back to that. Now, I'm happy with myself. I live my life to the fullest and enjoy every twist and turn along the way."

Dess's gray eyes darkened. "But you're a cop—you've got to be chasing down criminals and figuring out murders and the rest all the time. How can you enjoy life like that?"

The question sounded genuine, and it tugged at my heart. "There's more to life than work. I'm sitting here chatting with you right now, aren't I? And I chose this career because I get a thrill out of a lot of it too—tracking people down, figuring out what they're up to." We'd just avoid the subject of what the crew *really* did with that information.

Dess nodded, but her expression stayed bemused. The idea seemed foreign to her, almost like a fantasy novel full of fictional characters that could never exist in reality.

Did she really have no concept of how to enjoy herself? God, what a number that prick of an ex-boyfriend had done on her.

"I'm sure you can enjoy your life too, Dess," I had to say. "I don't know the details of what you went through before you ended up with us, but after this case is over, you can go do whatever you want. It'll be your choice now."

Assuming the client didn't decide she was a loose end we had to deal with.

Dess smiled, but a trace of sadness lingered in it. What had she endured that made her believe that life wasn't worth taking pleasure in?

I knew so little about her. She'd mentioned a bad relationship, and we'd killed her friend during Viper's job, but that was it. I knew nothing about her past, and I had no idea what could make things better for her.

I examined her stormy eyes and found a restlessness and... something else I couldn't identify.

"I guess I've always been focused on satisfying other people's expectations," she said slowly. "Doing what they asked me to do as well as I could. And sometimes I liked that. But I've never really had a chance to make all that many decisions on my own."

I could hear the honesty in her voice, and it brought an ache into my chest, bittersweet. No one should have a life like that, but she'd trusted me enough to open up to me.

I leaned toward her, intending to grab her hand but stopping myself. She didn't like being touched, so I wouldn't touch her. But I could still help.

"Well, what's something that makes you happy?" I asked. "Just for you, not because you know someone else will be happy about it too."

"Just for me…" She trailed off, and I could see the wheels turning in her mind. Again, unwavering sadness washed through me as she struggled to come up with a single thing that made her happy for its own sake.

"I like chocolate," she declared, a smile springing to her face that looked almost triumphant, as if it was a victory for her to land on that one thing. Maybe it was.

I remembered the hot chocolate that Garrison had made and shared with her. She *had* looked shocked and utterly delighted when he'd given her some. That was an easy thing for me to offer, whether Garrison liked me dipping into his collection or not, and I had every intention of making sure she had plenty for as long as she stayed with us.

"What else?" I prodded.

She answered a little more quickly this time. "Exercising makes me happy. The adrenaline rush and feeling how much I can do with my body. Sparring and coming out on top."

Which I'd bet she did most of the time. I wished she'd pummeled that boyfriend of hers good before she'd taken off on him.

"What about entertainment?" I asked. "Like—movies, music, TV, books?"

She brightened up so fast my pulse skipped a beat. "Oh! There was this TV show I saw once… Years ago, and I think it was already kind of old. I just happened across it one day when I didn't have anything else to do at that moment, and then I got sucked in and couldn't help watching the whole thing. It was about a spy and her husband solving crimes." A crease formed in her forehead. "I missed the title sequence, though, and I never could find it again."

But it'd stuck with her all this time. I stood up, abruptly energized. This was something I could do for her, something no one else in the penthouse could, at least nowhere near as easily. And it'd be so worth it to give her a little more of the happiness she'd obviously been sorely lacking.

I beckoned for her to follow me. "Come on. We're going to find your spy show."

Dess leapt to her feet, her eyes widening. "Just like that? How—"

I grinned at her. "You'll see."

I marched back to the penthouse with Dess at my heels. Talon had moved to the kitchen where he was making himself a cup of coffee. He didn't comment when I grabbed my laptop and stole his spot on the sofa.

Dess sank down next to me. "Do you really think you can find it?"

There was something almost childlike about her hesitant excitement, something that contrasted sharply with the lethal fighter I'd witnessed in the safe-house attack. Yet again, I found myself wondering just how this woman had become who she was... whoever that was exactly.

"I know I can," I told her with total confidence, flexing my fingers over the keys. "All I need are a few details about the show—the plotline in the episode you saw, the characters, the setting—as specific as possible. We already know it had a woman who was a spy and her husband... was he a spy too?"

Dess frowned, tapping her lips. Somehow she got even more gorgeous when her expression went distant with thought, still lit with hope, the black waves of her hair tumbling around her face.

"I think he might have been a doctor?" she said hesitantly. "There was one part where she got shot and her arm was bleeding, and he had to give her stitches. He had some kind of medical experience, anyway." An amused gleam came into her eyes. "Maybe he picked it up in the army like Julius."

"Could be." I added that note to my first search string. "Did you recognize any of the actors? That would help narrow it down too."

She shook her head with a sheepish grimace. "I'm not very up on celebrities and that sort of thing. I remember she was blond, and he had dark hair. Both slim and fit. I think..." Her eyebrows drew together with concentration. "His name was Ron—Ronald. He hated it when she called him by his full name, so she did it to tease him sometimes. I can't remember what her name was... It might have started with H?"

Now we were getting somewhere. My fingers flew over the keyboard, typing in all that information, tweaking a word here and there as the search results spilled out across the screen, narrowing by date because she'd said the show had looked older—ah ha!

I clicked on an image of the DVD cover to enlarge it and turned the laptop toward Dess. It was a campy '60s show that'd only run two seasons, with a blond spy named Helen and her husband, a dark-haired paramedic named Ronald. They were posed in the image back-to-back beneath the title, *Spy Time*, her with her fingers held up in front of her in the shape of a gun and him looking shocked.

It wouldn't have struck me as the kind of show I'd expect Dess to be into, but her mouth dropped open immediately. "Wow. That's it. You just—it only took you a couple of minutes."

I waggled my fingers, flushing with pleasure. "The magic of the internet and a healthy respect for search algorithms. Now that we've found it, how'd you like to watch an episode?"

A small laugh tumbled out of her. "Can we really?"

"Of course. Your wish is my command. Just give me another minute or so…"

I sent my computer scanning through the hordes of legit and—being honest—mostly illegitimate media sites out there and found one that was streaming *Spy Time*. It was so simple I grabbed the TV remote and clicked it on at the same time. Dess scooted forward on the sofa, glancing between me and the TV. A couple more clicks, and…

The first episode started playing in front of us. Peppy '60s music spilled out of the speakers as the characters romped from one crazy scenario to another in the opening sequence.

Dess's lips parted. She gazed at the screen with an expression that could only be described as rapturous. Then she shot me a quick glance, her eyes shining. "Thank you. I really do appreciate it."

Her obvious delight sent a flutter through my chest. I'd done something good today.

"I was happy to," I said honestly. "Now watch!"

She smiled again, with a softness I wouldn't have expected to ever see from her either, and relaxed back into the corner of the sofa. She pulled up her knees in her usual closed-off way, but this time, she didn't seem like she was guarding herself, only getting comfortable. As she watched the show play out, the saddened expression that came from a life of hardships—I had to assume—transformed into perfect contentment.

What a sight.

One of the main characters cracked a joke on-screen,

and Dess laughed loudly, covering her mouth as if even she was startled by the sound. The smile didn't quite fade from her eyes.

She could watch her show all she liked. I couldn't stop watching *her*. I didn't know when I'd see that joy again, and while it lasted, I couldn't look away.

I'd embrace every last second of it, and I already knew I'd do whatever I could to make it happen again.

TWENTY-ONE

Decima

EVEN AS I lay on my cot perfectly still, my mind wouldn't stop shifting back and forth between thoughts. Maybe I needed to try some of that meditation stuff. Although Blaze had said it didn't actually help him to settle down but just to feel more in harmony with the rest of the world or something, so who knew if it'd work for me either?

He'd said a lot of things today. Things that had set my mind into this whirling of uncertainty. I'd felt so... so *good* watching that episode of *Spy Time*, everything else in my life falling away, laughs tumbling out of me like I couldn't remembering happening since I was a kid.

But then, as the credits had rolled, he'd turned to me and asked if I wanted to watch another, and reality had come crashing in. There *were* a hell of a lot of other things in my life, things I couldn't—shouldn't—forget. How could I sit there laughing at some silly TV show when Anna and everyone else in the household were dead, when I'd barely made any progress into figuring out who'd killed them, let alone bringing them justice?

Blaze could treat life as a game all he wanted, but he didn't know what mine was made up of. He didn't understand how important it'd been for me to stay focused and train as hard as I had. Every time I'd left the household, I'd been risking my life to take down a threat, with the whole household depending on me. Happiness was a distraction, not something I should have been chasing.

And yet... some part of me wanted so badly to go out there and beg him to put on that second episode. What was wrong with me?

I couldn't stand keeping my body motionless any longer. Pushing myself upright, I eyed the exercise equipment that filled the rest of the room the cops had given me. Working out had always been my surest method to blow off steam and regain my focus.

I needed to get my priorities straight, and all of the emotion boiling inside of me was accomplishing the opposite. It had to go.

A half-hour sprint on the treadmill would start the job well, and an extended arm workout after that—weights and maybe some bodyweight work—would finish the job. The prospect of exhausting myself thoroughly brought me a much more comfortable sense of relief.

I pulled my hair back from my face and went through several opening stretches. Getting on the treadmill, I allowed myself to ease into its grip and resistance before jogging on it. I'd used them before, but every machine was a little different. You could roll an ankle if you started at top speed on equipment you weren't familiar with.

Once I'd set my ideal pace, I flew. Remembering Noelle's coaching, I willed my breathing to remain steady until the entire process became a constant thrum of instinct and will. The running drove me forward, my legs and lungs started to burn, and the long days of emotion-filled events peeled away from me one layer at a time.

I turned the treadmill up another notch, adjusting my form and easily keeping pace. My heartbeat increased in tempo with it. My ribs thrummed with each hard pound of my feet, but they were nearly healed. The pain was mild enough that I could breathe right through it in a matter of minutes.

Just how I liked it.

When the burn started to prick at my muscles, switching from exhilaration to exhaustion, I slowed my sprint to a fast lope and continued, closing my eyes. I'd seen normal women jogging along the city streets before, passing by me while I was immersed in a mission. Did they get the same release out of it that I did, or did they run for some other reason?

The door to the workout room opened with a squeak of the hinges, and I spared a glance behind me. Talon stood in the doorway, a towel slung over his shoulder and a jug of water dangling from his hand. I tilted my head up in greeting but didn't give him more of an acknowledgment than that.

"I heard you going at it and figured I'd join you," he said. "The others have all headed out, and I could use something to keep me occupied." He paused as if waiting for my approval.

I wondered if he'd turn around and leave if I told him to. Had it been anyone else, I might have tested that question, but I knew Talon wouldn't attempt to make small talk while he worked out. Anyway, it was his exercise room. I was just an interloper here.

I gave him a sharp nod, and he didn't say another word as he walked over to the rack of dumbbells. The weights clinked as he lifted a couple. I waited until his sounds of effort filled the room before I slowed to a fast walk and caught my breath.

My legs ached beautifully, and a thin layer of sweat covered my entire body. I raised the hem of my shirt and wiped the sweat from my face as my heart regained a normal, steady tempo. As I came down from the high of the exertion, my gaze traveled over to Talon, just as he lifted the weights he'd picked up.

Oh, fuck. I'd already known he was an immaculate specimen of manhood, but watching the muscles all through his shoulders, arms, and back flex to perfect effect made my sex clench. As he raised and lowered the weights with absolute control, the image rose up in my mind of what it would feel like to be held against that body, handled with the same muscular precision.

If watching a TV show could bring some kind of bliss, imagine how good indulging in *that* kind of "enjoyment" could be.

My lips tightened as I registered the thought that had just crossed my mind. I'd come in here to burn away my unwanted emotions, not stir up more of them. Apparently, I hadn't run myself ragged enough on the treadmill.

With a groan, Talon placed his weights back on the rack and met my eyes, the blue of his as intense as ever. Sweat glistened atop his shaved scalp, enticing me to run my hands over the smooth skin.

"Are you done?" he asked. "I thought maybe we could spar."

I raised my eyebrows. "Eager to show off your skills at dominating an injured opponent again?"

He gave me an even look, unfazed by my jab. "I find it's the best kind of workout. Keeps the mind sharp as well as the body in shape. And you're a good challenge even when injured. But I wasn't planning on dominating."

He strode to the chest at the side of the room and opened it, pulling out a pair of boxing gloves and sparring pads, creased with use but still shinier than the ones at the safe house.

He passed the boxing gloves to me, and I tapped his arm with one after I took them. "You should wear gloves too. You're not my teacher, and I don't need you to go easy on me. If we're going to spar, let's actually spar."

He eyed me, still holding the pads that he'd planned on using to direct and deflect my hits. "You don't want to box with me."

"Don't I?"

Whatever Talon found in my glance must have convinced him, because he dropped the pads and lifted his own pair of boxing gloves. "You don't want me to go easy on you, huh?" he asked, falling into a fighting stance.

The pose came to him so naturally that I almost questioned my decision. Not because I didn't think I could take him, but because something low in my belly liquified at the sight of his confident power.

No. I wasn't going to stand here and drool over him like some kind of nitwit. I tugged both boxing gloves onto my hands, one over the damned brace that I often contemplated chucking out the window. "Do your worst."

He shook his head. "I'm not doing my worst with you. An easy warm-up first, then we can get into light boxing." I *swore* I detected a hint of humor in his tone.

I didn't want to warm up more. I wanted to get rid of all those pesky feelings that continued to multiply in his presence. Didn't he understand that?

Of course, he didn't. He barely ever showed so much as a flicker of emotion. In a way that was good. I wasn't the slightest bit worried that he'd put on a cajoling front and turn on the sweet talk that would bring up horrible memories rather than desire. He wasn't *trying* to seduce me. But I still had the urge to provoke him in other ways.

If I pushed hard enough, I could get something from

him. He was a man, after all, and even the most stoic ones could be pushed to their breaking points.

I should know.

Rather than starting easy, I swung my left fist with all the intensity I could, and Talon quickly deflected it.

"What kind of cops are you, anyway?" I asked, throwing another punch. I'd either get some information out of him or rile him up. I'd be fine with either outcome. "Living together undercover, breaking all kinds of rules— you've got to be some special type. FBI? CIA? Some other string of three letters?"

Talon shook his head. "Just the usual kind."

"Do you deal with a lot of cases like what happened at my friend's house? How often do total massacres happen around here anyway?"

He went quiet, and I ducked one of his slower punches, elbowing him hard in the gut when he left a small opening. A burst of air shot out of him, and he clenched his jaw as he jerked back.

"Take it easy," he said firmly, leaving no room for argument. He clearly didn't know me as well as he hoped.

I moved in with a swift one-two, ignoring the twinge in my bad hand when he batted it aside—because that gave me a chance to shove my other fist into his stomach.

The glove's padding muted the impact, but Talon still groaned from the force of the blow. The frustration that blazed in his eyes for just an instant left me a little giddy. One point to me.

"That's it? You're just going to ignore my questions?" I said.

His blows remained easy, practically mocking, as if he still didn't believe I could keep up. "There's nothing to say. You know that we can't discuss our other cases."

"Fine, what about *this* case?" I insisted, bouncing from foot to foot and awaiting another opening. He had his face guarded with ironclad defenses, but his abdomen—the same spot I continued assaulting—couldn't be defended properly with our height difference. I hit him there again and deflected his returning blow.

Cool. Calm. Collected. I needed to break him out of his careful control.

"No," he said, and his tone left little room for argument. "It's classified."

"Yes, so you all keep saying," I shot back. "I think you just don't want to admit how stumped you are. I told you more in that one little trip by the house than the bunch of you had figured out on your own, didn't I?"

I threw a combination of punches to Talon's abdomen, looping one around and hitting him in the side. His mouth twitched toward a frown.

"Enough talking," he demanded, and I knew I was getting somewhere. "This is sparring, not an interrogation."

"Why can't it be both?" I taunted, bobbing and weaving around him. "Prove that you've figured out *anything at all* about the people who murdered my friend. Give me some hope that you're going to find the pricks who did that to her. Do you have any idea what it's like, seeing someone you care about slaughtered like that? Haven't you ever given a shit about a single person in your life?"

His eyes flashed again, searing hotter as he glared at me. I'd hit a nerve, a good one, but I wasn't done. "What, is it because nobody ever loved you? Is that your excuse for being cold as an ice cube—why you can't be bothered to give me even one ounce of closure? Why the fuck should you care about anyone other than yourself?"

His defenses dropped just a fraction, and I struck. I smacked him hard across the face, and his head seemed to whip to the side in slow motion.

Then everything sped up to a blur. In a single moment, he shook off his gloves and snatched both my wrists in his hands. He shoved me, and I could do nothing but backstep with him until my back was pressed flush against the cool wall. His body caged me there as he pinned my arms above my head.

The musky scent of his sweat and a feral tang that was all him washed over me. He leaned so close his breath grazed my face. "Give it up," he snarled, his voice deeper and more threatening. "You're not getting anything out of me."

The pure masculinity that oozed from him—the fierceness in his stance, the power in his hold even though I knew I could break it if I tried hard enough— sparked an uncontrollable, insatiable flare of desire that couldn't be suppressed. His mouth had come so close to mine, and all at once I could think of nothing but closing that distance.

My brain short-circuited—that's the only way I can explain it. I lunged, not to break free but to steal a kiss.

My mouth met Talon's roughly. He froze, his grip loosening in shock, his lips surprisingly soft but unmoving beneath mine. Panic flashed through the flood of my desire. Had I wrongly assumed there'd been interest on his side?

Just as I started to pull back, embarrassment flushing my cheeks, Talon shoved his body more solidly against mine and kissed me back hard.

His grip on my pinned wrists tightened, but somehow that only made the kiss more delicious. I groaned against his lips, and he all but devoured me. His tongue swept into my mouth, his teeth grazing my lips, all the muscular planes of his body pressing up against me. The power radiating from him brought me to my metaphorical knees.

As he kissed me again, our mouths crashing together even more violently, I brought my own tongue out to play. I'd never known how thrilling it would be to spar like this instead. His hips rocked into me, a hard bulge brushing my lower belly, and every nerve in my body clanged with need.

His lips moved to my neck, nipping and licking and claiming every inch of skin. Abruptly, he released my wrists, grasping my thighs instead. He pushed me up the wall just high enough so that the hard length of him could settle against my sex.

Oh my fucking God. The friction of it drove me wild, making me want to claw at him until I'd torn off all the layers of clothes between me and him, until he could be plunging right inside me.

What had gotten into me?

The thought had only just flitted through my head when the ravaging of my neck transformed into kisses that were almost tender. An image flashed through my mind— teasing words in a sweet voice, gentle caresses, never letting up, never stopping no matter how much I tried to wrench myself away—

I stiffened, transported out of the moment and back to that other time and place I wished I could forget.

I closed my eyes tightly, trying to ground myself back in the present. It'd felt so *good* a second ago. But I couldn't get back to that place where this intimacy felt like a gift rather than an assault, not when Talon had gone soft on me.

Maybe that was crazy, but I already knew I wasn't a normal woman. My body needed what it needed.

I flung both boxing gloves to the ground alongside his and gripped his shirt with a clenched fist, yanking on it until he raised his head to meet my eyes. The lust hazing the icy blue irises had me soaking my panties. But I had to make this clear, or we couldn't go any farther. And holy fuck did I want to find out how far this could go.

"I'm not a porcelain doll," I said, low and determined. "So don't treat me like I'm one. Give me everything you've fucking got. Make it war, not love."

Something flickered in his gaze. Then he reached a hand behind me and wrapped it around my ponytail, pulling my head back and exposing my throat to him. He bit hard on the side of my throat, and I gasped, a slight moan escaping my lips.

Yes, that was what worked. I felt my entire body melt at the gesture. This was nothing like the asshole who'd violated me with false sweetness before. This was something totally different—different and fucking amazing.

Talon shoved his free hand down my pants, palming my pussy, and a jolt of blissful heat rushed through me. My breaths fractured into panting.

"How rough do you want it?" he said into my ear, tugging back on my ponytail with more force.

I let out a strangled sound as his finger flicked over the sensitive spot between my thighs. One touch set off a quiver of pleasure that took my breath away completely. Was this what sex was supposed to feel like? What it normally felt like for most people? If so, how the hell did they manage to do anything else?

"I want you to make me scream," I whispered, and slammed my mouth into his once more.

Talon's next move nearly accomplished my request in one go. He plunged two fingers into me, still stroking the place right at the core of me that made me squirm and whimper with need. The place that had been too long deprived of a touch other than my own. The way he touched me there—the roughly oscillating motions he made combined with the crush of his lips against mine—flooded me with so much giddy heat I could barely think.

I broke away from his lips long enough to rip my shirt off over my head, leaving only my sports bra. Talon dove in to leave tingling bites up and down my neck, finally dipping his head to the exposed hollow of my cleavage as his fingers kept pumping in and out of me. I writhed against the wall, desperate to reach some point I couldn't even explain. One of my hands dropped to that tempting bulge behind the fabric of his pants.

Talon jerked back with a muttered curse. He withdrew his hand from my own pants and lifted his fingers slick with the proof of my hunger. Holding my gaze, he licked my arousal off him, and I just about went up in flames.

The smile that pulled to his face was pure, unadulterated masculine assurance. A heady tremor rippled through me even with him barely touching me.

He took a step back. "Don't move," he ordered.

I had absolutely no desire to be anywhere but here. Where the hell was *he* going, though?

He all but hurtled out of the room and barreled back in mere seconds later with a foil wrapper in his hand. Understanding clicked in my head. Of course. I hadn't even thought—

But why would I? I'd never gotten this close to any man except the one who'd taken what I hadn't wanted to give. And besides, Noelle had brought me to get a birth control implant inserted into my arm years ago, after that incident—one of the most effective ones, if she was to be believed. Just in case.

It didn't protect against everything, though. Who knew how many women Talon had been with before me? I didn't bother to mention my own version of protection as he prowled toward me. Every thought but the act we were about to commit fled my mind.

Talon hooked his fingers around my bra and yanked it off me. Before he could close his hands over my bare breasts, I wrenched at his T-shirt. He tossed it aside, and I took in the expanse of black and gray lines. Intricately woven tattoos covered his chest and his broad shoulders. It was an utter masterpiece of guns, bones, and military tags, shaded to a terrifying perfection, mesmerizing and beautiful.

No, *beautiful* wasn't the right word for the grandeur of Talon's naked torso.

He was a mountain of sculpted scars and tattoos, muscles bulging through all of them and tanned skin weaving it all together. His body was a fine piece of art. From the ragged scar poking up from his hip to the small, thin lines that ran across his biceps, he stood as a living, mesmerizing sculpture.

That masterpiece lifted me onto a clear section of the weight rack and peeled off my pants and panties with one swift gesture that left me even wetter than before. As he dropped his own pants, I couldn't take my eyes off the thick, corded length of his cock.

He smoothed the condom over the hard shaft and then

pinned my arms over my head again. I arched my back instinctively, and he looked over my entire exposed body —every small scar and curve.

He lowered his head to suck one and then the other nipple into his mouth, tugging with his teeth on the release. A gasp tumbled out of me at the shock of combined pain and pleasure. Then he lined himself up and thrust into me, balls deep.

With that motion, he fulfilled my request. He made me scream. The sound reverberated through me alongside the electric burst of bliss. No sensation I'd ever been able to produce with my hand had come close to this.

Talon hesitated, examining my features, and a prickle of panic rose up again. I hissed through my teeth. "Fuck me hard."

Something flared in his eyes. He pulled back and thrust into me again, dipping his head to reclaim the peak of one of my breasts in tandem. Each roll of his hips brought a delicious burn between my thighs that spread all through my torso.

He was big, but I'd been so wet and ready I could take him. The stretch was nothing short of paradise.

Talon could still have hurt me if he'd been too rough about it. I could tell he restrained himself just slightly, adding a little twist here, shifting his angle there, in ways that made me moan. But through it all the force of his thrusts and the scrape of his teeth against my skin kept all sensation except enjoyment at bay.

As he found his rhythm and saw what I could handle,

he picked up his pace to a brutal speed. I bucked into him, riding the surge of sensations, gasping at the pleasure that shot through me every time he buried himself inside me. It washed through every inch of my body, every part of my soul. And then, with one final plunge, he shattered me.

Ecstasy tore through my body, leaving me shaking and clenching around him. A cry burst from my throat. Talon continued his relentless rhythm, drawing every ounce of writhing lust from me.

He didn't take long to follow, tipping his head back when the orgasm swept through his body. He let go of my wrists and gripped both of my hips, his thrusts growing sporadic as he finished his release. Then he bowed over me.

We stared at each other, damp with not just our own sweat but each other's now. Talon's face remained as impenetrable as ever. I couldn't even tell whether he was happy we'd crashed into each other like this or upset. Or whether he really didn't care at all.

"Well, that was one way to keep ourselves occupied," I said in a rough attempt at a joke, playing off his earlier comment.

Talon didn't even acknowledge my words. He withdrew and touched me only enough to help me down from the rack. "I'd better shower," was all he said. Then he picked up his clothes and walked out.

Okay, then. I sat down on my cot, hugging myself. Had I made a mistake?

It hadn't felt like a mistake at the time. Remembering

the way he'd hammered into me, the feel of his hands and his teeth, I bit my bottom lip. My sex was already throbbing at the idea of having another go.

If it'd been a mistake, then it was one I wasn't sure I could avoid repeating. I'd had no idea—I mean, obviously sex had to feel pretty good if people bothered at all, but for it to be *that* amazing...

I shook off those thoughts and grabbed my own clothes. As fantastic as it'd been, it obviously wasn't happening again today. Possibly not *ever* again with Talon, depending on what was going on in his head right now.

As I pulled on my shirt, a faint rattling sound reached my ears. What was that?

Then it hit me. The phone. I'd left it on vibrate.

I dashed over to the trunk where I'd stashed it and tugged it out from behind. Thank God it hadn't gone off while Talon was here. I flipped it open in my hand—and then just stared at the text message that had popped up on the screen.

This is Noelle. When you see this, respond immediately.

That was it. No expression of concern or acknowledgment of the horror I'd witnessed in the mansion, no curiosity about where I might be. Just a simple demand.

Something about it made my hackles rise. *Was* it even Noelle? Scarlett hadn't known who'd left the phone for her, or at least that's what she'd claimed. She hadn't acted as if it was someone she trusted.

And—Noelle was *dead*, wasn't she? I'd seen that woman with the right sort of hair and build in the middle of the massacre...

But of course, the corpse's face had been too mutilated to identify. I wasn't sure it'd been my trainer.

Where would she have been if not at the household, though?

Too many questions cluttered my head. If I even confirmed that I'd gotten the phone, would I be alerting someone I didn't actually want to tangle with, at least not yet? Maybe this was some kind of trap arranged by the same people who'd rampaged through the mansion.

Whether it was them or it really was Noelle, I'd find out. I could use this connection. I just needed a day or two to think to be sure I made the right decision. I was running this mission on my own, making the calls. When I'd acted hastily before, I'd nearly screwed myself over.

Taking a deep breath and ignoring the tension clamped around my stomach, I turned off the phone and shoved it back into its hiding place.

TWENTY-TWO

Decima

I ENDED up throwing myself into another workout, pushing the muscles in my arms and legs to the limit, until the tension inside me faded again. Every now and then, my mind flashed to the other release I'd gotten not long ago, to the way Talon's hands had held my body and his hips had thrust into me, and my panties dampened all over again. I pushed myself harder.

I'd learned something from him, something about myself and what my body was capable of that I hadn't known. That was the important part. It wasn't as if I could pursue any kind of *relationship* with him, not that he seemed likely to want that. He was a cop, and I killed people on a regular basis. Also, he and his friends had essentially kidnapped me, even if I'd sort of allowed them to the last time.

But I couldn't say I had any regrets about the interlude we'd shared. If nothing else, it'd give me plenty of fodder when I took matters into my own hands in the future.

When I was done, feeling looser than I had in ages, I ducked into the bathroom, because I could definitely use a shower too. I lingered there for longer than usual, scrubbing all the sweat from my skin and working a lather through my hair. The soap I grabbed had a bit of Talon's tang to its scent—it must have been his. There was a weird intimacy to having it wrapped around me alongside the water streaming over my body.

When I'd dried off and dressed in a fresh pair of clothes—Steffie had run my discarded outfits through the laundry like she did for the guys, which I couldn't complain about—I stepped into the main room to find that all four of the men were now home.

They'd gathered around Julius's small table next to the whiteboard, and the man in charge was pointing out a few details in a sketch he'd made that looked roughly like the layout of a building. He had several army figures set out on the table. He motioned to them, moving a few, knocking one over, and the other men nodded. Blaze tapped away on the laptop he had balanced against his lean chest, his expression unusually serious.

They were up to something, making plans—I could taste it in the energy in the atmosphere as well as their body language. But other than a quick glance Garrison and then Julius shot my way, they didn't acknowledge me. They didn't intend to loop me in on this particular plan.

I could pretend I hadn't realized that, though. I ambled over with an air of casual curiosity. "What are you all up to, tucked away in the corner like this?"

"Discussing business," Julius said in that commanding tone of his. "Why don't you relax in your room until it's dinner time?"

I folded my arms over my chest. "If it's about the massacre at Anna's house, it involves me too. I want to know what's going on."

"It's got nothing to do with your friend," he said, but his expression was so impervious I couldn't tell whether I should believe him.

They'd all fallen silent, waiting for me to leave. Talon looked at me briefly with no sign he even remembered how tightly we'd been entwined a couple of hours ago. What would his colleagues have thought of him if they'd known?

I didn't have any interest in throwing him under the bus, though. That'd just destroy any chance there was of getting a second opportunity to enjoy the intense pleasures he could offer. Still, the thought of going back into the exercise room where the smell of sweat and him still hung in the air made my skin itch.

"I'll just go hang out on the sofa," I said, turning away, thinking I might get a chance to spy on them like I had before, but Julius cleared his throat.

"No, I think it's better if we have the room completely to ourselves."

Damn it. I held back a frown, not wanting him to

realize how much I'd been counting on learning more about their mysterious mission.

Glancing around, I realized that I might be able to turn this into a different sort of opportunity. "Fine. Can I go up to the roof instead? I'd rather get some fresh air if you're going to insist on me being out of your way."

Julius's gaze followed mine in a moment of contemplation. I braced myself for a refusal, but he nodded. "I don't see how that could hurt anything."

He didn't think I had a hope in hell of escaping the apartment that way, he meant. We'd see about that. It'd be far from the first time someone had underestimated me.

I followed Julius as he strode to the locked door. He typed the code into the numeric lock quickly, angling his body to prevent me from seeing the numbers, and I made a show of not caring anyway. If they were going to let me go up on my own, I didn't need to sneak up there. I just needed to figure out what I'd do once I had the whole outdoor space at my disposal.

The door opened with a click. Julius pushed it wide and gestured to the stairwell. "I'll leave it unlocked so you can get back in when you're ready."

A small act of generosity. I gave him a similarly small smile. As I marched up the stairs, I felt his eyes on my back until the door thumped shut behind me.

Emerging onto the rooftop deck, I simply stood there for a few moments, looking at the bright blue sky and sucking in the fresh afternoon air. I hadn't been lying when

I'd said I enjoyed it. Another thing to add to my list for Blaze. *Air* made me happy.

How pathetic was that?

But then, I hadn't gotten to savor the outside air very often. I'd stayed in my rooms in the household for days at a time in between missions or the occasional outdoor training session. My section of the mansion hadn't even had windows. The household had wanted to ensure no one could possibly find out I was living there, their secret weapon. The secrecy protected both them and me.

It made sense. But that didn't mean I couldn't enjoy this sort-of freedom while I had it, right?

The solitude was nice too. Other than when I'd been in one bedroom or another, this was the first time I'd been totally, blissfully *alone* since the moment the men had surrounded me after I'd crashed the car.

It probably wouldn't last. How long did I have before one of them came to check on me or tell me to get back downstairs?

That thought brought my mind back into full alertness. I had a small mission of my own here, and I needed to see it through before I was interrupted. I wasn't sure I'd want to take off on the men right now, still with no real sense of direction, but it'd be good to be prepared in case I decided I needed to make a quick escape later.

I started by walking the entire length of the wooden wall, feeling for imperfections or rot. No surprise, the wall was as secure as it was tall. When I returned to the spot beside the door, I stepped back, analyzing the barrier from more of a distance.

It was taller than the wall around the household by a few feet, so jumping it would be impossible without help, but with a chair stacked on top of the patio table, I knew I could make it to the top. But from there... I didn't know exactly how high up we were, but the length of the elevator ride and the absence of any taller buildings in view suggested it was at least ten stories. I'd bet more.

With a grappling hook and a good length of rope, I'd have been just fine regardless of what the outer walls looked like. Somehow I didn't think I could ask the cops to pick up those items for me at the store. Tying sheets and other items together was always an option, but I didn't think there were enough in the apartment to guarantee I'd make it close enough to the ground to jump the rest of the way.

Maybe there was another building nearby, or a tree or cables or some other object I could make use of. I wouldn't know until I got up to the top, though, and if they caught me clambering along the wall, they'd never let me up here alone again. I had to be sure I was ready.

Lost in thought, I ran my tongue over my teeth and found myself meandering over to the telescope I'd examined earlier with Blaze. I drummed my fingers on the smooth metal. Too bad it wasn't an X-ray machine like one of the gadgets in *Spy Time*, built to let me see right through the wall.

Who said it might not show me something in the sky

that would be useful, though? A more distant building or some other landmark? That would help me orient myself and the apartment in the city.

I bent down, leaning toward the place where I assumed I needed to put my eye.

A snarky voice carried from behind me. "Most people know not to touch other people's belongings without asking. Hands off the telescope."

I jerked back and whirled around to find Garrison stepping out onto the deck. I'd let myself get so lost in thought I hadn't heard the door open. *Sloppy*, Noelle said in my head with a tsk of her tongue.

Blaze had mentioned that the telescope was Garrison's. Garrison stood watching me with his hands slung in his pockets in a careless pose, but his expression was chilly. Why did he have to be such an ass all the time?

Well, there was nothing stopping me from poking the bear and seeing what came out.

With a taunting smile, I lowered my fingers to the telescope and stroked it. "Get my hands off of this?"

Garrison tilted his head and looked between me and the telescope, his hands not leaving his pockets. "Do you know how to use it?"

"Not particularly."

"Then I'm sticking to my demand. Hands. Off."

I rolled my eyes and folded my arms over my chest, stepping toward him. "Buzzkill."

Not dropping eye contact, he sank onto one of the lawn chairs surrounding a small coffee-style table. He stretched out his legs and leaned his head back as if making a statement about how little he was intimidated by me.

He just didn't know better.

"Let's not pretend you're actually up here to stargaze," he said.

I made a sweeping gesture toward him. "Feel free to enlighten me about my own motivations, then."

He glowered at me. "You're looking for escape routes. Hopefully you're smart enough to have figured out by now that it's hopeless."

I let the corner of my lips quirk upward. "You think I'm smart, huh?"

Garrison let out a huff of annoyance. "That wasn't what I was getting at."

"But you said it anyway." I plopped down onto the chair kitty-corner to him, matching his careless demeanor. I didn't think I'd given away anything about my intentions. He was just guessing, and when I'd tried to run off on them a few times already, guessing that I might be thinking about doing it again didn't exactly require major brain power. "What makes you so sure I'm in a hurry to get out of here?"

"You've been trying to take off since the first day. What makes today any different?"

I could think of a few things that made today different, but I wasn't going to mention them to him. Instead, I scooted to the edge of the chair and leaned forward. If I'd slid my foot out, I could have brushed it against his ankle.

"What's wrong?" I teased. "Are you worried you'd miss me if I got away?"

I could see his hackles rise—the way he sat up straighter and the cunning smirk on his face tightened, remaining only because of his iron will to remain cool and collected.

"If you got away," he said, "it would solve every single problem I've had over the past week."

I smiled and pushed him further. "You've been worried about me *that* much? I'm flattered."

Garrison scoffed and gripped the armrest. "You'd like to think so, wouldn't you? Having someone worry about you instead of giving you reasons to worry would be a nice change of events."

Wow, if I really had been fleeing an abusive boyfriend, that would have been a low blow. I feigned a wince. "Ouch. Well, maybe it takes one to know one."

His eyes flashed, and I restrained an outright grin. Another item to add to my happiness list—I enjoyed this back and forth with Garrison. Rolling with his verbal punches, finding the best way to throw the jabs back at him. It was like a different kind of sparring. Not quite as thrilling as the way I'd tangled with Talon but exhilarating in its own right.

Garrison considered me with a scowl. "Why *did* you come up here then, Dess?"

"Like I told Julius, I wanted some fresh air." What else could I say to shut down that subject? I tipped back my head. "And maybe I wanted to sunbathe too. Got to look pretty when I have four manly men studying me all day."

I flicked at my hair in what I hoped looked like a flirtatious gesture. Unfortunately, flirting was *not* my thing, and only half the hair I flicked went over my shoulder, the other half catching in the breeze and flying back into my face. I swiped it aside as if I'd meant to do that.

"Something tells me that you don't particularly care about looking pretty for us," Garrison said, looking me over.

With anyone else, I'd have worried it was an insult, but with Garrison, I couldn't totally tell. He wasn't wrong, after all.

I raised my eyebrows. "Are you saying that I haven't been meeting your exacting standards? Feel free to tell me where I've fallen short."

His mouth twisted, and I knew that I'd made it difficult to respond. He could purposely offend me, and I had no doubt that he was considering doing just that. But if I knew Garrison at all, and I had a feeling that I was quickly learning his preferred method of snark, he wouldn't go for the obvious insult.

He liked the challenge of our conversations too, even if he pretended they irritated him. Why would he have kept up the snark with me if he didn't? He could have just ignored me.

My mind flashed to Talon and the aggressive, dominating way he'd taken me in the exercise room. What would it be like to "spar" with Garrison *that* way? An image darted through my mind of us continuing our battle in the bedroom, fighting to claim our pleasure.

Maybe it was the thrill that came with the thought that propelled me onward, a spark of inspiration lighting in my mind. I didn't give him a chance to spit out the response he was brewing. Instead, I took charge.

I sighed dramatically. "It's okay if you don't find me pretty. There's more to me than looks. I wonder if the same can be said about you?" I cocked my head to one side. "I'm starting to think not so much."

Garrison's eyes blazed, and I knew part of him was seeping through the mask he wore so well. "I'll have you know—"

"That your sharp tongue is only to deflect attention from your many flaws? That's what I thought."

He uncrossed his legs and brought himself slowly to his feet, standing over me in a way that would have intimidated a lesser woman. I'd expected it. I could see the way his frustration with me and his fascination roared inside him, battling for dominance.

He didn't hate me. Not really.

"I think we're done here," he said. "Time to go downstairs."

Oh, no, he wasn't getting out of this that easily. I pushed myself off the chair, planting myself just inches away from him.

"Don't be silly," I said with a sly smile. "We're just getting started."

Then I grabbed the front of his shirt and tugged him toward me so I could capture his lips.

I hadn't been sure if he'd kiss me back. I'd only been counting on a startled moment or two before he pushed me away. But the next thing I knew, Garrison was gripping the back of my head, molding his mouth to mine. A torrent of hidden emotion flowed into me with the fervor of his kiss.

Oh, he didn't hate me at all.

As if he'd realized what he'd given away in the same instant I had, Garrison jerked back. His cheeks had flushed, but his eyes glinted with annoyance.

"Don't fucking do that again," he spat, running a hand through his shaggy blond hair.

I gazed back at him innocently. "Really? You didn't exactly seem to mind in the—"

"I said don't." He took another step away, as if he needed the distance between us to control himself. Which maybe was true. Then he jabbed his hand toward the stairs. "Get back inside where you'll make less trouble."

He ushered me down the stairs, staying a few feet behind the whole time, and then stalked off toward his bedroom the second we'd come into the apartment. Blaze and Julius were still discussing something by the whiteboard. Talon had gone into the kitchen to heat up the dinner Steffie had left for us.

Perfect.

I turned toward Blaze's workstation as if eyeing it curiously—and pulled out the phone I'd snatched from Garrison's pocket while he was distracted by the press of my lips. A satisfied smile tugged at those lips now. He'd had no idea I'd made off with it.

But now I had to search it for what I needed before he or any of the others noticed.

I tapped in the passcode I'd observed through the kettle's reflection. A part of me expected it not to work, but when the entire phone opened to me, I couldn't help outright grinning. Jackpot.

I went immediately to the recent text messages, scanning them for anything important, though I had little context for most of them. The only message that really caught my eye was from Julius, sent this morning, and it was basic—*102 Freeton Ave*, which was an address I didn't recognize, and the words, *Blaze says this is the one.*

Was this the address that they'd be visiting later? For their plans that supposedly had nothing to do with the household case?

The address was easy enough to commit to memory. Then I opened the browser history and knew my mistake the moment the page loaded.

A porn site was the last opened page, a woman and her pussy exposed wide to the camera. I rolled my eyes. Typical.

I opened the other tabs, finding only unimportant questions he'd typed into the browser. Nothing substantial.

Every second I had the phone on me was a risk. I closed all the apps I'd opened and turned it off, then ambled over to the sofa. When I sat down there, I let the phone slide between the cushions.

He'd assume it'd fallen out of his pocket sometime earlier. Nothing at all to do with me.

Now I just had to figure out why Blaze said that address was "the one" and what exactly the guys meant to do there.

TWENTY-THREE

Decima

I LAY awake on my cot long after I'd supposedly turned in for the night. The men had made a show of turning off all but the dim security light that shone over the front door and heading toward their own bedrooms, but I hadn't believed their act for a second. They were just dodging any more questions I might have asked.

It might have been two hours or maybe three when my perked ears caught the faintest rustle of movement in the main room. I retrieved my new phone from where I'd stashed it under my pillow tonight and slunk to the door. There, I eased it open the slightest crack.

The four cops had already gathered near the entrance. They weren't talking, just equipping themselves with a few last weapons—Talon tucked a pistol out of sight by his waist; Blaze checked a holster strapped to his calf and then tugged his pantleg over it. Julius stood closest to the door.

The flip phone was an old model, but it still had basic camera functions. I pressed the button to zoom the screen in as much as it'd allow me, just as Julius reached to tap in the lock code. He didn't bother to hide it now, since he had no idea I was watching. Most people wouldn't have been able to pick out the numbers he'd pressed at that angle in the dim light, but my well-honed eyes translated the movements into a sequence I immediately memorized.

It was far from the first code I'd had to stealthily obtain, and I doubted it'd be the last.

As soon as I'd seen that, I let my door ease all the way shut again. No point in risking them noticing the tiny gap when I didn't need to.

I sat on the floor next to the door with my ear tipped close. There were a few more rustling sounds, and then the soft click of the door shutting behind them. I waited several more minutes to be sure they didn't unexpectedly come right back. Then I nudged my bedroom door carefully open and slipped out into the main room.

There was no sign of any of them. I checked each of their bedrooms to be sure, getting whiffs of their varying scents that brought a tendril of heat into my belly alongside my eager anticipation.

Tonight, I was going to get some real answers.

I ducked back into my room to stuff my remaining cash and the phone into my pockets. I'd need both out there in the big bad world sooner or later, depending on what I ran into on the way.

My reaching hands hesitated over my tote bag. The stuffed tiger's worn head poked out the top.

Part of me wanted to snatch it up, but that was ridiculous. I couldn't bring it along on a mission. Even if I'd had a bag that wouldn't get in the way, there'd still be a small chance of it throwing me off balance or snagging in a tight space.

We go into every mission with just the bare bones, Noelle used to say. *That way we can stay focused on what we really need and what's really important.*

What the hell did I want a toy for anyway? I might be back. And if I wasn't, oh well.

But for some silly reason, a weird pang shot through my chest as I stood up and walked away from it.

I didn't like going out unarmed, but the sharpest thing I could find in the kitchen was a dinner knife. Did the guys just never use anything sharper with their food or had they hidden them all after I'd arrived? I frowned at it, and then my gaze slid toward the sofa.

There was a different kind of weapon here.

With a wry smile, I marched over to Talon's knitting bag and dug out a spare needle. I could wield that more effective than the blunt knife. He could get a little satisfaction from knowing I'd taken his comments to heart even if the theft annoyed him.

Tucking the needle into my pocket, where a few inches

of it still protruded, I strode over to the front door and typed in the code. The bolt thudded over in an instant. Another smile sprang to my face, my triumph washing away any lingering uneasiness about what I was leaving behind.

The short hall outside held only an elevator, no entrance to a stairway that I could see. That seemed like one hell of a fire hazard, but I wasn't here to complain about how up to code the building was. I pressed the button to summon the elevator.

It whirred to a halt, and the doors parted. When I stepped in, my first time riding it without a blindfold, I noted the rows of buttons on the righthand side. Fourteen floors. I'd estimated well.

But none of them were lit up, and the little screen over the door that usually would have shown the current floor was blank. Interesting. Another mystery I didn't have time to investigate now.

There were a couple of underground levels for a parking garage, but I didn't know how to find the guys' secret passage that most likely involved a subway tunnel. The main entrance should work just fine. I hit the button for the lobby.

As the elevator descended, the carpeted floor under my feet thrummed. I shifted my weight, staying limber and on guard.

There were an awful lot of things I didn't know in my current situation, but that was okay. I'd get through it. I had an address, and I knew at least a few of the people I expected to see there. I'd completed plenty of assignments with no more information than that.

There was nothing all that impressive about the lobby the elevator let me out into. The paisley-print carpet looked clean, the glass doors that led out past the mailboxes to the street unsmudged, but it didn't hold the same sense of wealth that the household's mansion did. It actually reminded me more of my own rooms in that house: simple and practical but well-made and maintained. Somehow that brought back the pang in my gut.

I was going to avenge all those lives lost. Tonight might be my first step to really achieving that vengeance.

As I pushed past the outer door, the night air washed over me, refreshingly cool but tinged with the familiar reek of gasoline and tar you couldn't escape down here on the street. No wonder the guys liked their rooftop deck.

I hurried away from the apartment building, scanning the darkened road. It was past midnight now, only a few cars rumbling by on the street. I'd have looked for a quiet side-street where I could have stolen one, but I wasn't familiar with the street I was heading to or what part of the city it was in. I wasn't sure where I was going.

I headed toward a busier street up ahead. Just as I came around the corner, I caught sight of a cab with its available light on. At my wave, it pulled up by the curb, and I hopped in, calculating what would be a safe distance from my actual location.

"55 Freeton Avenue," I said, figuring that'd drop me a couple of blocks from 102. The cabbie nodded and gunned the engine. I settled into my seat, glad to see he didn't appear to be much for small talk.

Even with barely any traffic, it took about thirty minutes to reach my destination: a grim street of dingy office buildings and warehouses not all that far from the mall where I'd met Scarlett. When the driver stopped outside number 55, a medical supply outlet store that was obviously closed, he gave me a skeptical glance over his shoulder. "Are you sure this is the right place?"

I smiled brightly at him. "This is it." Then I handed him enough cash to cover twice the amount on the meter. He didn't complain after that.

I watched him drive off and then set off toward 102, crossing the street and sticking close to the fronts of the buildings. Half of the streetlamps were broken or burned out, which made keeping to the shadows easier. When I reached the right address, I slowed, studying the building.

It was a little smaller than the others, squat and windowless other than a small pane of glass next to the door. The grout between the bricks was crumbling. No sign hung over the door to suggest what purpose the place served.

I slunk over and tested the front door handle tentatively, careful to stay silent. It resisted my hand, locked. That was fine. The men hadn't looked as if they were going somewhere they expected to be met with open arms.

Had they even gotten here already, or had I managed to

beat them to it? Maybe they'd made another stop on the way.

For all I knew, they weren't coming here tonight at all and this was a target for later. It might be even better if I could poke around uninterrupted.

Slipping around to the back of the building, I found another regular door as well as a garage-style one, which suggested this was some kind of shipping warehouse. Both were closed, a tiny window in between them pasted over with faded newspaper. Whatever the place was used for, it didn't look as if it was used very much.

What could it have to do with the household? Or was it really part of some other case?

I worried my lower lip under my teeth for a moment and then tried the back door. To my surprise, that handle turned in my grasp.

Just as I nudged the door open, the muffled bangs of a pistol with a silencer reached my ears.

My pulse jumped. Someone was here, all right, and they weren't happy. Were the cops in there shooting at someone or having criminals shoot at them?

The murderers I'd been searching for might be right here in front of me.

Along with my body's innate apprehension about walking into danger, a thrill of adrenaline coursed through my veins. I stepped into the short, dark hall on the other side of the door, my gaze fixing on the streaks of light showing around a corner just up ahead. Grunts, moans, and more gunfire reached my ears from the room beyond my view.

I'd recognize those noises anywhere. Men were dying over there.

I darted toward the sounds with a growing sense of protectiveness. If the bastards who'd mowed down everyone in the household were trying to slaughter my men now too, I'd make them doubly regret everything they'd done. Hopefully I could get my hands on a better weapon than Talon's knitting needle first.

When I peeked around the bend, all I could make out were a couple of shipping crates at this end of what appeared to be a much larger room, illuminated by thin yellow light. The lids of the crates had been popped off haphazardly, them and a few crumpled beer cans lay on the floor near the wall. Holding my breath, I dashed behind the nearest crate, dodging the debris, and peered around it to get my first real look at the scene.

It was nothing like I'd anticipated.

Blood splattered every wall—every possible surface in the main warehouse room. Bodies slumped on the floor and against a table heaped with bulging baggies—some kind of drug operation, from the looks of it. Figures moved through the darker areas around the edges of the room.

One of the bodies wasn't a corpse quite yet. The fallen man groped for a gun that'd fallen a few feet from his hand, and another bullet slammed into his skull, making him crumple. Blood was already flowing from a wound across his wrist, staining the cement floor red.

Why would you shoot someone in the *wrist* first and not the head to begin with?

My gaze caught on one of the figures circling the room, and a jolt of recognition shot through me. I'd have known the graceful, deadly way Talon moved anywhere. His honed brutality had drawn my attention from the first moment I'd met him, and I'd only become more familiar with it in our various sorts of sparring.

Before my eyes, he lunged behind a delivery truck parked at the side of the room and hauled out a guy who'd been crouched there. A curved knife gleamed in his other hand. Without hesitation, Talon plunged the blade into the man's chest, jerking it upward in a zigzag motion that sent even more blood spraying across the side of the truck.

My eyes stayed glued to the slash as he tossed the guy aside to crumple on the floor. That jagged line across the throat and upper chest... I'd never seen anyone make a kill like that. But I had seen a matching wound.

My stomach lurched. I yanked my gaze away to scan the other bodies with sharper attention.

It wasn't just that corpse, or the one who'd taken a shot to his wrist that'd opened his artery. I spotted two other men who'd gotten Talon's knife treatment, and another who'd been shot across the forearm in just the right way. Others were sprawled in positions that hid their wounds, but from the amount of blood all over this place, letting off a meaty stench into the stuffy air, every kill had been carried out by a meticulous plan to maximize the gore.

It was brutal.

It was utter *chaos*, perfectly constructed to achieve that effect.

And I'd stumbled on a scene so very much like it just days ago.

One last guy made a dash toward the other end of the room, and Blaze stepped into view, the jaundiced light turning his pale red hair orange. He raised his gun and shot the wannabe escapee in the face.

A satisfied smile crossed his lips. He'd pulled off the kill as if he did it every day before breakfast, just for fun.

Who the hell *were* these men who'd dragged me into their lives? What kind of cops would take down a drug operation like this? Shouldn't they... shouldn't they only shoot people in self-defense? Where were the handcuffs and the announcements of people's rights? Didn't they want to, like, question any of them or something?

No. This was all very, very wrong.

The groans and the gunshots faded from my ears. I'd arrived at the tail end of the massacre, and it appeared to be finished. The silence that descended over the room turned the thump of my heartbeat in my ears almost deafening.

Garrison ambled out of the shadows, bending to check the bodies and pull wallets, phones, and weapons from their pockets. I'd seen the results of his meticulousness in the past too. He glanced over his shoulder, and Julius strode out to where the lights were brighter, just tucking his gun into its holster under his arm.

"I thought they'd put up more of a fight," Garrison

remarked, tossing another phone into the plastic sack he was carrying.

"Drug dealers are sitting ducks most of the time," Julius said, just as casually. He swiped at his forehead with the sleeve of his shirt. Despite all the blood around me, the four men had managed to stay impressively clean. I noted only a few flecks on Julius's shirt and one splash on Talon's, which he was already peeling off.

He tossed it into Garrison's bag. "Are we done here?"

"Just got to take a few more pictures," Blaze announced. He was patrolling the room in his usual energetic way, now snapping photos with his phone.

A sickening certainty coiled around my stomach. These men weren't any kind of cops. They were outright killers.

And this wasn't the first kill scene of theirs I'd witnessed.

At the household—those zigzag cuts, the clipped arteries, the spectacle of blood... I'd never seen it before, and I hadn't again until right now.

There was no way it could be a coincidence. Julius and his gang had slaughtered everyone in the household and then tracked me down and taken me... as some kind of prize? To toy with me for fun while they decided what to do with me next?

That part didn't make sense to me. I couldn't wrap my head around why they'd have brought me into their lives the way they had. They would have just shot or stabbed me at the scene of my car accident.

But who the hell knew what went through their heads?

I'd had no idea who these guys were, so I couldn't go by my original impressions.

I'd come here hoping I'd get a clue about who'd destroyed the household, and I'd gotten a hell of a lot more than that, so much that I didn't have any idea what to think. My head was spinning.

I drew back behind the crate. It was all right. I couldn't take them on here, with no real weapons and no preparation—but I knew where they lived. I knew how they worked. I could sneak back there and lie in wait for when they returned...

But the unexpected revelation had set me more off-balance than I'd realized. As I backed toward the hall, preparing to make my escape, my heel smacked one of the beer cans I'd forgotten to watch out for.

It rattled across the floor into the wall, and footsteps pounded toward me in an instant. I bolted for the hallway, bracing for a shot—

The footsteps stopped. "Dess?"

I should have kept running. But the sound of Julius's commanding voice was so familiar, so *normal*, that I couldn't help spinning around as I reached the hall. Tucking myself around the corner so my body was shielded, I stared at him, wondering what he could possibly plan on saying to me.

He was holding his gun, but he'd lowered it to his side. Talon, coming up beside him, had dropped his weapon too. They both looked utterly shocked—even... horrified? A lot more upset than they'd been about the actual horror they'd just carried out.

I wanted to vomit. My lips clamped shut against the urge.

"How did you—" Julius cut himself off with a shake of his head. He glanced behind him and winced as he turned back to me. "Let me explain. I know it looks bad, but—"

Looks *bad*? An incredulous guffaw tumbled out of me. "*You* killed them," I snapped. "You killed Anna."

And then, because my brain had finally started working again, I whipped around and pelted toward the back door.

Julius hollered my name. Shoes scraped against the concrete floor behind me. But I rammed the back door open and sprinted down the alley, rounding the corner onto the sidewalk before I even heard the squeak of the door opening again behind me.

I kept running on and on, spikes of adrenaline propelling me forward. Nausea twisted my gut.

I'd quite literally slept with the enemy. I'd been *living* with them. I'd sworn to avenge the household, and instead, I'd shared my body with one of the men who killed the people there. I'd befriended another.

I ran harder, and all those roaring emotions built to an apex, flooding over in a trickle of tears. Noelle's voice rose up from long ago in my childhood training sessions. *Crying is a weakness. Crying is a weakness.*

The chiding statement echoed in my mind over and

over, but it didn't stop the tears from spilling fast and violently down my cheeks.

I knew I was far enough away that the men shouldn't be able to track me now, but I couldn't bring myself to stop running—not until I found myself nearing a residential section of town where porchlights beamed through the night.

The last thing I needed was a suburban mother calling the real cops on me, so I slowed to a brisk walk, still breathing heavily. I dropped my arms, and my left wrist brushed against my pocket. I stopped and looked down at the bulge.

The phone.

Noelle had always been the voice of reason in my life. If the men I'd thought were on the side of the law were actually my enemies... then maybe the person who'd reached out to me was my friend after all.

I forced myself to place one foot in front of the other as I strode onward and pulled the phone from my pocket. Bringing up the message from last time, I examined it for several minutes.

What did I have to lose? Julius and the others knew that I'd seen them. No way was I getting back into their apartment undetected. All I had was a shrinking ball of cash, the clothes on my back, and this phone some mysterious benefactor had left for me.

I spotted a small shed to the side of one of the houses, and I veered in that direction, walking as if I belonged on the property. I shook the shed's handle, and when it didn't open, I slammed my brace down on it.

It snapped with a crack. One glance over my shoulder was all I allowed before I ducked inside and closed the shed door behind me.

A lawnmower and some gardening tools sat inside, but it was mostly empty. Plenty of room to hunker down and gather myself. It felt safer than walking the empty streets.

I dragged in a breath and typed out a short reply on the phone—an adequate one. The question I should have asked to begin with, knowing anything offered through Noelle's contacts was more trustworthy than a bunch of strangers who'd all but kidnapped me.

How do I know it's you?

I hit send before I could second-guess my decision, and then I waited. My mind ran rampant, the events of the past several days flickering past me. How had I been stupid enough to trust the very people I'd meant to hunt down?

The incoming text arrived with a vibration of the phone. My gaze jerked to the screen.

Meet me at the Volcano Aquarium tomorrow morning at 7am.

I stared at the words, and they clicked in my mind. Anyone from around here would know that there were no volcanos or aquariums nearby. It shouldn't have made sense, but to me and Noelle, it did.

A sewer tunnel—hot as the inside of a volcano, I'd grumbled more than once—ran parallel to the duck pond in the center of the town. It was an emergency meetup point, one set aside only to be used in the direst circumstances.

Only Noelle and I knew about it. Only the two of us knew the quirky name I'd given it as a preteen—The Volcano Aquarium, named after the heat, the location, and the smell of dead, rotting fish.

It was Noelle. I knew it was. We'd never had to use it before. But if there'd ever been dire circumstances, it was now.

TWENTY-FOUR

Talon

"WHAT GOOD IS your fucking facial recognition if it can't find who we're looking for?" Garrison groused at Blaze, who was typing on his laptop frantically in the back seat next to me.

"I'm working on it."

Julius turned in the driver's seat, his eyes smoldering with tension in the darkness. Only a faint glow reached the inside of the car from distant streetlamps at the edge of the vacant lot we'd parked in.

"Work *faster*," he demanded. "That's your job, isn't it?"

Our leader always kept a controlled front, but I knew Julius well enough to tell he was struggling as much as any of us, maybe more. He expected perfection. He took pride in our missions, worked out every minute detail of the operation, and they *always* went according to plan. We made sure of it.

Then Dess had come into the picture, and nothing had gone completely according to plan since.

Blaze stopped and looked at Julius with a cold expression that rarely came over his face. "If you can get the job done better, do it yourself."

I'd never seen Blaze talk to anyone—let alone Julius—that way. Maybe we were all unhinged by Dess's intrusion tonight. She must have been distressed by the bloodbath that she'd seen, but when she'd spoken her final words to us, she hadn't been staring at the corpses that littered the floor. She'd stared right into Julius's eyes, and we'd all seen the fury there.

She knew it'd been us who killed her friend and everyone else in the mansion. She knew that we'd been lying to her from the start.

It wasn't a total surprise that Blaze's nerves were frayed. He'd seemed to be forming some kind of friendship with her—and he'd spoken up for her from the beginning. I'd almost have said his eyes had been brighter and his steps a little lighter after they'd spent time together yesterday morning.

What did surprise me were the shifting tides inside *me*. I hadn't said a word since Dess had run off, and I wasn't sure I could even if I wanted to. The strange pang inside me wasn't anywhere near crippling, but... I couldn't remember the last time I'd felt even that much about anything.

Julius inhaled slowly as if gathering his cool. He spoke more evenly than before. "Why isn't it working?"

Blaze didn't bother looking up. "The same reason it wasn't working an hour ago and three hours before that. I can't scan faces in the dark, so unless she walks right below a streetlamp and looks toward the camera at the same time, we're not going to find her until dawn. Which is... about a half hour off still."

"We'll find her," Julius said. "We have to. We don't leave loose ends."

"Assuming she's even still in the city, let alone the state," Garrison muttered.

There it came again—the slight discomfort in my chest that grew each time I thought about Dess hating us. Leaving us. As if I'd *lost* something.

But that didn't make sense. As close as we'd gotten during our heated encounter in the exercise room, as much as I'd enjoyed it, it'd been purely physical. We'd barely talked, and she hadn't seemed to mind that.

Blaze jerked his head toward Garrison. "If she isn't, then I'll find her wherever she went. But there's no reason to assume she's gone that far."

Garrison raised his hands. "I'm just saying, no one would stick around here knowing that we're going to come after them, having seen what we can do. Even I can admit she's smarter than that."

"She's obviously smarter than any of us gave her credit for," Julius said, raking his hand through his hair. "How the hell did she even manage to follow us?

Did you see anything out of the ordinary during the drive?"

Blaze shook his head. "I saw you lock the penthouse behind us. She couldn't get into the passages without us noticing, let alone the garage. I've already checked the cameras down there—no sign of her."

"Then she went out the main entrance. But how the hell did she get there, and how did she know where to go afterward?"

"What does it matter?" Garrison asked. "She *did* find us, she's seen what we can do, and now we're screwed."

"She only knows our aliases," I pointed out. "Not our real names or anything that would identify us to the actual cops." Talking eased the discomfort inside me just a little, as if it helped that I was contributing. But a small ache remained. Exactly as if a hole had been carved out of my chest, one only she could fill.

No, it didn't make sense at all. It would probably fade in a matter of hours anyway.

"If she got out of the building, then she knows where the penthouse is," Blaze pointed out. "So much for that being our secure base."

"And she can pass on physical descriptions to the police." Julius scowled. "Or whoever else she might want to tell about this. I'm even more sure now that we never got the full story about who *she* is and how she's involved. Which is why we need to track her down, fast."

"I'm trying," Blaze grumbled.

Watching them debate our situation and Dess's part in

it brought the pang back into sharper clarity. I couldn't decide if it bothered me or if it was kind of a relief to know I was capable of that kind of emotion.

I didn't *need* to feel things. I got by just fine in my usual unaffected state. A lot of guys would have scoffed at the idea of feelings and acted as if they were a weakness anyway.

The ache for Dess didn't seem like a weakness, though. It felt like a sense of direction, propelling me forward.

Despite Julius's determined words, Garrison's snark, and Blaze's frustration, I got the sense that this wasn't just about loose ends for them either. No, we didn't want to deal with the fallout if we couldn't contain what she knew... but she'd intrigued all of us in different ways.

"We never should have brought her to the penthouse to begin with," Garrison said, tipping his head back with a groan.

A growl came into Julius's voice. "Don't you dare say 'I told you so.'"

Garrison glowered at him. "Fine, I won't say it. I'll just think it very loudly. We have a loose cannon running around—one who knows our address, our occupation, and the fact that we killed her friend. If she tells even one person, any person, our job just got a hundred times harder." He paused, and his mouth twisted. "Also, I liked that apartment."

"We might still get to keep it," Blaze said, always the most optimistic of us.

A haze of pre-dawn sunlight was beginning to glaze

the horizon beyond the windshield. Blaze stayed ready for his facial recognition program to kick in, not daring to look away from his laptop. "It didn't seem like she had anyone *to* tell. Maybe we can…"

He trailed off, obviously knowing there weren't many solutions that involved us finding her and ensuring she didn't talk that wouldn't involve her as dead as the drug dealers we'd just mowed down.

"I don't think she'll go to the police," I said slowly. Julius and Garrison looked at me, seeming surprised that I'd jumped in. I continued, expanding on my reasoning so they knew I wasn't just shooting my mouth off. "She stole a car when we first met her. She was running from something, and she was trying to avoid leaving a paper trail at a hospital. When she thought we were cops, she held herself back from telling us anything."

Garrison grimaced. "Considering the stuff her boyfriend was mixed up in, if any of that was even true, she might tip off some other criminal crew instead. That'd be a whole different kind of headache. I think I'd rather deal with cops. At least they're a little more predictable."

"None of that matters until we find her and—and see what she has to say," Blaze said, as if she was likely to say anything at all and not fight us tooth and nail.

We all fell silent, the others possibly thinking the exact same thing I just had. Julius sighed. "We can't know for sure how it'll play out until we get to that point. The one thing I'm sure of is that we definitely don't know everything there is to know about Dess. I don't think we've even scraped the surface."

Nobody could argue that claim.

He looked down at his hands, the knuckles marked by a few small scars, and flexed his fingers before going on. "If she has ties to a criminal syndicate, we'll use her as a message. She can't be left alive if she's with one of our enemies. If we decide she's a risk in other ways, we'll deal with it appropriately. I think we can all agree on that. But we have to wait and see."

The ache inside me dug a little deeper at the thought of ending Dess's life. An image flashed through my mind from one of the movies I'd watched—secretly in my room on the small TV I had in there, studying the actors' faces and body language as they played out some heartbreak. Trying to understand the pain they were going through that was unconnected to any actual wound. My hand rose to my chest, putting the slightest pressure there, like I'd seen the characters do sometimes.

I couldn't tell if it helped.

I thought back to sex with Dess—to how hungry she'd seemed for the physical connection once we'd collided. There'd been nothing artful or scheming about our coming together, just pure bodily lust, so much it'd seemed to unnerve her in brief moments when I'd caught a flicker of uneasiness in her eyes. And yet she'd kept going. She'd clung to me, urged me on. And when she'd come apart, it'd been like she'd ascended to the heavens.

She'd lost something too—and not just her friend.

There'd been an emptiness inside her she'd been longing to heal. And for just a little while, I'd been able to fulfill that need.

I'd fucked bad people. I'd talked to them and worked with them my entire life. Dess was wounded in a way I couldn't explain, but she wasn't like those people at all.

"I don't think she'd be out to hurt us vindictively," I said. "She's scared, and who wouldn't be after what she saw?"

Julius looked at me, studying my expression. Maybe picking up on the fact that I had experiences with her I hadn't shared. But he didn't prod me about them.

"We can't know that for sure," he said, "but I hope you're right."

Blaze's demeanor changed like the flick of a switch. He sat up straighter and pointed to his screen. "I've got her. She's on the move."

We all peered at the grainy image of a figure striding into what looked like a city park. There was no denying it. That was Dess, and she walked with purpose.

"Let's go round her up," Julius said, and slammed the car into drive.

TWENTY-FIVE

Decima

I EASED down into the sewer tunnel on the far side of the pond, using an entrance behind a small maintenance building. The stench hit me fast. I started breathing strictly from my mouth as I eased my way down the ladder and into the humid corridors.

Thank God it hadn't rained in the past week, or this excursion could have been a lot messier.

The heat sent sweat trickling down my back. My shoes squelched onto the ledge alongside the channel of sludge, but I didn't allow myself to glance at whatever nasty things I'd stepped on.

It didn't matter. All that mattered was confirming that Noelle was alive—and then working with her to carry out the mission I'd first set out on: destroying the people who'd slaughtered the closest thing we had to a family.

Those people being the four men I'd spent most of the past week with.

My stomach tied itself into knots. I wasn't usually all that anxious when I got down to work, not after all my years of practice, but this situation was like nothing I'd dealt with before.

Noelle would straighten it all out. Noelle would see the way through. She'd always been there to point me in the right direction and make sure I was prepared. Why would now be any different?

Assuming it really was Noelle, and this wasn't some horrible trick.

I approached the meeting spot quietly, avoiding piles of waste that'd collected along the edges of the rounded tunnel. I wanted to get a good look at whoever was waiting for me before I showed myself. My footfalls were silent, so as a slender, muscular woman's figure came into sight in the wide alcove up ahead where a few different tunnels joined, I had time to analyze her.

While I remained cloaked in darkness, hazy light seeped over the woman from a grate high overhead. From the back, her shoulder-length salt-and-pepper hair looked just as familiar as it always had. She stood with a typically rigid posture, both hands clasped behind her back. Then she turned her head, revealing her profile, and my shoulders sagged with pure relief.

There was no doubt that the woman before me was Noelle. I wasn't alone in this mess. Everything could go back to—well, not normal, but closer to normal than the craziness of recent days.

"Noelle," I called out, stepping closer.

She whipped around, and her cool, hardened eyes—so ready to take down any threat—soothed me. Finally, I had someone on my side.

My steps sped up as she looked me up and down.

"Where have you been all this time?" she asked in her usual demanding tone, as if this were a regular meeting and I'd shown up late for a training session. "It took *days* for you to get your hands on that phone, and practically another day to answer me."

Her voice echoed through the tunnel, and I nearly flinched at the accusation I heard in it. I stopped in my tracks, still several feet away from her. "I didn't have the opportunity right away," I said. "There's a lot I need to tell—"

Noelle didn't let me continue. "Why did you leave the household at all? Your orders are always to remain in your rooms unless otherwise instructed."

The knots in my stomach came back, tighter than before. This wasn't the reunion I'd pictured. I hadn't expected hugs and fawning praise, of course, because that'd never been Noelle's approach, but I'd thought she'd be relieved to see me too. Concerned about what I'd been through. Upset about the deaths we hadn't been able to prevent. Angry, yes, but at the people who'd carried out the massacre.

Instead, she only appeared to be annoyed with *me*, as if

I'd veered off track on an assignment I'd already had a playbook for. As if nothing had been lost but my obedience to instructions she'd never actually given me.

It felt... wrong.

My legs stayed locked in place. "I didn't have a choice. Everyone was dead. I couldn't save any of them. I thought you were dead too. The only thing I could think to do was track down the people responsible."

Isn't that what you'd have wanted? something in me said, but I didn't ask the question out loud. The answer was obviously no.

Anger crackled through Noelle's words now, but it was directed at me. "One of the first lessons you learned was to keep to your part of the house. You weren't given permission."

Given *permission*? Did she really think I should have stayed put after I'd seen what had happened in the rest of the mansion—that any sane person would have pretended all was well? How could I have known there was anything or anyone to wait for?

My uneasiness prickled deeper into my skin. I shifted my weight from one foot to the other, instinctively testing the surface beneath me. "I didn't think I needed permission in a situation like that," I said. "And—and I had it anyway. Anna opened my door. She *told* me to leave."

Leave. Find somewhere safe. I hadn't followed the second part of those orders all that well, but I wasn't sure that was my fault.

Noelle's lips curled into what I could only describe as a

sneer. "Anna wasn't responsible for your security. Anna was your cook and your housekeeper. She was useless. I'm the one who makes the real calls about where you go and what you do."

I knew that Noelle was a cold woman, but I'd always thought that if my life were in danger—if I were in a perilous situation—she'd be there to help me. Judging by the way she looked at me now, that wasn't the case after all. She didn't seem to care about *anyone.*

"Anna was my friend," I said. "Your colleague. And she died making sure that I lived."

Noelle must have picked up on the horror in my tone. She placed a hand on each of her hips and offered a small gesture toward sympathy. "Her loss was unfortunate. As were the losses of all the faithful people who worked for the household. However, they're not important now. They're dead. You're alive, and your deviation from protocol could have gotten you killed."

I didn't bother reminding her again that I hadn't disobeyed anybody. In fact, I'd been nothing but obedient by leaving the household at Anna's command.

Why the hell would I have stayed there when leaving and finding the killers was an option? I'd been trained for years to hunt down targets, and now, when I'd put those skills to use against the people who'd not only threatened but destroyed the household, Noelle was chastising me for it?

I stayed silent and gritted my teeth. How had I been so wrong? I'd looked at her as a guide—as someone I could trust and whom I'd protect with my life. She was talking like... like I was a misbehaved pet, or a possession that'd purposefully been misplaced. Not a person at all.

The respect I'd felt for her didn't seem to go both ways.

But she still had to know more than I did. It wasn't as if I could walk away.

"Why did it happen?" I asked. "Why did someone kill the whole household and leave them like that?" There was no point in mentioning right now that I knew who'd done it. I still didn't understand why the men I'd spent the last few days with would have. Had they been long-time enemies of the household? Had it been some kind of *game* to them? They'd acted so casual about the shootout in the drug den, even taking pictures...

The pieces didn't fit together.

Noelle released a hoarse laugh. "Why? Decima, dear, I'm not the one who killed them. You would need to ask the assholes who did that question."

I frowned. What had *she* been doing for the past week, then? "Haven't you been investigating to figure out who did this and why?"

"No, I've been busy trying to track *you* down and confirm you weren't actually caught in the crossfire. Nothing else was as important as that."

Nothing else was as important as finding me, but she'd spent the entire time since I'd turned up berating me? My head was starting to ache.

Abruptly, I found myself thinking of the men—the

fake cops. The way I'd seen them work together, a perfectly cohesive unit when they needed to be even if they bantered and snarked at other times.

I had no doubt at all that if one of them were killed, the other three would go to the ends of the earth to get justice for that death. I'd always given the same loyalty to the household, and I assumed that everyone who was part of it held the same sentiment.

Noelle had brushed it off like an afterthought.

How could the people who were obviously the bad guys make me feel safer than the woman who'd made me who I was? And yet, ridiculously, I couldn't help craving the men's presence around me: Julius's impervious authority, Talon's cool strength, Blaze's hyperactive cheer, and, hell, even Garrison's defensive snark.

"You really have no idea why an attack like that would have happened?" I tried again. "Did we have so many enemies that there's no way of knowing who would have had the resources?"

Noelle sighed. "We can get into all of that later, Decima. It's time to leave. We can regroup, and then I'll tell you everything you need to know."

Everything she decided I needed to know, not everything I wanted to. The same frustration I'd felt when the guys had stonewalled me surged up again, twice as strong when it was coming from her. "I want to know now."

She scoffed. "You would be smart to listen to me if you

want to live. The dangers of the real world are worse than I could ever explain to you, and some of those dangers are after both of us for being part of the household. The longer you sit here and argue with me, the more likely it is that they'll find us and kill us both."

Would they? Julius and the others had obviously known something about how I was connected to the household all along. But they'd given me a bed and good meals and space to move around in. If they'd wanted me dead, I had to admit they could have killed me a dozen times, at least in the first day when I'd been disoriented and hadn't realized how formidable a force they were.

How well did Noelle really know what she was talking about?

I squared my shoulders. "If you would just tell me—"

"You know what? I'm done with you disobeying me." Noelle snapped her fingers. "Garlic milkshake," she said, emphasizing both words in that odd combination.

Something inside me clicked, my mind going just a little dull and hazy, detached from the rest of my body.

"Garlic milkshake," Noelle repeated. Despite my resistance, my posture snapped to attention, my limbs tensing with readiness. She smiled. "Good. No more questions."

I tried to open my mouth anyway, but my jaw refused to budge. What the fuck? I stared at Noelle, backing up one step and then another.

Her eyes narrowed. "Stay where you are."

My feet seemed to meld with the ground. My heart thumped faster. How was she doing that?

Noelle ran a hand through her hair and took a deep breath. "You used to try my patience like this when you were much younger, you know. You had a phase where you had to ask 'why' about everything, and it was *infuriating.* Good little killers don't ask questions." She chuckled darkly, striding toward me and walking around my stiff body. "But with the right words, we can be sure you don't get too caught up in your own initiative."

I didn't remember hearing the phrase she'd used before —except I did. It hit me with a sudden chill. Those nonsensical words had fallen from Anna's lips as she attempted to suck in her last breaths, to save me.

An even more chilling thought hit me. If Noelle could control me like this, would I even have been able to step outside my rooms without Anna saying that special code?

Noelle smirked, taking in my stillness. "Now, take a step forward."

I willed myself not to do it. With every single ounce of restraint I had left, I rallied against the order and told myself not to obey. But my left foot—of its own accord— swung forward to plant itself farther forward before my right foot came to meet it.

"Good. Now follow me. We're leaving."

Noelle turned, and without any control over my own limbs, I trailed behind her. One foot after the other. On into the dim light of the alcove toward a metal ladder against the far wall that Noelle was approaching.

Panic rose in my chest. I was locked inside my own mind, unable to send any signal to the rest of me. I pounded on the internal wall that stood between me and my bodily functions, but it didn't break. It didn't *move.*

I didn't recall a specific memory, but a sensation from a long, long time ago flooded me—one of helplessness. I could remember another time when I'd been out of control of my movements. I was young, and my limbs were restrained as my body was taken... taken somewhere I didn't want to go.

As quickly as the memory came, it flashed out of focus, back into the depths of my mind. The reminder sent a jolt of fear and iron will through me, and I stumbled over my next step.

I couldn't remember the last time I'd been able to make a choice for myself in the household, but right now, I had to resist. Noelle couldn't do this to me. I *wasn't* her pet or her possession.

I was my own person—a person who loved chocolate and the TV show *Spy Time*, who could take happiness from the simple pleasure of a breath of fresh air, who craved the brutal intimacy a man like Talon could offer. I was *me*, and no random combination of words could give her ownership over me.

With the force of that defiant thought, I came to a halt. I looked down at myself with a thrill racing through me.

I'd done it. I'd broken her control. I'd made my own decision.

I'd been directed by Noelle my entire life, but for the

last week, even with the men deciding where we went and what they'd tell me, I'd been freer than I'd ever been before. I *wouldn't* go back to being a puppet. I owed the household their justice.

I'd give them that. But I'd give it to them on my terms.

"No," I whispered, my voice still difficult to use.

Noelle spun around and narrowed her eyes at me.

"Garlic. Milkshake."

My body stiffened, but I forced it to relax. I was free. I would stay that way. I'd thought I could trust Noelle—I'd put all my faith in that fact—but I'd been wrong.

Trusting Noelle was worse than trusting the men. At least they were loyal to their own. After what she'd just done, I'd count on them to give me the real story about why they'd attacked the household before I believed any story she spun for me.

"*No*," I said again, louder. "I have a say in what happens here too. I don't belong to you."

Noelle let out a sharp guffaw that made me want to punch her. As my hand clenched, she shook her head.

"We could have done this the easy way, but you've given me no choice."

I widened my stance automatically, preparing for a fight. Noelle wouldn't be easy to take down. I'd been able to for a few years now, but it'd often been tricky. And those times I hadn't been working around a still partly sprained wrist. She might have weapons on her too.

I hadn't considered that it might not be her fighting me at all.

Noelle made a brisk gesture with her hand, and ten menacing figures sprang out of the tunnels on either side of her, charging straight at me.

TWENTY-SIX

Decima

NOELLE STAYED EXACTLY where she was, totally unfazed by the new arrivals. Of course. They were running toward me, obviously on her command.

As I backed up, looking to put myself in a better defensive position, my thoughts whirled. Why would Noelle have come with trained fighters ready to attack me —to capture me—when I'd shown up with every intention of following her out of this tunnel? If she'd approached me with an ounce of concern, I would have followed her demands to the ends of the earth. I'd done that for so long that breaking the trend tugged at something inside of me.

But I refused to be a slave.

Two of the men, one on either side, drew ahead of the others to reach me first. I didn't see guns or knives in any of their hands—no, they didn't want to kill me. Only to force me to obey where Noelle's special phrase had failed.

Then I couldn't think at all, my body switching over into the grips of my well-honed combat instincts. I squatted and veered, raising my brace to deflect a blow aimed at the side of my head, ducking away from grasping hands.

The men were obviously well-trained, but nowhere near as practiced as me. Too bad they had the numbers to make up for it.

My arm didn't ache in the way it had on the day I'd sprained it, and the pain in my ribs was barely detectable, but there was enough of the injury left to slow my motions. I caught a glancing blow to my cheekbone—avoiding the full brunt of it by pure luck. The other men were pressing in on me, ducking and weaving around each other to snatch at me in an attempt to gain the upper hand. I was outnumbered severely, and I couldn't dream of winning this fight if I fought fair.

It was a good thing that I knew how to fight dirty.

My fingers closed around the knitting needle I'd wedged into my pocket. I slashed out with it, slicing the tip through one man's palm, jabbing it at another's gut. It stabbed into his flesh, and he grunted in pain, but then he jerked it out and tossed it aside, out of my reach.

Fuck. I dropped down again and scanned the ground for any debris that could be used as a weapon. It was hard to make out much in the hazy light with attackers coming at me from left, right, and in front. I spun and kicked one way while aiming an uppercut in the opposite direction, moving my body at the fastest possible speed, scrambling to find an advantage.

In another scenario, I'd have been looking for my best chance to make a break for it. There was no point in fighting a battle where the odds were stacked against you if you could get out of it. But fleeing would mean losing track of Noelle. I hadn't wanted to go with her like a puppy on a leash, but she knew *something* about the murders at the household. She was the only connection to my old life that I still had.

If I left here with just as few answers as I'd turned up with, I'd be even more stuck than before.

As I whirled, wincing when a blow I couldn't completely deflect caught me in my ribs, my gaze caught on a chunk of broken concrete about the size of a fist. I dove for it, snatched it up, and swung it at the nearest head. It slammed into the man's skull with a crack of breaking bone. He dropped, and I knew he wouldn't be getting back up again.

That left… way too many more fighters.

My other hand groped and collided with a rusted pipe protruding from the wall. I yanked at it, only intending to use it for leverage, but it snapped off in my hand. Water gushed from the wall in a powerful burst.

The spray hit two of my attackers. I darted under the arc of water and swiveled to come at them from behind, but my left foot landed on a blob of slick sewage material —okay, being totally accurate, I stepped on shit—and slid.

I barely caught my balance, and then the nine remaining men were closing in on me again.

I tried to dodge around them or dash between them to get at Noelle. Maybe if I could take her hostage—if I even could overpower her—her attack dogs would back off. It wasn't a strategy I'd used often, but I was running out of options.

I dipped and wove, jabbed out with an elbow and snatched a handful of hair to ram one head into another. Tripping one guy, I used his back as a springboard to launch me free of their tightening ring.

The move would have worked perfectly if I hadn't hit my landing right on another gross glob.

My feet skidded, my torso jerked around in an attempt to catch my balance, and pain flared through my freshly banged ribs. A solid body rammed into me, tossing me onto the ground where even more putrid liquid soaked into my shirt. My groan was both pain and disgust.

"Got her!" my attacker shouted.

Oh, he thought so, did he?

In a motion that Noelle had drilled into my mind years ago, I hooked my foot over his leg and pivoted my hips. The man lost his balance, falling off me and allowing me to switch our positions. I sat atop him, and he reached for me, but I pushed his hands under my knees, grabbed his head, and snapped his neck in one swift motion.

I was tempted to slam it into the muck for good measure, just for being such a prick, but the other men were hurtling toward me.

Snatching up the nearest of my makeshift weapons, I sprang to my feet, wobbled, and heaved off the wall to add power to my heel kick. I lashed out with the broken pipe end at the same time. It carved a gash in one guy's cheek, but all he did was wince and keep coming.

I'd ended up out in the open with no wall to protect my back. My breath was coming in short spurts now, burning in my throat, and not just with the stench. I flung another punch, ducked, and slipped right onto my ass.

In an instant, four hands gripped my arms. I thrashed between the two men who'd grabbed me, but another wrapped his arms around my torso. They dragged me toward Noelle, one clamping his hand around my wrist brace so tight the tendons pinched with a lancing agony.

The same feeling from before—the utter helplessness I'd felt when Noelle had given her hypnotic command— seeped back into me. "No," I whispered, not able to prevent the word from leaving my lips. I *never* begged. Never. I'd sooner die than let someone hear me plead for my life.

But Noelle had no plans to kill me. It wasn't my life I was begging for; it was my freedom. That was... new. I'd never experienced the sweetness of freedom before, and losing it—losing the small taste of making my own choices—wrenched me to the core.

I slammed my foot back, and it made contact with someone's shin, but his hold on me didn't release. The iron grip on my arms didn't slacken no matter how I twisted and heaved. There were too many of them.

"Good," Noelle said. "Bring her to the truck."

My captors dragged me one more step—and the *bang* of a gunshot reverberated from the nearest tunnel.

The man at my left jerked, blood blooming in the middle of his forehead. As he toppled, I dropped as low as I could go, lifting my legs so my weight would put more strain on the men who held me. I didn't know what the hell was going on now, but I didn't plan on being caught in any crossfire.

"Seven more," an oddly familiar voice hollered. "No, eight. Take them all down—just be careful of Dess."

My gaze shot up to see Julius emerging from the shadows of the tunnel, pistol in hand. Garrison came into view just behind him, clutching his own gun, his nose wrinkled but his eyes as intense as his boss's. Talon marched out of one of the other tunnels, his muscles taut, a knife in one hand and a pistol in the other, with Blaze at his heels. The hacker let out a low laugh and raised his gun.

Someone swore. The two men who held me kept their grip tight, their hands digging into my flesh. The others hurled themselves at the newcomers.

My attackers had been unarmed—it would have been too risky trying to subdue me with any kind of weapons on them that I could have grabbed and used against them— and now that meant they were screwed unless they could take control of the battle at close contact.

Having seen Julius and his crew in action, I could have

told them they were screwed either way. But I kept my mouth shut.

Shots blasted through the alcove. Noelle's voice broke through the thundering sounds: "Get her out of here, now, *now*!"

My captors tried to haul me the way she was beckoning them, but with only two of them, I found a weak spot as soon as they were in motion. I swung my legs up again but this time rammed them into two kneecaps.

One of the men took the blow hard enough to stagger, and the second he was off-balance, I bounded off his body into a backflip. The hold on my arms and waist snapped. As I landed, I rammed the other man into the wall of the tunnel where another pipe protruded. It neatly cracked his spine.

As he crumpled, I rotated toward the man who was clutching his knee. "You're next," I murmured.

He had the good sense to look afraid. I *wasn't* helpless, and no one around here was going to control me.

When the man tried to lunge at me, I dodged and then came at him with a hail of punches. One, two, three, clocking him across the head, smacking him in the jaw, swinging out with my leg next and knocking him right off his feet. As he sprawled, I leapt over him and stomped on his throat with all my might. He gagged for a second before I crushed his windpipe completely.

My ears were ringing with the gunshots that had careened through the space around me. It was silent now.

The other five of Noelle's men lay in pools of blood mingling with the puddles of sewer water.

Julius and his men stepped toward me—and toward Noelle herself, who was standing there by the narrowest tunnel, staring at the guys with her lips pressed flat.

She looked... afraid. She took a step backward, glancing behind her. I knew there was nobody else—only her and the ten men she'd brought who'd all been disposed of.

She'd brought that huge force just to take me down, to compel me to come with her. I needed to know why. What was really going on here?

I saw the second Noelle made her decision in the flick of her eyes. She whipped around and sprinted into the nearest tunnel. I swiveled to chase after her, and Julius's voice rang out at the same time.

"Talon. No one leaves."

The other man was a few steps closer. He reached the entrance of the tunnel before I did.

"No!" I shouted, just as Julius grabbed my arms. Before I could break free, Talon had already fired the shot.

There was a thump from down the tunnel that must have been Noelle's falling body. My gut clenched.

"You asshole," I yelled as Talon stalked down the tunnel to check. "I needed her alive! She's the only one who knows—who knows anything..."

But maybe that didn't matter, not when the four men who'd already slaughtered everyone else I'd ever depended on had me surrounded.

I yanked myself out of Julius's hold and spun around, my back prickling with the awareness of Talon somewhere behind me. When I shifted to the side, that put Garrison behind me, still with a gun in his hand, but I liked my odds slightly better that way.

Julius watched me with a thoughtful expression. "Are you okay?" he asked. As if that mattered to him. As if they'd come—

Why *had* they come? They'd killed everyone... except me.

Talon emerged from the tunnel and gave Julius a brisk nod. "No one left who can say Dess was with us."

"*With* you?" I demanded. "Who says I'm going anywhere with you? What the hell is going on?"

"We just saved your life, sweetheart," Garrison said. "What does it look like?"

But *why?* I met Julius's steady gaze, confused and ready to do battle all over again, even if I didn't stand a chance against four fully armed, highly skilled killers. But it was Blaze who spoke.

"You don't need that woman," he said softly. "She'd only have lied to you anyway. I'm pretty sure that's what she's been doing your whole life. If you'll give us a chance to explain, I think I've found something that'll give you the answers you need."

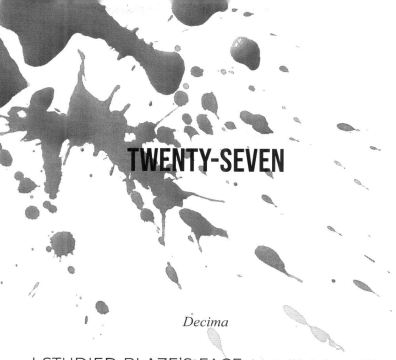

TWENTY-SEVEN

Decima

I STUDIED BLAZE'S FACE, but I didn't know if I could trust my instincts when it came to him. He looked as genuine as he always had. And he'd been lying to me the whole time, just like the others.

My gaze slid between the other three men. They watched me warily, but they were holstering their guns. I didn't appear to be next on their list of targets.

But that didn't change the crimes they'd already committed.

"Why should I listen to or believe anything you say?" I asked, annoyed at how rough my voice sounded. "You killed everyone in the household—you killed them *horribly...*"

"Hey," Garrison said, "I think we actually did a very nice job with that one."

"Shut up, kid," Julius said, sounding weary. He turned back to me. "We had nothing against the people in your house, whoever they really were to you. It was a job. We work for hire. Someone paid us to go in and deal out our specific brand of chaos, so we did."

A job. They hadn't even known Anna or the rest of them?

I glared at him. "So you slaughtered them for money? Is that supposed to make me feel better about it?"

"They weren't good people," Blaze piped up. "What Garrison said before about human trafficking was true. They were a branch of some secretive criminal syndicate —secretive enough that it was hard for me to dig up much about them, but I found enough. I always confirm that we're only taking on targets society is probably better off without."

I guessed to someone else's eyes *I* might be a criminal. My kills had all been for the protection of the household, but their enemies wouldn't have seen it that way. And somehow I had trouble summoning my usual conviction about the people I'd been protecting after the way Noelle had just tried to haul me away.

"What about me?" I said. "You didn't kill me."

"You weren't there when we were carrying out the job," Julius said, and I realized they honestly didn't know I'd lived there. I'd lied plenty to them too. "You weren't on the manifest. I don't know why or how you ended up in the building or what your relation is to those people, but our client didn't want you dead. It's possible you're the missing thing he expected to find, but he hasn't specified, so we can't be sure."

He paused, as if waiting for me to fill in a few of the blanks for them. I crossed my arms over my chest. "I don't need to tell you anything."

They were my enemies... weren't they? I'd sworn to kill the people who'd slaughtered the household.

But this wasn't quite the situation I'd pictured. If the men before me had been hired, if they hadn't held any grudge or had personal reasons for taking all those people down... then the real villain was whoever had hired them. *That* was who I should take my revenge on.

In a way, Julius and his crew had simply been a weapon wielded by someone else to wreak their intended havoc. What good would destroying the weapon do when the person behind it could just pick up another one?

Maybe they were my enemies, maybe they weren't, but they were definitely my only tie to the person responsible.

"Who hired you?" I demanded.

"We don't know," Garrison said, setting aside the snark for once. "Everyone goes by code names. All communication is highly secure. They don't know who we are, and we don't know who they are, not really."

They obviously had some means of communicating with them, though. I wet my lips.

"We don't have anything against you, Dess," Julius said. "We don't want to hurt you. But we need to understand how you fit in so we can make that call. What we've found… It's raised a hell of a lot of questions."

I swallowed hard, thinking of Noelle's betrayal. Of the way she'd talked to me, of the secret phrase I hadn't known was programmed into my brain to make me obey.

"After what happened here today, I'm not totally sure how it all comes together either," I admitted. I wasn't ready to tell them more than that.

"Can I show you something on my phone?" Blaze asked. "I was able to pick up a signal from a laptop in that woman's vehicle, and I scraped a bunch of the files. A lot of them relate to you. It might give you a starting point."

I stared at him. What could he possibly have found?

What could I lose by letting him show me? I nodded tentatively, still braced to defend myself.

Blaze slid his phone from his pocket and began typing. "There were a bunch of videos. I only had a chance to glance at one of them before we came down here—I wouldn't even have stopped to do that if we'd known how much trouble you were in. But that one reveals a lot all on its own. I can play it for you."

He was talking to me as if I were fragile. He *knew* I wasn't. The unease that roiled in my stomach begged for me to turn down the offer, but the part of my mind that yearned for information took control of my voice. "Show me."

He nodded and turned the phone to face me, the video already playing. He stretched out his arm, and I allowed myself to walk a couple of steps closer, drawn in by the images moving on the screen.

A little girl, no more than a toddler, stood in a blank white room. Her wavy black hair was strewn around her face, and her eyes were red-rimmed. Tears streaked down her cheeks.

She didn't look much like the face I saw in the mirror these days, but I recognized her immediately. It was me. In my training room in the household. What the—

A man stepped into view, dressed in sweats, his hands wrapped. "Fists up," he said. "We'll go through it again. You need to focus, and then you'll get to have your playtime."

Child-me sobbed and shook her head. "I want Mommy and Daddy. I want to go home. Please, I want to see them. Please, please, please."

My heart wrenched. Mommy and Daddy? I didn't remember this at all. I didn't remember ever thinking I had parents I could have seen if I asked. And the household had always been my home.

Hadn't it?

A woman came into the frame with brisk strides I recognized immediately. She was younger, no gray in her hair and her face unlined, but there was no mistaking Noelle.

She looked down at child-me with a cold expression so much like the one she'd aimed at me just minutes ago. "You can't see them. They're gone. This is your home from here on. You belong to us now, and we're shaping you up so that the bad things that happened to them *never* happen to you. Now listen!"

The little girl's sniffling intensified, but the loud sobs stopped as she hung her head. With obvious reluctance, she raised her tiny fists.

My throat constricted. What the hell was going on there? It didn't fit with anything I knew.

"I don't remember this," I admitted. "I don't remember anything before being part of the household."

"Kids don't typically keep their memories from that young," Julius said. "It's not surprising. But from the looks of it, you didn't have much choice about the company you were keeping."

My voice came out in a whisper. "I had no idea."

"You didn't know they took you from your family?" Blaze said, sympathy filling his eyes.

"No, I thought—I thought my parents were gone, like Noelle said there. But that they'd been part of the household before. That I'd always been part of it."

But that wasn't true. The child me hadn't acted as if I'd already known Noelle or the man. I'd asked for some other home where I thought my parents would be. And Noelle had talked as if they'd only recently taken me in. *You belong to us now.*

My legs wobbled under me as I grappled with the questions spinning in my head. Was Blaze right? Had I been stolen away from some family who had nothing to do with Noelle and the others?

Who was I really? And why would the people in the

household have kidnapped a terrified little girl... and shaped her into the killer I was today?

I looked at Blaze and then Julius, and they gazed steadily back at me. I didn't know where we'd go from here, but for at least the next little while, I had no interest in fighting them.

I nodded toward Blaze's phone. "I need to see more."

How would you like a bonus scene from Julius's POV, showing his perspective when Dess stumbles on their murder scene and when Blaze uncovers the videos of her as a child? Grab it by going to this URL or using the QR code below: https://BookHip.com/CHMRZVD

ABOUT THE AUTHORS

Eva Chance is a pen name for contemporary romance written by Amazon top 100 bestselling author Eva Chase. If you love gritty romance, dominant men, and fierce women who never have to choose, look no further.

Eva lives in Canada with her family. She loves stories both swoony and supernatural, and strong women and the men who appreciate them.

Connect with Eva online:
www.evachase.com
eva@evachase.com

Harlow King is a long-time fan of all things dark, edgy, and steamy. She can't wait to share her contemporary reverse harem stories.

Printed in Great Britain
by Amazon